IT NEVER RAINS IN LOS ANGELES

The Thomas R. Coward Prize Novel

It Never Rains in Los Angeles

by Charles Flowers

Coward-McCann, Inc.

New York

For Rhea and Beulah, for Luscious and
Ricky and Paul, for both Barbaras and
both Eddies, this is written, in
remembrance of things which cannot
be written

This is a novel, a work of the imagination.

All characters portrayed in it are fictitious.

—The Author

IT NEVER RAINS IN LOS ANGELES

CHAPTER I

THERE is no immigration treaty between Los Angeles and the United States. There is no Ellis Island. Aliens swarm in from the Midwest, the East, but principally the dead South—like looters in a riot-bombed discount store.

The people of Los Angeles are red, yellow, brown, black and white—in reverse order. These are the colors of flesh, and of hearts; the dye has seeped through to the core.

It never rains in Los Angeles. Except by exception. "An unusual junction of metereological phenomena." These phenomena conjoin several times a year, but only the unsophisticated tourist imagines he sees rain. It never rains in Los Angeles. He is drenched to his filaments by a historical event. Something to write home about.

Such an event has been chronicled for a Tuesday night in November. Residents signaled their surprise with a hundred-car pileup on a major freeway, as they had three months before, and a year before that. Thrifti-mart ordered umbrellas; old women prayed. It was a hard, fast, angry black rain—drops that battered down the sleeping ivy on a patio in Beverly Hills. It hit hardest in Watts, where windows cannot always be closed.

On Wednesday many black children were marked absent from school. Some feared their new clothes would be ruined; some feared their "naturals" would frizz; recent Southerners feared the thunder. Two little boys slipped into a culvert and were drowned. They had nothing more to fear. All were given a pink slip for unexcused absence.

By midafternoon, the event had spent its revolutionary force. It was a light-brown, sepia rain, polite but insistent. It drizzled with the ancient composure of a riddle no one had ever been able to answer. A Mexican rain . . . Chicano rain. It blew in feathery sheets, mud-streaked, across the dull plains of the south-central-Los Angeles black ghetto. In the distance, the shiny steel mountains of the rich city's business district caught rare gleams from the returning sun.

The brown rain lay upon William McAdoo High School. It melted into the rusty mud of the school courtyard; it congealed in gray pools on the asphalt parking lot. It was a school built with bricks forty years earlier to look like a school, and so it was hardly less cheerful than an abandoned factory, more secure than a state prison. It was the ghetto's grove of academe. Its students, said an educator, were "high-priority disadvantaged"; he disappeared toward Harvard before anyone asked what he meant. Funds dropped in his wake, sufficient to lay new carpeting in the faculty lounge.

Montana Neversmith, who looked at her scarred face in a cracked mirror in the wall of the second-floor girls' restroom, did not know she was "high-priority disadvantaged." Had anyone told her, she would not have understood what he meant; that was the consequence of her condition. But she would have hit him up the side of the head.

Miss Neversmith was sixteen and talked to herself through the tangled cracks in the glass. She was alone in the dirty room; school had let out half an hour before.

She did not say to herself, "I am Montana Neversmith and I am high-priority disadvantaged."

She said, "I am Montana Neversmith and I am the sexiest young lady in Los Angeles. Shit! I ain't no pasty ofay chick. I be black and proud!"

The face in the mirror seemed to agree. It was dark and stubborn, crouched in a verdant nest of crinkling wires. Its eyes flashed. A disembodied hand, with a pale underbelly like that of a mouse, drew a brazen white streak under stark lower lashes.

Miss Neversmith washed her hand under the only faucet that worked. The water was cold. The sink said, FUCK UNCLE TOM ORSON. She frowned to herself. *Niggers don't know how to act.* She scratched away the crusty message.

The brown afternoon turned yellow in the stale urine of the air, but the weak light did not bleach the highlights of her face. She remembered Benedict Williams and the party last Saturday night. He had seen her staring from a corner and struck a match against the wall.

"Just wanted to see what that black face looked like." He had laughed. "Get on," she had answered. That Benedict Williams, he was some cool dude. He wasn't a boy, like some she could name. He was a young man. Skin like blond mahogany, nose straight as any honky's, a proud and firm ass she longed to dig her fingers into.

She cinched in her belt, gave her own rear some room to talk. With a pink Kleenex, she wiped the daysweat from her cleavage. Gently, generously, she patted there a few drops of a mail-order fragrance, Madame Scrofum's Hindu Love Oil. She could get her money back if it didn't work.

It didn't.

When, at four-fifteen, Montana pretended to rearrange the mangled old textbooks in her locker, Benedict Williams strode by with his mind on higher things. He did not remember her. When he spoke, it was with the instinctive *noblesse oblige* of the young stud who knows every woman wants him. He took no note of Montana's special virtues.

"Say, hey, pretty!" he said, and barely nodded his head. Behind the black shades, his eyes said nothing; the solid frame beneath his light-green fatigue uniform bounced easily on stiff black paratrooper boots. His only smile lay in the ivory necklace of leopard's teeth around his lithe neck.

"Shut you mouth, boy!" shouted nervous Montana. This was the mating ritual of the streets they called Dogtown.

"Boy?" answered Benedict, his mouth curled in mock surprise. "Boy?" He stopped; he would take his part. He looked
back at the short figure with a hand on its feisty hips. He
wondered if he had ever seen it before, decided he hadn't.
Still, no reason to be rude. The revolution had time for the
little people.

"You heard me," the young lady growled. She looked at
the ground, but her heart sang like Marvin Gaye.

Benedict looked her up. He looked her down.

"Does a 'boy' hit you up the side of the head?" he asked.
Montana slammed the locker shut. She bent down to pick up
her furry purse. Benedict whistled. "Man. Does a 'boy' make
your heart flutter, young lady?"

Montana swung round to meet him with ice in her eye.

"You think you cool, honey?" she said sweetly. "My, my,
be a funny world, when a uppity little nigger think he ready to
catch. Uh-huh." *Oh, God in heaven!* she crooned to herself.
Benedict Williams. Talking to me. "Just any old pointy-headed
skinny-assed little thing. Pity, I do believe."

"You looking, ain't you?" He smiled. The elegant sweep of
his natural was like the kiss of the gods on a powerful king. He
was animal and soul.

"Ain't got time for fools," Montana answered. She was
getting someplace. She started down the hall. Tomorrow was
another day.

Then Benedict moved.

"Hey, young lady. Just a minute."

She stopped. *Already? Coming after me already?* She held
her breath, lifted the curve of her nose.

He smiled again. "Got a little milk on the corner of your
chin. See there?" Montana Neversmith jumped, startled, and
fell into his trap. She wiped furiously. *Sweet Jesus! he wasn't
fooling.* She collapsed beneath the skin. "Got to be
progressive, you hear? Revolution's coming. Niggers got to get
themselves together."

Benedict Williams went off down the hall. Montana sighed.

It had been a draw.

But not a failure. When she coyly turned to see that young man go off on his own, Montana Neversmith knew she would see him the next day. When she watched him slide out of sight down the stairs to the first floor, she did not know she had just seen something which would put her name on the front page of the newspaper. She did not yet know what she would remember all the days of her life: she was the last person to see Benedict Williams alive.

The first-floor hall was empty; Benedict was alone.

Quickly, but not furtively, he walked over to Room 105, the journalism room. He unlocked the door with a master key stolen for him by one of the night janitors. Benedict knew how to make friends.

He locked himself in the empty room and barricaded the door with a student's desk. He looked around.

Young Mr. Finch, a honky, had scored the peeling walls with mod posters. Angry giants like Malcom X and Huey Newton looked down on the young black man. Cassius Clay smiled; Brother Stokeley shouted; Rap looked supercool. Strange in that company, the Supremes chirped, with their pressed-down, assimilated hair, and a grand mother named Leontyne Price, whom nobody knew, gazed disdainfully like the last queen of a lost continent.

Yeah, thought Benedict. *These are my people. The greatest race on earth.* He smiled at the idea of Finch, whom he thought of as Emory. Benedict felt it was revolutionary to treat his teachers as no less than equals. *Emory's together, a cool white man.* Benedict loved the strange little man; it was a sentiment which clashed violently with the manuscript he took now from his jacket.

It had been written in a furious slash.

Benedict read it over, while the gentle brown rain lulled the world outside to doze; the sound touched the angry beating of his heart. Benedict was made miserable and proud by the terror of his own words:

BROTHERS, GET TOGETHER! KILL THE PIGS! Now! Got to be REVOLUTION now! The torture of our mothers, the rape of our pure black sisters must cease! Now!
UNITE AGAINST OPPRESSION! FIGHT THE HONKIES! Kill for FREEDOM! No more UNCLE TOMS! Be BLACK, be COOL, be REVOLUTION-ARY! COME to a BLACK PRIDE RALLY at Thad-deus Stevens Park—Saturday at FOUR P.M.

Benedict laughed out loud. If only that old Tom Orson could see him now. Food of the revolution being milled out in his own school, behind his ass-licking back. Orson, a black principal with a white gut. A real black man promoted by the system?

No way, thought Benedict. *Ain't no way.*

Orson had been brought in because the students had refused to attend classes under a white principal. The board of education had disagreed; they had their own rights. There had been fire bombs, walkouts, outbreaks of vandalism, a couple of injured teachers. The board had agreed. Now Orson had called a moratorium on "revolutionary activity." Benedict smirked. The students had made him; they could break him.

Now he checked all the windows in the lonely room. They were locked. The pale rain hung a veil between passersby and his dim movements.

No one could get in. No one would discover him.

Benedict walked over to the ditto machine in the back of the classroom. It looked as if it had not been used for some days.

Wasting taxpayers' money, he joked with himself. *I'll warm it up for them.* He rummaged through the absent-minded Finch's storage cabinet, found a ditto stencil under a copy of the Black Panther weekly. A large metal button clattered to the floor. FREE BOBBY, it cried on the way down.

Finch is all right, thought Benedict, *but I got to warn him about the Panthers. They're bad. They're out for themselves. Old Emory can get hurt.* Neatly, as he had been taught by a fat woman in the third grade, Benedict Williams printed his message on the master sheet. He saw the black letters form sense out of the blank whiteness.

He worked, unthinking, and there was beauty in the tough grace of his young movements.

In some dusty cell of his quick brain, an old movie replayed: Benedict, thirteen, the soft-spoken idol of his class; clever as a mongoose on the basketball court; given used copies of *Sports Illustrated* by a white teacher who had his own son; refused entrance to that son's house because "Gee, Benedict boy, you know it's not me (you're like a son to me, boy!), but I have to think of my wife and children, you know?" And Benedict, at thirteen, strangely, did know—for what seemed to be the first time in his life. And he was sure that he didn't want to be a bad nigger and cause the nice white folks any trouble.

Things had changed.

This'll shake them up, he thought, and wondered whether to emend "fight" to a more common four-letter Anglo-Saxon imperative. *Speak their own language.* He almost giggled; had that been the moral of Finch's etymological studies? *They choke their own sick tongue down our throats, then call us niggers for using it.*

The stencil was finished; he was ready. There was enough paper there to blanket the streets before the morning. The clear plastic dispenser was nearly full. Luck had always strung along with Benedict.

He looked once more about the graying room, like a wary hunter in a virgin forest. The windows were locked; the door was locked and blockaded; darkness had sprung like a trap. In the street outside, in the long hallways outside, in the great desert of the ghetto, there was no noise but the inscrutable brown rain.

Benedict pressed down the metal lever which would start

the flow of impression fluid.

It clicked sharply.

And that was the last sound Benedict Williams would hear.

He did not hear the shattering of glass which gouged the life out of his young and beautiful throat. He did not even hear the solicitous brown rain, which caressed the thick sweat and blood from his smooth and magnificent face.

CHAPTER II

EMORY Finch, no woman's dream of a moonlight lover, was nonetheless pleased with himself this morning.

He was at peace in his old gray VW. As one of those who believe that pleasure is nothing but the avoidance of pain, he was getting his reward. There was little traffic on the old boulevards he took to avoid congested freeways. It was early, but that was the price one paid; the air seemed almost clear. There was no smog to burn his sleep-laden eyes.

Carefully, as he did everything, he gauged his speed to hit the green lights, avoid the reds. How simple life could be, he yawned.

Gradually, as he left behind the beach city where he lived, the pavement grew rougher, the houses became sadder and more chill. Crudely painted signs promised potency, salvation and other bargains.

No matter. He was no longer a foreigner to the ghetto. He thought himself accepted, or perhaps, if it was not too much, loved. The first dread weeks were over. There were no more threats. He liked his job; it was too much fun to be called work. He thought himself happy.

Traffic became heavier; he began to see children walking to school; he left the last wide avenue, the last drying palm behind. Claustrophobia, like an early-morning flower, scented the ghetto air.

No matter. Finch thought he knew himself, his students. He thought he had found a place where his existence made sense.

The first hint that he was wrong jolted him wide awake. He saw it as he turned onto Fort Sumter Street.

Something was definitely the matter.

Why was there an angry crowd gathered outside his classroom window?

Detective Sergeant Jimbo Gannett slammed the classroom door. He frowned because it was eight in the morning and he had drunk too much the night before.

"Jesus Christ," he said reverently. "These . . . uh, blacks make the Viet Cong look like the DAR." He shrugged. "I guess violence becomes . . . uh, a way of life."

Emory Finch did not reply. He was trying not to get sick. From Gannett. From the rust stains of blood which splayed over the broken window and the dirty floor. His student's blood. The blood of Benedict Williams slashed across the torn Malcolm X poster which lay crumpled among the overturned desks.

Finch sat at his teacher's desk, sick with the emptiness of the room. Sick, because he knew he could do nothing but grade papers and fill out attendance slips. Sick from the sight of Sergeant Gannett, who did not belong there, interfering with the regular weekly test. Finch stared at the cheap planks of the floor; his thick spectacles misted in the smoggy hot morning.

Indeed, he was the myopic stereotype of a thousand comic books and beach-party movies; he was not the All-American Male expected on a coast where men read their only lessons from prevailing winds and surf, not from books. But his myopia was merely physical; he saw himself clearly. Somehow, he had faded into his thirties without ever doing anything he could call important, or even interesting. He was thirty-five, and the age itself seemed as pale as his colorless skin.

He saw clearly that he was only incidental to Gannett's investigation. His attachment to the murdered young man, his dedication to his teaching job—these meant nothing to the detective. Or to a society that had numbered and fingerprinted Finch along with hundreds of thousands of other state employees.

Let it be so, he thought. He could think of no single talent or accomplishment that should distinguish him from the herd.

And, as if to underscore the insignificance of his personal grief in this death, the detective assigned was only a sergeant. This, too, Finch saw clearly. It Benedict had been a student at Pacific Palisades, or even in the Valley, simple routine would have brought a lieutenant. And what that meant, Finch also saw clearly.

Gannett took out a notebook. He was worried.

Jimbo Gannett was known in the force as "the enlightened one." He had, on his own initiative, taken a night course in sociology at Los Angeles City College. He subscribed to *Psychology Today* and *Trans-Action,* and read the letters to the editor in both. A distant cousin had worked with the poverty program in New Jersey. Gannett never spoke against the Supreme Court and never searched without a warrant; he let patrolmen do that, and reprimanded them each time. He often smiled and was never brutal in public; he had also taken a course in radio broadcasting and had rouged his voice with deep sincerity.

But he was no milksop. His friends lovingly called him "Barge" Gannett. He was short, but powerful, although the spring waters of light Western beers had left sedimentary deposits around his middle. He was a crew-cut blond, less than forty, and his eyes were blank and gray as slate. He moved fast; he talked little. He was no man's fool, and on his way up. He had a trapper's nose for political winds. His wife, who had read books and once gone to the opera at the Hollywood Bowl, called him an "enlightened despot." In short, this violent murder could not have happened in his precinct. But it had. And now he must be patient with putty-hearted "liberals" like this man Finch.

It would be like humoring a baby.

"Pretty tough to teach down here, isn't it?" he tried. "Lot of flak, little appreciation."

Emory Finch said nothing. Perhaps the shock had paralyzed him; perhaps he feared for his own life.

"Don't worry," said the soothing Barge. "We're going to slam a lid on this school until we find the killers. No one else is going to get hurt, I can promise you that."

Finch smiled. His thin fingers played against the sallow desk. He looked at the detective as if through a language barrier. There was no wisdom in his face, no shock; he looked harmless and foolish, as his slight back bent like a cringing puppy's. Emory Finch would never lead troops to battle.

The Barge sighed. He remained patient. These were the times when he wished he had not been too gentle and too thick-waisted to become a karate instructor.

"Well, now," he said, with the forced cheerfulness of a dyke nurse bringing a bedpan, "we do have to get certain things out of the way. Nothing . . . uh, sordid. Just the background. I knew Benedict, by the way."

Finch did not seem to understand.

"One of our community-relations programs. Try to give the bo . . . the young men the inside view of the way we work. They think we're all pigs, but there's . . . uh, two sides to that problem." He got to the point. "I just need to know about the room. Who had keys, that kind of thing. All right?"

Emory Finch looked through the capable sergeant. Finch could have been mistaken for a mindless immigrant caught in the hold of a World War II freighter. He was that far out of it.

"Sergeant Gannett," he said, "I am not a fool."

The Barge coughed. Why did everyone invariably take offense?

"Ask. I'll answer." There was life in Finch's left eye. "Find out who killed Benedict. Find out before I do, or you will have two murders in the papers." He loosened into an unexpected smile. "I sound like a Frank Sinatra movie, too. Must be catching."

Gannett would have answered, and put him in his place, but the door suddenly burst open with a shout from violent throats.

"Can't let you—" stammered a flush-faced policeman as he nearly fell from the impact.

"Damn," said the Barge.

"Get on, Pig!" screamed a short young Negro. "That's my brother you killed!" A mob of students heaved behind him—faces hostile, set. They crushed the nervous cop against the wall, but stopped a couple of feet within the room. Finch had not moved.

Their leader shoved a desk out of his way; it cracked against another.

The Barge had leapt to his feet. "Mr. Roberson," he almost shouted, "this is a police investigation."

"Pig treachery!" replied the young man. "You think we don't know who killed the brother? No black man, I can tell you. Benedict was black and proud, and you hated him because he wasn't a Tom. You killed my brother, cop." There was a high-pitched wail somewhere deep beneath his voice; it played old rhythms of sorrow beneath the cadences of anger.

"I know you," said the Barge. "You're Scrounge Roberson. You know I know you. He's not your brother."

"He's my brother, white man!" The crowd at the door mumbled curses, but something in Roberson's manner held them in check. The hapless policeman turned incarnadine under his sergeant's bleak stare; he foresaw crude jokes at the station.

"All right, Mr. Roberson," the sergeant agreed in his most assuring radio tones. "Can we discuss this without your cheering section?" He smiled broadly toward the door. "I'll . . . uh, brief you on the facts. Nothing held back."

"That's my defense," answered Roberson. "They go where I go. I got no secrets from the brothers and sisters."

"Right on!" shouted someone in the crowd. "That's telling him!"

"Keep cool," said Roberson.

The Barge fiddled with his heavy brown belt. He glanced toward Finch. "Just asking a few questions of the teacher here," he said, as if shifting the blame. "I'm sure you can respect his right to privacy."

The young man ignored him. He was a pale reflection of Benedict—slighter, perhaps tougher. He was not controlled or devious; hate fell in showers from his stare. His natural, next to Benedict's, would have seemed stubby; a tooth had been broken. He was the courtier, not the king, and now the king was dead. He had to fumble where Benedict would have skated. And the Barge knew it.

"Roberson," he said, "I've been patient—"

"I've been patient for four hundred years, white man," answered the black youth. He faked the caw of a field hand in the movies, belied by the scar of his sneer. "I'se gwine get god-almighty tahred a' waitin', Massa Charlie." Someone tittered. "I swears I is, shore nuff!"

"Teach it!" shouted another voice at the door.

Roberson waved a stubborn fist. "So I reckon we'll jest get ourselves together and burn down this fucking world, white man, until you and your kind leave us alone!" He ignored the chorus of yeahs which seconded him.

"This is a school," the Barge began.

"An agency of the imperialists!" interrupted Roberson.

"And I suppose you have classes to go to."

"Where we learn about Washington and Lincoln and Roosevelt and all the other honkies who stabbed the black man in the back."

"That's politics," smiled the sergeant. "I just have a job to do. I'm trying to help."

"Oh, man, sing it to me! A job! A job oppressing every black man you can beat down. A cover-up, like you're trying to cover up the killing of our brother. Who you trying to fool, man? I ain't some field nigger just off the farm in Mississippi; I know you. I want to know, right now, what you're going to do about this. You going to find the cop that murdered Benedict?"

"Aren't you a little . . . uh, prejudiced, Mr. Roberson? You don't know that—"

"Prejudiced, huh? Man, that's funny. That really is. Real comical. I read you, dig?" And then the tears came. Brief, but strong. The young man looked away.

"Well," said the sergeant. "You don't seem to be in condition to run an investigation." He paused. "I am."

Roberson spoke very slowly. "I could kill you, pig! You don't give a damn. It's just another dirty nigger messing up your beat." He looked the detective full in the eyes. "You think I'm ashamed to cry for my brother? That's feeling, man. That's soul." The small crowd at the door said nothing.

"Scrounge," said Emory Finch, and suddenly everyone in the room realized that he was there, and that he had said nothing before.

The young man made a difficult choice; he answered without rancor. "Yes?"

"Strong men would cry for Benedict. If I were strong enough, I would cry." The broken voice sounded lonely in the silent room. "I think . . . Benedict trusted me."

"He was your friend, man," said Roberson.

"He was my friend." Finch looked hard at the bloodstained floor. "This man is looking for his murderer. I want the killer found."

"Dig," answered the angry boy.

"Trust me for an hour."

"Ain't no white man to trust, Scrounge," said a tall girl at the door. "Don't listen to no snake tongue."

"Shut up, sister," said Roberson. "I can think for myself."

Finch motioned toward the sergeant, who did not like being upstaged. "I'm going to help him find the murderer, Scrounge. I don't want the man to have any excuses, to say we didn't cooperate with him. That make sense?"

"But he's dead."

Finch looked up, shrugged his shoulders.

"Benedict said you were okay."

"Thanks," said Finch.

"I never trusted a white man," said Roberson. "I don't now." He turned to his friends. "We're late to first period. Let's not give those honky teachers a chance to say we're rowdy niggers. Let's go to class like dignified black young men and ladies, because that's what we are."

"Thanks," said Finch. The young leader did not reply. His followers walked away quietly; he followed. The Barge muttered something civil about reasonable behavior and the acceptance of responsibility; he meant to flatter.

Roberson turned at the door. He stared back at the Barge.

"Go to hell, pig," he said and slammed the door behind him.

"Sir, I—"

"That's all right, Manning," the sergeant said curtly to his stranded underling. "You just go on out there, if you're not too nervous, and try again."

"Yes, sir." The man started out.

"And . . . uh, Manning."

"Yes, sir?"

"Next time, see if maybe you can at least warn us before you invite another crowd in. We'd like to know when you plan a little party for us. Knock, maybe, or tattoo out some kind of call for help, okay?"

The man did not look happy. "Yes, sir," he said and went out.

"Thanks, Finch, for helping out."

"Cruelty, Sergeant Gannett, has never amused me. Perhaps I'm a weak man."

"Aw, that good-for-nothing cop? Don't waste tears on him; he expects it."

"Probably. That's what I find so cruel. A man trained to expect cruelty and insult. Like Roberson. Like Williams. And who's to blame? None of us? And who's to change it? None of us. Let's get on with it, Sergeant Gannett. We can't find the killer; he's too powerful and has lasted too many hundreds of years. But we can find his agent in this particular murder." A strange tic whipped across the muscles of his pale jaw. "And I'm as much a barbarian as you, Sergeant; I want to see the killer burn. Benedict deserved life; not many people do."

The Barge took a deep breath. The kooks you have to deal with. All in a day's work.

To clear the air, he told him the hard facts of the case. It was all beautifully simple. And short. There were no mysterious clues; there was no room for romantic suppositions. The few essential circumstances added up easily, without leaving any holes. And the answer made no sense at all.

Benedict Williams had been found dead at six in the morning by a janitor who had seen the broken window from the street outside. He had not come very close then, or he would have already known that the dark object which had apparently been pushed through the pane was Benedict's head. He had called the Black Panthers, who decided to steer clear. They called the police.

All the windows had been locked from the inside; the door had been locked, with a desk shoved against it. The janitor had needed help to break in.

The ditto machine sat as the young boy had left it. Fresh paper lay in the chute; the stencil had not been wet. There were no signs of violence in the immediate area.

But near the third window from the front, where Benedict's body had hung on the restraining shards of glass, there was still a tangle of overturned desks and splintered wood. It looked as if the desks had come to life and beaten him with their own force. His blood painted their cheap pine and metal; the bruises on his chest and face matched their blunt angles. He had died, or so it seemed, when they rose up and pitched him through the window; they had pressed him down on the old glass until the ripe youth had flooded red from his jugular. He had submitted and bled to death, unprotesting.

"It is very simple," said the Barge.

"And impossible."

The detective was not interested in observations from Finch. "That needn't concern you. I just want you to know how it happened so you can explain to your . . . uh, suspicious students. And I want you to tell me who had access to this room even if—"

"Even if it doesn't seem important?" Finch smiled weakly.

"Even if it doesn't seem important." Gannett had better things to do, and he was beginning to feel impeded. He and the teacher should be natural allies in the ghetto; they should be working together. He wondered if they were.

"It isn't my business, Sergeant Gannett, but what does access matter if the doors are locked?"

"It isn't your business, Mr. Finch. You teach, we solve crimes." Finch apologized with a deprecating wave. "Believe me, we need to know. After all, we're dealing with a clever murderer; that is, murderers. Or isn't it obvious that this must be the work of a gang?"

"It wasn't."

The Barge smiled in triumph. "Remember who was murdered here, Finch. Benedict Williams. I remember that cat. He wouldn't go down to one man, or even two. It would take three or four tough . . . uh, blacks to take him. Much less hold him on that glass until he bled to death." Finch shrugged. "And they're damned sharp, no fifth-rate slummers. They cleaned up. We found no fingerprints except Benedict's on the ditto machine, and there are so many confused prints in the room, of course, because of all your students and—"

"What?" Finch jerked up, electric. "What did you say?"

Gannett smiled benevolently. "Well, you see, even if they did leave prints, we'd never find them in all that—"

"No, no." Finch sounded fairly imperious. He was the teacher who had been offered the wrong answer. "The ditto machine. There were no prints but Benedict's. Isn't that what you said?"

"Of course, because—"

"Of course, Sergeant." Finch appeared ready to grant his interlocutor an A. "Of course. And now you see that it was only a human murderer, after all."

The Barge groaned. Television had made crime detection an easy-chair avocation. If it were only as pat as all that; if there were only no people to deal with. For one thing, he would have been promoted long ago.

The Barge smiled.

"We do appreciate all the help we can get," he said. "We do. My . . . uh detective's nose tells me it's a gang murder. It's a hound's instinct, I know, but it's all a poor cop has. Leave me my illusions." He meant to be sophisticated, charming. He meant to move on to the next question.

Finch, lamentably, had ignored his efforts.

"What I don't see," he whined, "is exactly how." He pulled at a pimple on his wan face; his brow furrowed under thinning brown hair. "I don't see how."

Strange, thought Gannett; they usually advance a complicated hypothesis, especially with a locked room. A gold mine for amateurs. Strings, and homemade traps, and curious clockworks. Give him time. Better, don't give him time. Just get out of there and leave him to his little adventure.

"Thank you," he said, and rose to leave the room.

Finch looked drugged.

The Barge thought of an important reminder; it would cover his exit.

"By the way," he said, "you know, of course, that you can't have class today. Right? We'll be needing to come back and check things. I'll leave my man outside to watch it. Okay?"

Finch had not heard him.

"Sergeant," he said, "you must check the machine again. Every part of it." He hummed a phrase which Gannett, from his one year at college, recognized vaguely as baroque. "Yes, it's the part that matters. There's bound to be a mistake."

The Barge started for the door.

I wonder, said the journalism teacher to himself; *I wonder how much knowledge it would take . . .* He looked up at the detective, as if handing out the night's homework assignment. "A technical mind. It would have to be someone with a technical mind. And educated. Cold, clever, and educated."

"Murderers," answered Gannett involuntarily, "are never any of those things. But thanks, anyway."

"Vicious," said Finch. "To do that to a young boy. A vicious mind that should die the same way. That would be justice, Sergeant. And we've never seen it on the face of this earth. But I'm crippled by lack of knowledge. If you're sure there are no fingerprints . . . but I don't know enough about—" He stopped. He was alone in his bloody classroom. The detective had left; there was no one at the door. Emory Finch was alone with the memory of a student he had loved.

He walked over to the broken window. He made himself finger the bloody edges.

"Yes," he murmured, "I won't walk away from it. I'm in it to the end." He walked back toward the little gray ditto machine. *I've read of such things. It's possible. But I need to find someone who knows . . .*

The explosion made him jump. Finch heard screams down the hall and stampeding thunder of frightened students. He knew the smell of acrid smoke would sift up through the door. He looked back at the place of his student's death.

It's starting, Benedict; it's starting. And it's not the way you wanted it. He knew what Gannett didn't, that there was no time for mistakes. *And you're not here to stop it. Or keep it sane.*

Finch left his room. He avoided the confusion near the explosion. It had been a piddling smoke bomb; others could handle this one. There would be worse to come.

He headed toward the science building and, he hoped, the key to Benedict's murder.

CHAPTER III

FIVE minutes later, Principal Orson had everything under control. Students went back to class; janitors scoured the blackened lockers. The long hallways became as quiet as the valleys of dead kings.

A rare man, a black high school principal, Orson now hurried back to the one conference that might save or lose him the job. It all depended on his powers of diplomacy with one woman teacher.

He was powerful, built like a wrestler. His feet were doormats; his hands made fists like boulders. But his wobbly gait was the awkward waddle of a tenant farmer in Alabama, and that was the real lie.

For he had grown up in Alabama, and his father, like his father before him, had been a tenant farmer, and the young Orson had hated it all. He had never walked that way; he had never talked that way. Orson had run out of the dreary South as soon as he was able; he had never looked back to that shabby cabin.

But in these days of black power and negritude, it would not be well for a black man to seem ashamed of his origins. Even the Superintendent had served him hog jowl and black-eyed peas, both of which he loathed. He had smiled like a tramp coming home, and furtively gagged. It was equally onerous for him to conform with the throwback ruralities of the new black mythology in the ghetto. He certainly did not think of himself as having "soul." He preferred Mozart to Otis

Redding; James Brown gave him heartburn. Orson's skin was very dark. But he hated Negro music; he hated Negro humor; he hated Negro shouts and gestures and jive slang. He hated the sexual accident which had made him a Negro.

And Beverly Minere, who taught Afro-American literature and sponsored the Black Student Union, knew. She was dangerous.

To the world, Orson was first of all a black man. To his wife, he was strangely successful, for a black man; to his superiors, he was strangely clever, for a black man; to his students, he was strangely confident, for a black man. But Orson was one thing, above all. He was cold.

And Beverly Minere was getting in the way.

"Sister," laughed Orson, as he ambled over to his desk, "looks like we got a fire on our hands."

Beverly laughed; it was a short, derisive snort. She could have said, "Your hands," but she knew she didn't need to. He knew what she thought of him.

Orson smiled broadly, with what he thought of as his watermelon smile.

"Thing is," he said pleasantly, "we got to burn whitey down without . . . getting scorched ourselves. We got to work together; and your militants have—"

"Not *my* militants." Her voice was a metal sliver. "Black young men who have minds of their own. Minds that haven't been muddled, or taken over, by the white man."

Orson still smiled. He would not give up.

His friendly mask hid well the contempt which he felt for this "girl." Beverly Minere was a twenty-eight-year-old black woman with a master's degree from Berkeley; she stared back at him with the surly frown of a recalcitrant teen-ager. She was tall and graceful, and she wore a sculptured natural with the freedom of a goddess; but she slouched in the cheap plastic chair opposite his desk, her proud shoulders collapsed in a pout.

She may talk of racial pride and the beauty of blackness,

thought Orson; *yes, she may talk of the Great Day Coming—but she looks now like a jive-time chambermaid on the carpet for stealing rhinestones.* His contempt almost escaped in a laugh.

"Okay, Beverly," he said calmly. "Okay. You don't trust me; I'm the white man's boy. Orson, the Uncle Tom to beat all Uncle Toms. I've sold out, okay?"

She did not relax. *He'll have to do better than that,* she thought. *Traitor to his race.* She resolved again that no student of hers would ever turn out this way. She'd kill them first, and good riddance.

"Maybe you'll get rid of me someday, maybe someday soon. But not yet." Her eyes had not left his; no part of her moved. "You aren't strong enough yet. And when you are, if it comes to that, I'll pick up my coat (which I keep right by the door)—"

Beverly Minere smiled in spite of herself.

"Right? Principals don't last long these days, and I'm not stupid or stubborn enough to fight the inevitable. Not even, if you are thinking so, for the Board of Education. I'm thinking of Number One first. So when you win, if that's the way you want to play it, I'll pick up my coat and walk out of William McAdoo High School." He paused, then ruined it. "And I hope I will have done my best as long as I am here."

Damn, thought Beverly. Why does he always have to drag in some bit of white middle-class morality? Doing my best, like some ofay Boy Scout oath.

"James," she said.

He opened his face, as if accepting a bribe.

"Cut the cute darkie grin, okay?"

He did. Not in surrender, not with embarrassment. Just because she made sense, and he knew it. Beverly listened to fools, but she was no fool herself.

Damned nigger woman, he thought. *Should have fucked her that night two months ago. All they ever wanted. A few good twists and hot groans, and even Beverly Minere, scholar and savant, would forget the revolution.* He looked at the rich breasts, slumped still in the centuries-old slave's attitude of defiance. She didn't have any trouble getting it, he was sure. And he was sure that she never got enough of it.

"Fire me," she said.

Orson sighed as he stood up. He walked to the window and looked out on the slummy street. Dope addicts, pushers, hustlers, pimps—his people out there, waiting in the open for the lunch break and the ripe pastures of his students. He felt again the heavy weight he often felt around his neck.

"Is that the way you want it, Beverly?"

"Fire me," she said. "Are you afraid to take the chance?"

Orson watched an old wino stagger into an unpainted fence beside a shack across the street. Vague memories stirred.

"Yes," he said simply. "I'm not strong enough, not yet. I've only been here two months. You've got three years on me, Beverly, and the students would blow up the school, with me in it. You know that."

"What do you care about the school?" she snorted. Her fist struck the side of her chair. "What do you care about anything but your own career? A pat on the head from Mister Charlie for being a good boy and keeping the dirty niggers in their places."

"I care," he said. "But you'll never see it."

"Right on!"

"I'll wait. I'll get stronger." He turned to look down at her. "And when I'm strong enough, I will fire you. When we're even."

Her laugh was bitter.

"Thanks, James. It's nice to get a straight answer from you. Why, you almost sound like a black man."

There was a belch from the intercom.

"Mr. Orson," said the shrill voice. "Mr. Orson, they're burning down the third-floor teachers' lounge! They've got—"

"They?" shouted Miss Minere. "Listen to that damned Mexican, will you? Who does she think 'they' is, and—"

"Quiet!" Orson took his priorities seriously. "No, not you, Marie. Just tell the vice-principals to handle it, you got that? No need for me to come running every time there's a little incident like this."

"But, sir, they say—"

"All right, Marie; I understand you. Just tell the vice-principals to handle it. Tell them that's what they're paid for around here." He switched her off angrily. He did not like the background music of Beverly's gay laughter.

"Too white to soil your big hands with the colored folks, honey?" Suddenly, she had become transformed into a woman who was alive and merry, almost abandoned. And attractive.

Orson snapped back at her. "You know that's not it."

"Go on." She delighted to find herself maddening to him. "Go on and say, 'You know who's behind all these things.' "

He looked at her. "Do you?"

Her cackles were drunken. "Why, sugar, that's just the way them little darkies are; don't know how to act. Ain't you heard? You give them a nice, fine school with nice, fine white teachers, and what do they do? Do they crawl around on their knees and give thanks to de Lawd? No! They mess it all up! Just don't know how to act, I reckon."

"This is serious, Beverly."

"Damn straight it is. This is revolution, brother, and you're on the wrong side. You better throw out your schoolbooks and learn your lessons from the real teach."

Orson was losing his aim.

"And what about Benedict? How far can you get without him?"

"Benedict! Man, you something else. Benedict wasn't the core of this thing. He was a front. He was a good speaker, and he brought in the women, but he was too much his own man to be a good leader for the people. He might have turned out like you." She laughed harshly. "And that's something else, believe me."

"So he was . . . counterrevolutionary." Orson fingered the cant as if it were rummage goods.

"If you like." She was standing now, thrilling to her own cold anger. "Will that be all, sir?"

The principal looked wearily down at his desk; memos lay there from a score of frightened teachers, not all of them white, by any means. He wished there could be a showdown. Right now. One stiff, furious fight, and the winner take all. But that would never happen. It would all go on and on, until one side weakened a little, and then there would be another two sides, and it would all go on and on again. He was very tired. He wanted to go home. But he didn't yet know where that was.

"Beverly," he said finally. "If Benedict Williams was so bad for the movement, you might have wanted him out of the way."

Even Beverly Minere, who expected the worst of this man, seemed shocked.

"You fool!" she hissed. "You big black goddamned fool." She walked deliberately over to Orson. "Benedict Williams was a man. A man!" Her last words could scarcely be heard. "Don't you know, boy, that Benedict and I were . . . lovers?"

She slapped him hard and walked slowly out of the room.

To Orson, in that moment, she seemed as proud and lonely as any empress in the dark continents of his past.

He flicked the intercom switch.

"Marie," he said, "is that detective still nosing around?"

She was obviously glad to hear his steady voice; hers was not. "I don't know, sir, but now the vice-prin—"

"Find him," said Orson. "Find him and bring him here."

He flicked her off and rubbed his cheek. It was stinging, tender, but it was alive. And Benedict Williams was not.

CHAPTER IV

OBADIAH Snatch actually did roll his eyes. Pimp of the old school, he was the tongue-clicking, foot-shuffling stereotype which turned Beverly Minere's stomach.

She had often told him so.

"Ye-as, sistuh, I ain't no Nat Turner, hee-hee, but I's livin'." She had been stunned to see him actually slap his knee. "I gets along, hee-hee." She had brushed him, like a gnat, from her mind.

Sergeant Gannett was less fastidious. No, he didn't like Snatch, nor did he respect him. But the detective was happy to do business with the old pimp that Wednesday morning; he was sure that each was helping the other when he slipped Obadiah Snatch the five-dollar bill. The old man fairly flew into a buck-and-wing.

Gannett laughed. "Hard times, Obadiah?"

"Yaa-aa-a-suh," whined Snatch. Skinny, stooped, he was to his friends and customers "that pointy-headed nigger from Darktown." He was a mummified relic of ancient Harlem—conked hair with lacquered glaze, dirty white bucks, black slacks and purple sateen shirt, White Owl cigars and Cooch Mountain red wine on his breath. Yet his miraculous voice had the range and color of a Wurlitzer: his tiny reeds wheedled from the boss-man, but his sharp brasses cut terrors through the hearts of his few enemies; he begged for mercy with a miserable croon that gave pleasure to cops who wanted to appear tough, but the lusty tom-toms of his seductive pitch

35

melted young girls' spines to molasses and surged warm trem-
ors through their fleshy parts. Obadiah was one of the last of a
dying breed. His passing would not be mourned by the new
generation. He was nearing retirement age in a profession
which had earned him no pension.

"That so?" The Barge smiled kindly, the concerned friend.
"Aren't your girls getting any business for you? Rain slow
them down?"

"Girls?" Snatch rolled his eyes, blinked the lids. "My girls?"
He stepped back and shot the detective an exaggerated frown.
"Why, Sergeant, some nigger been tellin' you I be a . . . pimp?
Old Obadiah? They be puttin' you on, yeeeees-suh. Why, man,
what I be pimpin' for, huh? You treats me right; my friends
treats me right; I got all I want in this wide world. Lawdy, I
do."

Gannett was laughing again; he enjoyed the performance.

"Okay, okay, Obadiah," he said. "I'll check my sources
next time."

"Don't have to do that," said Snatch seriously. "Just you
come and ask me. I won't lie to you, Sergeant; not even a little
fib. You can trust old Obadiah. Hell-fire and damnation! To
think some brother would tell you a story like that. Shows
you what kind of world we is a-livin' in, uh-huh. Can't believe
them niggers, no way, huh?" He winked.

The Barge winked happily back. And then he felt, for the
first time in his conscious life, that he had somehow been
tricked. He glared at the old huckster's face; it looked blank,
inane, mindless. The detective looked at the old man's garish
threads, remembered his own crisp button-down collar and
Brooks Brothers tie, and felt secure again. Everybody in his
proper sphere, and Gannett on top.

"Sure," he said. "You're straight, Obadiah."

"That's the truth," said Snatch. "I lay off the womens now.
'Sides, I be too old, Sergeant; them pretty little things don't
want nothing to do with a dried-up old piece like me." Snatch

winked conspiratorially, but this time the detective did not respond in kind. He could not say why.

"Five dollars isn't much," he began.

"Yeah," moaned the pimp. "I got my medicine to worry 'bout now, and all that doctoring. Life is hard on a old man, 'specially with bad people spreading lies and all. Five dollars ain't much; you ain't lying there."

"I've got more."

"Hee-hee! Ain't that rich? I bet you do; I bet you do."

Obadiah Snatch giggled, then his face grew strangely serious. "I swear, Sergeant, I swear I don't know how I'm going to get any more of that money. I swear I don't."

"We could talk a little," the detective said. He looked at the crowded street. They stood directly across from the high school; the swarm of hustlers flowed clear of them, but grouped in thick pools at the street corners. No one looked directly at Gannett, but they all knew him. The loud laughter and cursing from two run-down hamburger stands was more subdued than usual. Every cheap pimp, whore, hustler and pusher on the street knew Gannett, but they weren't worried today. They knew what he wanted.

"I do declare," said Snatch. "If I had a secret I be going to tell, I'd tell it right here on Fort Sumter Street, I swear I would." He waved to a young hustler who was shooting craps on the sidewalk; the boy ignored him. "Fact is, I don't know nothin' the man wants." He stared curiously at his lean feet. "If I did, Sergeant, I'd tell right here. Yeah, this be 'bout the best place I know for tellin' secrets." He grinned.

"I been recollectin' a mite this fine morning," said Obadiah. "And I be rememberin' my sweet Auntie Grace in Texas. Ever been to Dallas, Sergeant?"

Gannett grunted. He idly felt for his watch.

"Fine place. Nice and friendly." The sharp brown eyes flashed momentarily. "Old Auntie Grace be 'bout the baddest doo-mestic in that fine town. She say, 'Obadiah Snatch, you listen to me good and proper: ain't but one fool in this whole world, and that's a man what don't want to live.' And she say,

'No smart-ass nigger boy with him mouth too big gonna live past sundown.' Yeah, I think of old Auntie Grace this fine morning."

"Benedict?"

"No other."

"All right, Obadiah. Tell me plain. Who would want Benedict's mouth shut? And why?"

The old pimp looked honestly stunned. "Me? How'd I know that, Sergeant?" He lowered his voice to a husky whisper; he spoke in tones like sanded ebony. "I be assured, howsomever, that old Benedict he got some mean friends. You know? He talk big, gonna change things in this here ghet-to." Obadiah snickered. "Fancy talk all the time. I 'spect he made somebody awful mad."

"Stop playing, Snatch."

"Man, I ain't jivin'. This be for real."

"Who?"

"Do not know. Word of God. Do not know."

The Barge tediously unfolded the stained twenty as if running through an old parlor trick. He smoothed it out in the hazy sunlight; Snatch dutifully stared. The bill slipped back into the detective's walrus-leather wallet, a markdown in Bullock's College Shop. Snatch heaved a tubercular sigh.

"When you learn something, let me know," snapped the Barge. "I'll be around." He turned back toward William McAdoo High School.

"One thing," said Snatch. The detective stopped. The pimp teased out a grimy scarlet handkerchief and dabbed at saliva in the corners of his grin.

"Yes?"

"This here smog ain't fit for rats to breathe." He paused. "Makes a man choke up."

The detective frowned.

"Yeas-suh. Anyways, a strong dude with two lungs gonna choke on LA air, hee-hee."

"You'll live," answered Gannett, who thought Snatch was

building up a charity case. Five dollars had already been wasted; let the old shine live off his whores, and the voyeurs at his notorious motel.

"Right on! I'm not ready to die, Sergeant Gannett." Something hard lay under the old man's voice; something . . . cold. "I be hangin' on tight, and I got two hard-workin' lungs that ain't gonna sleep on me. No suh. But you take a young man like Benedict Williams now."

"Keep going, Snatch."

"Everybody know old Benedict he got only one breather."

"What?"

"Happen back in Alabama, 'bout the time old Miz' Parks sat herself down in the white folks' part of the bus. Young white doctor made him a little mistake. He be having a real nice party and they call him to the poor folks' ward on Saturday night. I swear, he do his best. Got to help one poor nigger boy breathe; one lung be better, praise God, then lyin' in a cold grave. Don't blame the doc, Sergeant; he do his best, I swear he did. That knife a-shakin' and all. Anyways, it be mostly Benedict's fault; be him that make his old Pa mad 'nough to cut him up the chest like that."

"So Benedict had only one lung. So what? He bled to death." But something said earlier that day gnawed at the backstairs of his brain.

"Yeah. Reckon as how you be right."

The Barge remembered other duties. I'll talk to you later," he said.

"No money for old Obadiah?" the pimp whined.

Gannett smiled as warmly as a Rotarian. "When you hear something helpful, I'll be eager to do business, Obadiah." His smile brightened. "You know all about business, don't you? And you know how bad business can get down at your motel when a police car parks down the block. That right?" He faded away into the idle traffic of the slum street, headed toward Orson's office. A Spanish type was waving frantically from the window there.

Obadiah Snatch watched him leave, then suddenly laughed out loud.

The pimp leaned back on his thin heels and looked up at the steamy morning. The white sun was stained brown by the dozing layer of smog. He smoothed down the greasy rivers of his dyed black · hair; a low-rider full of drinking teen-agers passed, and he heard an old song he could no longer dance to. Obadiah smiled and thought of the best things in life; he thought of the brief joy his young girls brought into a miserable world.

"Goddamn," he said. "That white man don't see his own shadow." He laughed again.

Obadiah Snatch shuffled down the cracked sidewalk that was his beat. He winked obsequiously at a couple of snazzy dudes who lounged against a mangled stop sign; they looked away. One beat out West Indian rhythms on his knee. Obadiah remembered his own youth back in Harlem, and was glad that he was old.

Small change tinkled like camel bells in his pocket, but he wasn't afraid. They might pretend to hate him, but they wouldn't roll him. He was needed.

He chose the rustiest dime for the telephone call.

With the familiar grin, he remembered a former conversation with Detective Sergeant Gannett: "Them Panthers be bad niggers, Sergeant! You watch out. Man who want to live long he stay away from them bloods."

The telephone stopped ringing; the receiver at the other end had been picked up. There was only silence. Chuzz Jackson, cleverest of the local Panthers, said nothing.

"Brother," said Obadiah, in a voice that was surprisingly clear and vibrant.

"Brother," answered Jackson. The black phone reflected the black of his leather jacket and the black lenses of his gold-rimmed shades.

"The man don't know nothin' 'bout Benedict."

"Hold on, brother. Keep it cool."

"Ain't nobody list—"

"Lay money on that? That funny clickin' noise you just heard ain't chitlins fryin', y'hear?" Chuzz Jackson, who had been raised in Los Angeles and missed no nuances in Marcuse, always wondered whether his down-home accent sounded fake. "Sounds to me like Charlie's boys got their wires on us again. Don't give 'em no peculiar ideas about our charitable establishment."

"Dig."

"No fish, no smells?"

"Uh-uh." Obadiah's answer was deliberate. "They nowhere, man."

"Yeah. So they'll be right here. Thanks. When the pigs got nothing, they come hustling us. We must be one passel of bad black boys, you reckon?"

Obadiah laughed.

"Listen, brother." Jackson's timbre made clear he was no longer playing. "You throw the man any little sardines, just to fatten him up? Ain't nothin' wrong with a brother gettin' a little scratch; times is hard. I'm just sittin' here wonderin' what you might know."

"Jus' what everybody know, brother." Obadiah Snatch, even dead serious, could not quite throw off the teasing come-on.

"And what might that be, old brother?" Jackson did not take offense so easily; his leather piece protected no thin skin.

"Old Bened . . . . our boy only got one lung."

"What?"

"Don't you know? That dude had himself carved up nice and proper, back on the farm. He only got one lung."

"Meaning?" Jackson well knew that Obadiah Snatch was no fool. It stretched his credence to follow the old man now.

Snatch collapsed in high titters. "Brother," he said, "you sounds just like old Gannett, I swear. Man, I ain't sharp in the head, you know? But I sits here and I'm thinkin', and I'm recollectin' what a tough boy that young man was, you know?

And I asks myself, just for askin', how come that bad dude was a sweet and lovely football player, and yet and still, he jus' lay back and let somebody kill him dead. I'm askin', and I swear I don't know no answer. And I'm rememberin' it takes a mighty long day to bleed out you life, and I'm rememberin' about that one lung. Funny things bound to happen in this old world."

"Yeah," breathed Jackson. "Right on."

He hung up, and then wondered what he had just heard.

After a moment, he gave it up. The realities would soon enough slap him awake; he would wait. Chuzz Jackson, alone in his bare office, turned to the secure effluvia of his neo-Marxist world. He found his place in the latest paperback collection of Castro's speeches. There's one brown brother, he thought, who is a real man. He floated into the long cadences of the translated rant.

Suddenly, a terrifying word transfixed his eye; implications stiffened his spine like lust.

"It's possible," he whispered. "Yes, it's possible. But who the fuck—?"

Chuzz Jackson threw down the book and grabbed the phone. He must check with his Minister of Defense.

CHAPTER V

"THE time is now, the day is here," shouted Scrounge Roberson to the crowded classroom. "The liberation of our oppressed people is assured and certain, dig? We will wipe out the racist imperialist pigs who have raped this great land."

The Black Student Union members applauded; this was worth skipping lunch.

But Beverly Minere winced. Her revolutionary sympathies were no stronger than her quick critical ear; Roberson's speeches always set her teeth on edge with his bizarre stylistic mishmash which could at once suggest Dr. King, Carmichael, Kennedy and Eisenhower. Not to mention the Bible. Still, this was the least of the problems brought on by Benedict's murder the night before. She clung to it because she was not ready to face the sick shock of full realization. He would never stand there, his regal body pulsing with the lush rhythms of negritude, and hammer out those splendid speeches which no man had made before him. He would never again dominate that dingy classroom. He would never again let fall his cool smile in her lap, or meet her eyes to ask if she was proud of him.

The revolution would go on. She would go on. And she would not forget. Beverly Minere sat at the front of the room, her head bowed toward Roberson, and regarded his enthusiastic audience with calm gravity. This was how Benedict had liked to see her. She would not let him down.

Roberson had dropped into a solemn baritone.

"Brothers and sisters," he said, "you've got soul. You know what's in my heart today." Silence smothered the angry young throats; eyes grew liquid. "Benedict Williams, our brother, is dead."

From outside, squeals of the lunch crowd fell awkwardly through the windows; it was lewd music of the foolish world, drunken, and moving out to sea.

"There are some," continued Roberson quietly, "who think a brother killed him."

"No!" came several angry shouts.

"There are some," said Roberson, undeterred, "who think he was the victim of factionalism. The divided movement. There are some, in high places, who think us niggers just can't get ourselves together."

"Fuckin' honky propaganda!" yelled a member of the defense squad guarding the door.

"Right on!" answered the crowd.

"Don't forget the Uncle Toms," a loud young woman intervened. "Some of whom . . . are not too far away, if you know what I mean." Her eyebrows arched; her voice had curdled.

"Orson, that sh—"

"Sisters, brothers," said the calmer Roberson. "Let's not get sidetracked; that's just what our enemies want."

"Right on!"

"One thing at a time—that's revolution. The Toms and the sellouts and the house niggers, why, we got plenty of time for them; we'll take care of business when the opportunity's right. First, we got one specific issue to settle, and we're going to settle it! We're going to settle it for Benedict!" He dropped from the high crest of emotional oratory to a choked rustle. "We're going to make those pigs give us the truth." He paused. "No more cover-ups. We make them an ultimatum."

"Yeah."

"They find the pig who murdered our brother . . . ." His sharp tears were not faked; Beverly Minere looked down.

"They find the pig who murdered our brother, and in twenty-four hours—or we gonna have ourselves a li'l fire."

The audience jumped to its feet. The applause was thrilling, to Roberson and Beverly Minere; or appalling, to Gannett's assistant listening from the next room; or simply loud and meaningless, to Emory Finch, who stood outside the locked door and waited for the lunch bell to ring.

He meant to see Beverly, though he suspected she probably hated him. In her scheme, he would be the white missionary, misguided purveyor of rotten exploitation.

Emory Finch had grown accustomed to being hated for his race; he rather enjoyed it. By a paradox typical of the involutions of his thinking, black hatred released him from the stomach cramps of his Anglo-Saxon Protestant guilt. If whites were to ridicule him as foolish, tedious, immoral or unsuccessful, it would seem a matter of personal inadequacy; the fault would be his. When blacks hated him, they were quite democratic about it; nothing personal was involved. It was not his fault; he could do nothing to improve. By indirection Finch could find some solace in the irreversibility of this universal distaste. As a child, he had dutifully believed that it was entirely unforgivable that he dropped dishes on the floor and missed short flies on the diamond.

When the bell rang, he instinctively stepped back from the door. He needn't have bothered. The members of the Black Student Union began chanting "Revolution Now." It took all of Roberson's persuasive powers to calm their ardor.

"Hold back," he said. "Don't play into whitey's hands. We'll show him we can stick to a deal, like lily-white gentlefolk, you see?"

"Aw, come on, Scrounge, we been waiting long enough."

"Yeah. We been waiting over four hundred years."

The spattering of cheers and giggles died out beneath Roberson's sober gaze.

"I'm hip," he said. "I'm hip. I've been waiting, too, ever since I got thrown, half-starved, off that slave ship. And ever since I was forced to stand by and watch the generations of my black women raped by the white pig."

"What we waitin' for, then?"

"Trust me, brothers and sisters. I was that close to our dead brother, Benedict. He would have wanted it this way. Trust me. We give Mister Charlie twenty-four hours, play by his rules. You go off to class, and take your white middle-class tests, and be real nice to your con-cerned white middle-class teachers while they re-late." There were friendly titters; Scrounge Roberson winked. Then his mood changed. "All right, now. Let us be young ladies and gentlemen, let us be black and proud, let us now walk out of here in a dignified manner and carry on the business of the day. Tomorrow, we'll see. May be another story."

Angry in their mourning, the band of young revolutionaries walked out into the mass of playful bodies that signals any high school's change of classes. Younger students deferred to them, gave them berth. In the ritual garb of green fatigues and black shades, they held the terror and majesty of wrinkled Inquisitors.

Roberson lingered, but not long, and when Beverly Minere looked up from her memories of another speaker, there stood Emory Finch.

"You free this period?" he asked.

She snorted. "Man, I ain't never been free. Don't you know that yet?" She sat down at her desk and shuffled papers. Let him squirm, she thought; this is my territory.

The tardy bell rang; the halls were strangely empty.

Finch closed her door; the two faced each other. "The children's hour is over," he said. "They've left it all in your lap." She looked away, annoyed.

"We have a dead brother to think about," said Beverly Minere.

"I'm an outsider," Finch said. She did not respond. "But I can guess what might happen tomorrow. I can guess that these students are angry and hurt enough to burn this school down."

"Well," laughed Beverly, "ain't you the clever one."

Finch walked over to a window; he gazed absently on the muddy quad. A sophomore he knew was carrying her baby home; it was the only thing in the world which gave her pride. She had brought it to school so her grandmother could walk to the grocery for relaxation. Now she would be late for fifth-period class.

"Beverly," he began, "I thin—"

"Your thoughts, white man, are irrelevant," she snapped. "And I'm not your mother's maid. We've never been introduced; I'm Miss Minere to you."

Emory glanced at the ancient windowsill. "Barbara McNair Power!" it shouted. He smiled in his pinched way. So much comedy, and so much tragedy at McAdoo High. And now there was danger.

"Miss Minere," he said, "you don't need any white man to tell you what to do. I suspect you don't need any man at all to tell you what to do."

She held back her first reaction. What exactly had he meant? She listened.

"You've got two strikes against you—you're black and you're a woman." He dabbled sallow fingers in his lusterless hair; it was a meaningless tic. "That makes me twice an enemy. All right, try it another way. I think we have the same aims."

Beverly Minere sighed deeply and leaned back to stare at the ceiling.

"I want what Benedict wanted. And so do you." She started. Ever so slightly. "I want his killer found; I want progress to come the way he wanted it."

"He was a brother," she said cautiously.

"He was my brother, too."

"What?" She fairly screeched. "Man, you something else. That's funny; that really is. What did he do, con you into thinking you're part black? That you've got soul somewhere beneath that pasty skin? Come on."

Finch answered very quietly. "No."

"Well, take it from me. Benedict Williams did not fawn upon any lackey of the system—"

"No, he did not."

"—and he knew who his real friends were. He knew he couldn't trust a white man. They come here, with their bleeding poor liberal hearts, ready to do good and sacrifice for the benighted black folks of the ghetto— Don't you think we know that? A nice little Peace Corps with a starting salary of seven hundred a month. That's really having your cake and eating it, too. Then they get 'frustrations' and see 'tensions building up' and decide they have to think of their families first."

"I don't have a family," said Emory Finch.

"You'll wind up in Pacific Palisades or in the Valley with all the rest. Until then, you can drive home to the beach and chug down a couple of Scotches. But this is my life, mister. I grew up here; I stay here; I'll die here. When the fighting starts, your skin puts you on one side, me on the other. And don't kid yourself; Benedict may have liked you; I don't know. But he knew, if you don't, that the showdown would come, and it would dig a no-man's-land between you."

"Maybe."

"Definitely."

The little man took off his glasses; he wiped the thick lenses. I never do anything right, he thought.

"Beverly," he said, "did you know that Benedict was sleeping with the head cheerleader?"

And then she knew that he knew. And she felt vaguely that he was dangerous. "Bastard," she breathed, and the jewels of her dark eyes sparkled with hatred and fear. "You sick little prying bastard. You knew . . . ."

"About you."

"Get out," said Beverly Minere. "Get out." She was suddenly too tired to say more. The anger had gone; the pride had grown stale in her fine mouth. She wanted to fly home and fall weeping on the pink chenille bedspread; she wanted to read LeRoi Jones and shout glories while Benedict Williams ran his knuckles down her smooth belly. She wanted to die.

"Get out," she said weakly. "Oh, please, get out."

"I'm very clumsy about things like this," responded Emory, who rarely understood emotions.

"Please. Just leave it."

"No. Hear me out. Just . . . be calm. Can I get you a glass of water?" Beverly stared drunkenly; he must be some kind of nut. She shook her head. He went blindly on. "The point is," he began, as if explaining a problem in grammar, "that you loved Benedict. In a different way, in my own way, so did I. Benedict had nature's gift, I suspect, of making a woman feel she was a woman—"

"Please shut up," whispered Beverly.

"—but he had another gift, and it's much more rare. He made a man become a man. Maybe . . . because he expected nothing less. And it worked. Benedict made me feel strong, and sure, and confident, and that, believe me, is a feat worthy of the gods. I was no longer afraid. I did not seem to wear glasses."

Miss Minere was confused. Why is he telling me all this? she wondered, and what is he telling me? He was certainly not the white man she had suspected.

"What do you want?" she asked.

"Will you help me?"

"I can't. I don't know what happened. Can't you see? I don't want to think about it."

For once, Emory Finch did see. "I have ideas," he said, "but I will need your help. You know things . . . about this place . . . that I don't. Will you help me? Will you help me find Benedict's murderer?"

"Later," she said.

"Later," he agreed. He left her in the lonely room.

He was not there when she stopped sobbing at her desk. He was not there when she stood up and brushed the wet stains from her face. He was not there to see the small bottle she took from her Ghanaian purse.

He would have been very much surprised.

CHAPTER VI

"**Y**OU-ALL have nothing to fear," said Miss Lee to her fifth-period history class. "If you did your work, this will be an easy test." Her students knew better.

"Yeah," groaned one. "The last easy test was so long I didn't finish reading the questions before the bell rang."

"Stop taking those little red pills, Paul, honey, and you just might be able to finish before the cows come home."

The class laughed; that Miss Lee was something else.

Paul pretended to scowl. "Lighten up on me, Miss Lee," he said. "Give me some slack."

"Gracious," she answered. "You've had enough slack for three morons, and it's a disgrace. Popping those pills and letting them eat up a good head like yours. Why, Paul, a boy with your—"

"Boy!" He grinned. "Boy?"

"My goodness." Miss Lee smiled. "I sure have one hard time learning to speak Californian." The class laughed again and she passed out the dittoed test papers.

"Ummmm!" said a fat girl. "These smell good."

"Don't trip out during class," returned Miss Lee. "These are fresh off the press and . . ." She stopped. They weren't that fresh. She had run them off the afternoon before—in Finch's room, because it was just across the hall. Miss Lee shuddered. There was something she did not want to remember.

The students became serious; they saw that the test was typically rigorous. Miss Lee was no slouch. She joked around,

50

but she never wasted a minute. She expected them to work harder, think deeper and learn faster than any class in the school; by and large, they did. Her pride in them leaked through her constant flippancy.

Miss Lee was white and Southern, but she was not hated. For one thing, she was raven-haired and twenty-three, and she groomed herself like an airline stewardess. Her dark eyes were large and seductive; her pink skin, smooth; her skirts, short. Her male students said she had "big legs," and she knew that was a compliment, whatever it meant.

The spring before, she had graduated in history from the University of Texas. She had gone there because all her girl-friends had, and because it was only twenty-five miles from the happy home she had never left before. She had been a good Baptist and believed in total immersion; she had not believed in smoking and drinking and mixed bathing, and she had thought marijuana was the stimulant of professional murderers. She had also believed that racism, like sex and other unfortunate realities, lay only in the imagination of very dirty-minded people, and would soon go away if no one ever thought of it.

Three months at William McAdoo High School had changed little Katie Lee a great deal. Even she did not yet know how much.

"This test be a bummer," whispered a young man in the back of the room.

"Yeah," answered his friend in the next desk, "but Miss Lee, she cool. I think she part black."

"You hush up!" hissed the first. "You want her to hear you? She won't like that."

"Both of you be quiet," said Miss Lee, who had very sharp ears. She sat at her desk and trudged through the intricacies of the standard Los Angeles City Schools roll book. Almost as if to herself, she went on, "My great-granny always said it was a Cherokee Indian, you know, but I don't rightly see how she could tell in the dark."

There were scattered giggles.

The door burst open; a cool young man strode into the room. "You Miss Lee?" he asked defiantly.

"My," she answered pleasantly, "can't we knock?"

"Look, teach," he began, but Paul angrily interrupted.

"You watch out," he said. "That's our teacher." "Yeah," agreed the back of the room.

"That how it is?" asked the newcomer.

"That's how it is," answered Paul.

"Keep cool, brother. I didn't mean nothing. I dig." He turned back to Miss Lee. "Sorry to lose my head," he said. "I've got this message for you."

She took the note and read it quickly; no rift in expression reflected the quickening of her pulse.

"Thank you," she said simply. "Please tell him I'll be right out." The young man left.

"Uh-huuuuuuh!" trilled a cheerful young lady in the front row. "Miss Lee got her a man!"

"You better believe it!" her teacher answered. "I got several. Now I know that you will sit right here and quietly take this test while I go outside a few minutes."

"Sure," said someone. "Specially 'cause you gonna leave the door open a crack and listen."

"You got it," said the teacher. "I got this business to take care of, and so do you." She winked at a grinning young girl. "Can't let this durned school interfere with my love life."

The class laughed happily as she went out, then dug into the test. They knew she was joking.

"Baby," said Chuzz Jackson, "I had to see you. Is it cool?"

"Right on," giggled Katie Lee, as pinpricks of fire teased her private places. She clutched her roll book to her breast and gazed serenely at the tight-muscled man before her. He leaned casually against the row of hall lockers, folded the leather-covered arms across his chest and winked at her through the smokescreen of his traditional black shades.

"Never seen anything like it," he said. "How do you get

away with it? Little white girl from Texas comes to the big
bad black city; mother predicts rape. Flash! She makes it in
the ghetto. Even with an accent that makes G. Harold Carswell
sound as if he can read and write." He lowered his voice to a
sensual purr. "Us black boys ain't supposed to think about
that white stuff; it be bad for us; give us sore necks." Chuzz
Jackson was not far from the sad fact of thirty, but he had, by
some trick of magic, kept a smile that was as guileless and
charming as the true laughter of children.

"Monster!" Miss Lee hissed. "But I just love you to death,
despite your dirty mouth."

"Sorry," answered Jackson. "It's my disadvantaged childhood rearing its ugly head."

"Besides," she went on, "I never noticed that any of these
(quote) racial considerations (unquote) kept your little black
thing at home."

"Miss Lee!" Chuzz almost screamed, mock-horror twisting
to his ears. "Honey, wash out you-all's mouth with some soap.
I declare, Los Angeles has corrr-rupted you, darlin'. You better
hie back home to Daddy's ranch. Hey, now! You been soci-
atin' with them uppity colored folks in the city? Tell Cousin
Jackson the truth now; you let one of them black boys see
you naked? Huh?"

Miss Lee laughed.

"State your business and leave, Mr. Jackson," she said. "Or
I'm going to throw in my roll book and run away with you.
Goodness, people sure would talk."

"You reckon?"

"I reckon." She paused. "Are you prowling around here
about Benedict's murder?"

"How did you guess?"

"Watch your tongue, smart-mouth. I can tell you this much:
nobody admits to knowing anything. The cops don't even
know how it was done, and nobody on campus wants to talk
about it. Strange, you know? Our daily bits of violence around
here usually keep my classes going full steam for a couple of

days—explanations, different versions, follow-ups. This time, nothing. No one understands it; no one wants to face it. Maybe it really didn't happen; maybe Benedict didn't really die."

"He's dead, all right. Obadiah Snatch walked right over and lifted the sheets this morning; it was Benedict, bloodier than we ever saw him."

Katie Lee smiled. "That's almost funny," she said. "Old Snatch. He makes his own rules." A small disturbance could be heard through the door to her classroom. "Uh-oh," she said. "Doesn't sound more serious than paperwads, but I better go back." She whispered. "Tonight?"

"Tonight. One other thing, Katie." The sound of her name on his lips was like exotic music; she knew the tune, but the instrument was like nothing she had ever heard in her life. Katie Lee knew she was doing a bad thing; she would have killed anyone who tried to stop her.

"What is it?" she nearly sang.

"What's the Bookworm up to?"

"Finch?"

"He's poking around, making strange noises about how the murder was done."

"Oh." She was interested. "And what has he found out?"

"That's just it, babe. Nothing. Nothing, exactly."

"I see." She turned toward her door. "He's harmless," she said slowly. She looked back at Chuzz Jackson, who still leaned against the wall. "Yes, I think he's harmless."

Jackson started. "What do you mean, harmless? Harmless to me? Baby, don't think I had anything to do with this. What put an idea like that in your pretty pink head?"

"Nothing." Miss Lee frowned, ever so slightly. "Still, it's kind of a lucky thing for both of us. Wouldn't be so cool for everybody to know a local Panther leader is shacking up with a honky chick, right?" Chuzz Jackson dropped his arms and stared. "Yes, Benedict knew, and he could have told Beverly-babe, who already hates my lily-white guts. I might add, it also

IT NEVER RAINS IN LOS ANGELES   55

wouldn't be too cool back in Texas if Mommy and Daddy found out about baby sister's little caper; they don't want grandchildren who look ready to shine shoes."

"Grandchildren?"

She laughed. "Don't turn purple; that's just a manner of speaking. Don't you worry; little Katie's been taking her pill."

"How did he know?"

"Benedict? Honey, you just ain't thinkin' straight today. He got it from Finch."

"The Bookworm?"

"The same. Those two traded secrets like kids with baseball cards, believe me. It must have something to do with Finch being the journalism teacher. Or with the more obvious fact that he has no personal life of his own, so he lives a bit of everyone else's. Psychology lesson for the day."

"Interesting."

"Anyway, if there's anything you want to know about William McAdoo High School, Finch knows it. After hours and during."

"Except the murderer's name."

Miss Lee showed no expression. "I have to get back to class," she said. "If I were you, I'd try to forget all this nasty talk of murders and stuff. We've got our own problems. I've been reading a book, all about how black men are forced by American society to think of white women as sexual ideals, doesn't matter who they are."

"Katie," Chuzz said huskily, "it's not like that between—"

"And white women grow up thinking black men are powerful rapists from the primeval jungle; fucking studs, as it were."

Chuzz said nothing.

"But it's cool," continued Miss Lee. "It's cool between us. All I'm saying is, we got other things to think about. Forget the murder. Finch doesn't know who did it; he won't find out. You and I, we've been playing behind the barn, and we've got to be careful."

Chuzz regarded her uneasily. She wasn't talking "up front."

Had she changed the subject as a diversionary tactic, or was it a tactic at all? He knew one thing; this sweet little thing was not so transparent as she pretended to be. And not slow on the uptake.

But he played along. Somehow, it was in the rules.

"Correction, ma'am, begging your pardon," he said. "You got to be careful. I'm just an irresponsible, fun-loving, banjo-twanging, childlike black boy; I just been dipping my wick, thanks to your charity."

"Think nothing of it," she said with mock condescension. *"Noblesse oblige.* One must fulfill one's debt to society, good fellow."

"Baby, you seem more interested in just fulfilling your little—" His obscene tease was suddenly drowned out by a burst of shrill hooting from the classroom; obviously, a student had committed an illegal, or unnatural, act.

"Uh-oh. Back to work." She smiled coyly, and let a hand flutter equivocally at her breast. "Thank the Lord, I am thus spared from whatever vulgar remark you were about to make." The hand dropped, but somehow graced against his thigh. "Back to the monsters," she said, in a different tone.

"Uh-huh. A real dedicated white liberal savior. Ain't we lucky?"

"You got no complaint." She couldn't suppress the giggle. "And . . . you won't have any tonight." Her wink was pure Tenderloin. "Besides," she said, now on a different tack, "they are monsters. I love them, but I know there's no truce between teacher and student. I ain't stupid."

No, he thought, that you aren't. And that could be good, or very risky. For somebody.

He watched her slip back into the classroom. For a moment, he listened to her voice on the other side of the door; it had become a sonorous instrument—firm, confident. The hilarity of the young mischief-makers subsided quickly to an aggrieved mumble. Miss Lee was coming down hard.

Chuzz Jackson, for a Panther, was more thinker than doer.

And he had many things to think about. Benedict's murder was an indication or a first step; the ultimate blows had yet to be dealt, and he foresaw a disintegration which was frightening to a man schooled in the orderly processes of revolution. This was something different, unmanageable.

Meanwhile, he was a bull elephant in another bull's territory. It was a matter of moments before word would leak to Orson. The principal, according to the code of their conflict, would be forced to call the police and have him removed.

He crept out toward the back exit, with a warm pat for the good friend in his shoulder holster.

CHAPTER VII

THE scream drove all thoughts of science from Finch's brain.

He was stunned. He had been meandering back toward his room, mulling over information gathered in the chemistry wing, when suddenly . . . The grave Finch chuckled. The scream had become the bellow of a wounded animal, and he thought he recognized the genus and species.

His first instincts were to pass on by, but he quickly changed his mind. This morning, he could use a little of the Marx Brothers, and he was sure the Barge would not disappoint him.

He opened his door to discover Gannett doubled over, sucking his thumb. This, at first glance, was startling. But no more startling than the grotesque device outside the window. It was contrived of old rope and wooden blocks and had obviously just collapsed, letting the frame fall on the detective's hand. Manning held the fragments up for inspection, and the weak grin on his face reeked of petty revenge.

"Can you bring yourself to clean that up?" Gannett shouted through the other window at his assistant. Fat lips skittered across his knuckes, as if kissing them back to life. He scowled. "Or would that be asking too much?"

"No sir," said Manning, and there was no expression to his pink Irish face.

Emory Finch fought back the silly grin that twitched at his lips. After a moment, he even succeeded in looking vaguely sympathetic.

"I don't think," he began.

"I know what you think, Finch," the Barge interrupted. "All right, so it didn't work. But a really clever murderer could have rigged up some device that would close the window behind him."

"Him?" teased the journalism teacher.

"Them, dammit!" The Barge began pacing the room. "I've read about such things. There was a famous case in Paris: the police were baffled. All it took was a long rope, a weight and a little hook of wire."

"No doubt," smiled Finch. "Still . . ."

"Still, you think the locked windows aren't important, and that's the craziest notion in this whole crazy case. If you'll forgive my saying so, Finch, you have the same hang-up as the pros in your business—reporters and TV men. You take the simple facts and blow them up. Distort them into fantastic stories. Good reading, but not the plain truth. The locked windows are the key to this case."

"In a way."

"And when we find out who—What did you say?"

"I agree, in a way. That is, it's not important to find out how someone could have gone through them. No one did—except, in a tragic way, Benedict."

"Christ," said Gannett.

Finch went blithely on. "But the fact of their being locked before Benedict came in, during the murder and after it, that fact stares us in the face."

Gannett was, in spite of himself, hooked. "You mean, they left through the door?"

"Hardly."

"Oh, I get it. A secret passageway. Well, come on, Finch, you've been holding out on us. Where is it?" Gannett comically tapped the chalkboard. "Do I look for a lever, a cleverly concealed button?"

Finch smiled pleasantly.

"The murderer, or murderers, if you like, were never in the room."

Gannett let his lower jaw fall. Then he slapped at his own ears, as if shaking out water. He grunted, and then laughed. And then laughed harder again.

"This some complicated intellectual joke?" he grinned, but with annoyance. He didn't like Finch's suggestions, or his manner, or his looks. He didn't like Finch. But he needed something, anything. He cursed his own sense of insecurity, which always made his spine turn to water in the presence of a college graduate.

"You're very patient with me, Sergeant," said a suddenly gentle Finch. In a rare moment of humanity, he had sensed the slower man's difficulty. "It's none of my business, and I'm not very clear. Further, I tend to be rather lacking in tact. I'm a bull in the china shop of other people's feelings."

He smirked at his little joke; the Barge was too stunned to answer. He shrugged limply.

"Still, certain things are obvious to the untrained mind. One, no human being entered or left this room between the moment Benedict locked the door behind him and that awful moment when the morning janitor discovered the body. Two, only one murderer was necessary, although there may have been a conspiracy. Three, the medical examination of the body ought to show something peculiar about Benedict's lungs. Four—"

"As for your third point," interrupted Gannett, who felt he must find a point of one-upmanship quickly. "We don't have to wait for the doctor." He smiled, laying his top card on the table. "Benedict had only one lung." He heaved a fat sigh of triumph. So everybody knew, did they, Snatch?

"Of course," answered Finch. "And that in itself is a clue, or at least an indication. After all, it's something that everybody knew about."

The Barge coughed.

"So that, as we all knew from the beginning, was his

Achilles heel. He was too clever for ambush, too strong for prudent men to risk a struggle. Finally, even when one considers his dignity and pride, it is too clear that, if he saw death bearing down on him, even Benedict Williams would have screamed."

"And how do you know he didn't?"

"I don't."

Gannett beamed. "Well, we do. We checked that. No one was around. Even the little Neversmith girl was clear down at the other end of the hall. And don't forget it was still raining."

Finch found this a tantalizing remark. "Strange," he said, "I always thought one became more sensitive to sound during a gentle rain." He was talking to himself. "You sit back, and listen for other voices, and you see the long dull years ahead of you, one by one, falling to the ground." Gannett looked bored. "In any case, it doesn't matter."

"But you said—"

"I said Benedict might have screamed for help. It doesn't matter whether he did or not; what would matter to the murderer is that he might have. And it would be too great a risk. The ghetto, Sergeant, often reminds me of my Fulbright year in India . . . ."

God-almighty! thought Gannett. *Does the little wimp really have brains? Recognized and sanctified by Act of Congress yet? Well, it just goes to show . . . all that education, and he winds up teaching in a fifth-rate school. Jesus.*

"You can never be alone. You walk in the forest, and there is a beggar's family sleeping under every bush. The streets are teeming, swarming, even in the middle of the night. In a way, McAdoo is like that; someone is always around, talking, or throwing dice, or just walking aimlessly. A murderer would know that, and think of it. He would plan a murder no one could hear through the cracks of this old building."

Gannett was scratching the tweed of his coat. "That's great, Finch; that's just great." As always, something in the teacher's nonsensical rambling held his attention, but he would not admit it. "You've given us a murder without a murderer."

"Exactly." Finch seemed pleased. "I knew you would see it."

But it was an undeserved A. The Barge almost choked. He crawled out on a limb. "How's that?"

"Add them together: Benedict's weakness, the one lung that made athletics pure torture for him; the locked room, where a murder took place without a murderer; the presupposition of silence, or, at the least, a brief struggle."

Gannett said nothing. He wrinkled his forehead. He had a headache.

Finch seemed reflective. "Even the broken window, when you look at it the right way, fits perfectly." He frowned. What was wrong with him? Why was he babbling on with such obvious pleasure in working out a logical solution to a misinterpreted problem? As if the problem were abstract. As if the problem were not the death of another human being, and that human being, a precious one. *Have I really been starved, and thus dried up of emotion,* wondered Finch, *or have I purposely abstained? I am a monster,* he thought; *a cold and toothless freak.* "And, then, Sergeant, you found the clue that pulled everything together." He smiled. Did he sound complimentary or simply offensive? Better explain quickly, before the detective dropped his jaw again. "No prints on the ditto machine. Of course, you couldn't know this, and I was too scatterbrained to tell you, but there should have been fingerprints. Lots of them. That machine is used all day, every day. It's the only one that works in this whole wing; it's the only one without parts missing."

Gannett was in a daze. His comments were automatic.

"A janitor?"

Finch laughed. "You don't know McAdoo. Getting a janitor to clean a room here takes a combination of nerve, influence and luck. It's easier to get an audience with the Pope. Besides, that's the business of the night shift, according to the faculty handbook, and they don't start work until eight."

For once, the Barge was with him, even sounded excited. "If that's true . . . ."

"Believe me, it is."

"Then the ditto machine was wiped clean for a reason." He suddenly foundered. "But what reason? How can—"

"It's possible, Sergeant; it's possible." Now Finch grew excited. "I wasn't sure until I checked with some of the chemistry teachers, but it's highly possible. Let me show you . . . ." He remembered the obvious. "Of course. You've taken it away. Damn! I hope no one has touched it."

Gannett had his feelings hurt. "We know our business, Finch. It hasn't been touched."

"Of course, of course."

"And what do you think we'll find on it?"

"Well, there are several possible methods, although I—"

"Sergeant!" shouted the breathless Manning, running into the room. Gannett wheeled savagely; it was the posture of a mad bull. The patrolman held a dying cigarette in his left hand.

"Put out the fag, Manning! What's got into you?"

His subordinate was not cowed. His news was too great; he was too pleased with himself.

"Look what we uncovered!" he said, still shouting. "Read this!" He handed the detective a dittoed sheet of paper; the ink was fresh and smelled of hospital. Faintly ether, and fresher than the smoggy afternoon outside.

"Uncovered?" grumbled Gannett. "There must be a thousand of these out on the streets by now."

"Yeah," responded Manning, who was not deflated by this observation. "But we're not supposed to see them. Read it."

Gannett did. It was a short announcement. Violent, and to the point. "Brothers," it began, and ended in suspicion and hate. He handed it over to Finch.

"They don't waste time," the Barge said grimly.

"We got to do something," interjected Manning.

"Manning," the patient superior said quietly. "I'm proud of

you." The patrolman smiled sheepishly. "Want to know how you can really help and . . . uh, benefit society?" Manning nodded. "Calm down. Calm yourself way down, and then walk right outside and try to guard the door." Manning looked disappointed, but the Barge knew how to cheer him up. "Remember," he continued, "you'll just try to look like a simple-minded policeman standing dumbly on duty. But we'll know better, won't we?" Manning seemed confused, wary. "We'll know that you're really posted out there to listen for . . . uh, clues. Yes, you just pretend you've got nothing better to do than stand there. But you'll really be on the lookout; see what you can pick up in the wind." He sighed.

Manning almost grinned; he walked proudly toward the door.

"Oh . . . uh, Manning?"

"Yessir?"

The Barge smiled. "Don't bust in again, okay? We . . . uh, don't want anyone to suspect you're sniffing around. Just you remember everything you hear, and we'll talk about it later."

"Right, Sarge." Gannett looked toward the ceiling, but Manning did not notice. He was fairly goose-stepping out.

"Where do we get them?" mumbled the Barge, but Finch was thinking of other things.

"Benedict wouldn't have let this happen," he was saying softly. "Even if Beverly . . ." He stopped. The remembrance of something she had said rippled cold through his veins.

"It won't happen," snapped the detective. "The tactical squad we got in LA is the best in the country. And these blacks know it. Just talk. Straight out of the rural tradition of gospel preaching." He was proud of himself.

"No," said a sober Finch. "They mean it."

"So what?" bellowed the Barge. "We can control them. We've got the means. If they want a showdown, we're ready for them. Not," he interrupted himself, "not that we want it that way."

"No, Sergeant? How do you want it?"

"Don't turn sob sister on me, Finch." The teacher shrugged. "You're too smart to believe all that police brutality crap." Finch made no response. "We're trying. We're really trying, and no one appreciates that."

"Lack of communication," Finch said idly.

"That's damned right. Here we are, trying to solve this killing of theirs, and they want to pull a fool stunt like this." He grabbed the dittoed paper off Finch's desk and ripped it in two.

"Theirs? Killing of theirs?" Finch shook his head sadly. "No. It belongs to all of us."

"We're all to blame," Gannett echoed snidely.

"We are." Finch took off his eyeglasses, hating them. "The weight of it will snap our proud spine, Sergeant."

"Let them try it tomorrow. We'll knock it down. And it's their own houses that burn first."

"They are strangers to those houses. They never owned them; they never chose them. They have nothing; they will destroy the something owned by someone else, and in that way, they will get something."

"There are laws," said Gannett, then almost bit off his tongue for falling into that trap.

"Yes," smiled Finch, who would not take an unfair advantage. "And one of them is, You can't kill a man until you kill him."

He's crazy, thought the detective. Smart, but crazy.

"Sergeant, it doesn't have to happen. At least, not tomorrow; not here. Their conditions are clear, although rather poorly expressed." He wondered whether Beverly never corrected the English of these inflammatory missives; she was a brilliant writer herself. Or would she consider formal English a condescension of the fabled white middle-class morality? "Find the killer by noon tomorrow, and they call the whole thing off."

"Sure," Gannett laughed. "That sounds fair enough."

"It can't be too difficult," said Finch. "How many people

would have the skill? More important, how many people would have access to the Theldhron?"

"The what?" shrilled the Barge.

"Theldhron. Theldhron 12." The teacher seemed puzzled by something. "At least, that seems to be the only one that would fit the symptoms. Here."

Finch took an old copy of the *New Republic* from a desk drawer and passed it to a surprised detective. A short article had been circled in red.

"Christ," breathed Gannett, as he read the article.

"I remembered it this morning, so I looked up this copy in the school library. I read it months ago, and thought of it as just another interesting fact. And yet it didn't seem real. At least, it seemed very far away from my little life."

"Jesus Christ."

"Yes," mused Emory Finch. "The miracles of modern science." Suddenly, he trembled. He threw his thick-lensed glasses against the wall; the plastic bridge snapped.

Gannett stared.

CHAPTER VIII

Principal Orson was a loner, a grave and secret man; he was no joiner. But he was a member of a select threesome that met every afternoon at 5:37 on the Hollywood Freeway.

Every day, foul weather or fair, their three cars choked to a halt behind the great bottleneck which fed the trim suburbs of the San Fernando Valley. The jam always lasted at least six minutes, often fifteen—sometimes more. Yet the pale frantic drivers who flanked him every day remained alert, nervous, eager for the bare inches that might open up at any moment. It amused Orson to suppose that his fellow travelers, already set on edge by the noise and the exhaust fumes and the delay, were all the more distressed to find a black man, like an omen of the fearful times, wedged in their own nest. They strained forward, seething at the cars ahead, drumming tense fingers against the dash; cool, calm, smiling, Orson leaned back, patient, and beat them to the next interchange every time. He was pleased to see this little game as an allegory of his life.

On his right, in a tough blue Mustang, something like a saleswoman frowned. She was less than forty, but too softly dressed to be in business, too nicely dressed to be a schoolteacher. Her lacquered red hair made a stupid face look mean. Maybe she was an accountant.

Orson smiled at her, as he always did, nodded and said, with a bemused shrug:

"Yes, I'm still here, you sloppy bitch."

She looked away, unwilling to admit he was there. Her windows were rolled tightly shut, her air-conditioning hummed full blast. Automatically, she checked the lock button on her door. She was too annoyed to try to read his lips.

Orson leaned back and let himself laugh.

The woman searched the wall of traffic for a possible break. If she nodded, it was not at Orson. It would be because someone on her radio, George Putnam or Paul Harvey or Garner Ted Armstrong, someone far away and on tape, had said that America was going to the dogs. She knew what that meant.

The man to Orson's left drove a low-priced Chevrolet, sensible as an English spinster's shoes. He was fifty, but not dead yet; loud silk ties complemented the dark conservative suits he wore. If he did not sell insurance, thought Orson, then nothing is sure in this world.

Orson made ghastly faces at this man, but the object of these attentions stared straight ahead. It was a remarkable gift. The black principal could have lit Molotov cocktails or rolled down his window and bayed lewd songs at the sinking sun, but the salesman would have continued to stare straight ahead. This man knew how to avoid trouble. Yet Orson knew that the white man was well aware of that Negro next to him; perhaps he varied his schedule a little each day, but still wound up, trapped by the inexorable new decade, with the same little clique at 5:37 on the Hollywood Freeway.

One thing was clear to Orson. That white man wondered why a well-dressed black man drove a Mercedes five years old, and not a Cadillac. And he wondered if that same black man owned a larger house than his in the San Fernando Valley.

But these interesting questions would never be asked. Distrust or worse, like another element in the dirty fumes around them, eddied up between the inert autos and left each driver in his own oubliette.

And that was fine with Orson.

He had no apologies for what he was, no doubts about what

he'd done. In a vague way, he could understand the idealism of his missionary white teacher, although he found it foolish; he even had a tenuous feel of the lacerated wounds that tortured Beverly and her young militants. But he had been born a century ago in a little town down South that knew lynching was not rhetoric, where rape was no metaphor. He had grown a hard shell over the vital parts of his soul; that's why he was alive.

That's why he was sitting on a hand-tufted leather seat headed for a comfortable brick house on the other side of the Hollywood Hills.

They can shout; they can posture, he thought with satisfaction. Let them. I know where the power lies.

No Great Day was coming. That had been his first lesson, and he was one hell of a fast learner.

Education meant nothing in itself; it had simply been the road out of the South, the ticket to the front seat in the bus. Racism did not gnaw at his belly. What was the love of a white, or of any man, to a boy who had clawed his way out of the smelly dungarees a society had pasted to his back? Even this job was a way station. He wouldn't fail; he never had before. He would be rewarded with higher pay, a better position, perhaps the presidency of a junior college. The title didn't matter. Just the progression. The moving upward. And he would never trip, because he had learned long ago exactly where he stood. If anything he had ever done was evil, it was also necessary. To his thinking, he was a wiser man than any who would follow Beverly's oratory. He would last.

An eager swell surged through the dispirited traffic, interrupting these thoughts. Roused cars nudged forward; headlights began to flick on, as if the vehicles had actually been awakened from slumber. Orson and his two companions rolled slowly ahead until suddenly, with a burst of enthusiasm, they were able to hit twenty per.

The relief was short-lived. Orson was surprised to see a young highway patrolman, on foot, waving him over to the side.

More of this Benedict business, he sighed. One of the "special problems" of his district.

With the quick reflexes of a man used to bouncing back from the mat, he slipped in behind the woman in the Mustang and wheeled into the breakdown lane. He just caught her triumphant, although slight, grin through her rearview mirror, as if she knew he was getting what he deserved.

"What is it, officer?" he asked politely.

"Sorry to bother you, mister. But I thought you might help." He pointed ahead, inarticulate, recently twenty-one.

For once, there seemed a definite reason for the freeway tie-up. In the outside lane, a few yards on, a rusty Buick of the forties had breathed its last. It had been smashed from behind. Even through the insistent cawing of a hundred car horns, Orson could hear the moans of a dying man. An old black woman, dressed in a flimsy print now hideously rent, stumbled crazily through a puddle of oil and blood; the purple ooze stuck to her white patent sandals and congealed in the snowy carpet of broken glass on the pavement. She sobbed as softly as a starving child. Habit. Without hope. A dark fluid bubbled at her battered lips.

Orson knew why he, the well-dressed Negro, had been stopped, but he liked his little joke.

"Do those people know me, officer?" he asked blandly.

The young patrolman tried to remain patient.

"No, of course not. But I thought you might be willing, as a private citizen, to help. It's easier, sometimes, if they can talk to—"

Orson helped him. "One of their own kind?"

"Look, mister, if you don't want to, just—"

"Glad to, officer, glad to," the principal beamed. "All part of my job, in a way." He was back in his role, and he was an expert. "I'm principal down at McAdoo High, you see, and you boys help me out a lot; you really do. We're all after the same thing, after all's said and done, and we need to—"

The patrolman, relieved, walked beside this charming man

with renewed confidence. In a short-fused world, he had evidently done the right thing. He didn't even notice the flickers of disgust in the older man's eyes.

It was six o'clock and Finch sat alone in his bachelor apartment, a single room with a view of an Italian family.

He wept soundlessly as he pulled the tinsel cover from a TV dinner. It was an automatic response. The flimsy tray, which came boxed in scenes of gay revelry and contented home life, was a symbol to him of the gray loneliness of his own life. He looked at the pale substances, gluey around the edges and pasty within. He reached out his hand, gently, to caress the knee of the woman who was not there.

He wiped his lusterless eyes with a fragment of paper toweling, and began licking at the scientifically planned pulp. His apartment produced no noise; television or radio would have been too concrete an admission of the emptiness he felt. Scrapes and bumps beckoned from the scores of cheap apartments around him; he heard giggles, and angry shouts, and he thought he was hearing the sounds of life. A young girl screamed with heady pleasure as her lover spun off in his revved-up Mustang, dappling the night air with the hiss of frying gravel.

Finch looked down at his bony white hands; he observed sadly an undernourished mole. I am hardly made in God's own image, he sighed. The plastic peas lumped in his throat.

The small apartment was furnished in Early Motel; a mottled gray mass carpeted the whole.

But the jumble of Finch's books made the place unmistakably his. Paperback, hardcover, lurid and faded and dusty, they bulged out from the wall bookshelves and made heaps in the corners. They were the only personal objects in the modern cubicle, the only decoration.

"My goodness!" his Irish landlady had once exclaimed. "You read all them books?"

Finch had smiled miserably. Of course he had; what else had he ever done? They were his life, his adventures. He looked at them now, and each of them reminded him of his private pleasures in reading: a quiet afternoon on a bench in the park, a steamy train in India, a telephone call in the midst of Chapter Three, an unexpectedly gentle smile from a salesgirl in the paperback store.

He finished the meal. He had dawdled as long as he could, but the little feast had inexorably, pitilessly dwindled, and finally disappeared. And now he was faced with the crisis of filling the cold empty hours between now and midnight. Usually, there were papers to grade, but Gannett had sabotaged that; none of Finch's classes had been held all day. He could visit friends, and be pitied by their wives; he could go to the movies, and buy his single ticket with embarrassment, and sit in the dark theater hoping no one would recognize him. Not that anyone ever did.

Strange. So much violence at school in one day, so much anger and sorrow. And now, after a short drive on the Harbor Freeway, nothing. His life was blank again. It was as if he had never taught at McAdoo, and no one there had ever known him. It was all unreal and could vanish in the instant. He was not a part of it, he was not needed; that whole world could die as suddenly as . . . Benedict Williams.

Emory Finch stiffened. You fool, he thought; at last, you can do something. Benedict was young, but he was a man, and he treated you as if you, too, were a man. Become a human being, fool; stop feeling sorry for yourself.

He was ripping a favorite paperback in two when the phone rang.

"Mr. Emory Finch?" queried the instrument. Its chameleon voice had become smooth, round and ingratiating.

"Yes," replied Finch, who did not like the voice. He asked it what it wanted; the voice turned creamier than ever and oozed into his ear. Finch felt he was being molested.

"You have nothing to worry about," crooned the voice. "We know how to respect a confidence."

"This is a mistake," snapped Finch. "I don't need a loan."

The voice fell over itself in lewd chuckles. "How nice to talk with someone so witty," it said. "I suppose that's necessary for a job as tough as yours."

"Who are you?" asked Finch.

"Oh, didn't I say?" The voice seemed sincerely apologetic. And then businesslike. "Steidman. Herm Steidman." Finch said nothing. "Your local newspaper." It apparently liked to be cute.

"Oh."

"Detective Sergeant Gannett, who works in your area, kept us away today. So I'm having to do my legwork . . . you might call it, by telephone." Finch waited. "Now, please understand that you won't be getting involved, in any way."

Involved? thought the teacher. He choked back a laugh. He certainly didn't want to get involved.

"A friend of mine downtown procured a list of the McAdoo faculty members, and I thought the journalism teacher might know the facts more clearly than most."

Sure, thought Finch. *And why didn't you really come down today and find out for yourself? Because you were afraid of getting your head blown off. Because every black man, woman and nursing child knew in his bones that you would listen, and smile sympathetically, and then rush off before the afternoon deadline to write lies that would please your eighteenth-century publishers. And just what do you want from me?*

"You people do a fine job in a difficult situation," continued Steidman. "And my paper's behind you all the way."

Yeah. And what about editorial policy on the proposed school budget? The enlightened view that placed new civic centers far ahead of school construction?

So you can trust us to print the real story. Don't worry; we protect our sources. Now, a few questions about the ghetto atmosphere. Do you feel threatened? Do you think other white teachers feel threatened by this latest violence? Be honest; I know how to put these feelings in perspective. After all, we can only expect teachers to be human. Do you feel threatened now more than ever?"

Finch heard a sharp noise behind him. He looked around; a short, squat black man eased shut the door and leveled a pistol at him.

"Our readers want the truth," Steidman coaxed.

Finch smiled. "Excuse me," he said to the phone. "There's a man leveling a pistol at me." The man frowned.

"What? Oh, I get you. Look, I told you, we protect—"

Finch hung up. He had better things to do.

His visitor smiled. "Man, you are really cold." He laughed. "You're something else." He seemed friendly; his pistol did not. Over tight black bell-bottoms, he wore a long yellow-and-vermilion dashiki. An ugly wooden lump hung on the leather cord about his thick neck. His skin was light; his trimmed beard, Oriental. But the most startling feature of this mysterious arrival was his round head; it had been shaved completely bald.

"Can I offer you a drink? Some palm wine?"

The man laughed again. "Not bad for a degenerate white imperialist," he said pleasantly.

"And poor white honky mother fucker," added Finch.

"You're being redundant." The little man reached for the doorknob.

"Do I know you?" asked Finch.

"I'm not important," the man answered. "I stay out of the light. I do errands."

"Yes," mused Emory Finch. "And I'm curious to know just exactly what kind."

"No doubt." The visitor bowed slightly, although his bright eyes never left the teacher's face. He almost chanted. "All will be revealed." He straightened. "Come."

Finch glanced at the shiny weapon. "And I thought it was going to be a dull evening."

"Come on."

"Are you going to hit me over the head?" For some reason, he wanted to be hit over the head. It would give some meaning to his life. He had never even been slapped in the face.

"Hardly." The man smiled. "We need your head in good condition. Sugawee," he said dramatically, "Sugawee wants to talk to you."

"Sugawee?" Finch was incredulous. "He's always in hiding. That is, seclusion." He didn't want to be offensive.

"Not tonight, brother."

The little man opened the door quietly. Finch walked out and led him, with the uncertain meander of leaders who are really following, to a glossy black limousine. It was empty. And so was the street around.

"Back or front?" asked Finch ludicrously. "I don't know the routine."

"Back," answered his companion.

He watched the journalism teacher open the door. He smiled sadly. It was all in the game.

He hit Finch hard in the back of the head.

CHAPTER IX

MISS Lee, ecstatic, fell back on her crushed pillow.
"My, my," she sighed. "I sure do like Los Angeles." She
tried to catch her breath. "I sure do like social revolution."

Her exhausted lover was less inclined to talk. Chuzz Jackson
had closed his eyes.

"Hey, boy," she giggled. "You ain't gonna crash on me, are
you?"

He gently took her right hand and moved it to his mouth.
Lazily, he bit a finger.

"Ouch," she said happily. She wrinkled her tiny nose obscenely. "Somebody around here sure sweats a heap," she said.

"Listen to the Virgin Spring," mumbled Chuzz.

Miss Lee laughed. "You better remember your place," she
said.

Chuzz tickled a nearby thigh. "I'm remembering yours."

"God," she said. "It's fun to talk dirty." In high school,
Katie Lee had been titillated to talk baby talk in the back seat
at the drive-in. She had grown up. Now it gave her sensual
pleasure to dip down into ghetto slang, or into East-Texas
farm dialect. Chuzz went along.

"Ain't no white boy ever stoke you up like that," he said.

"Ain't no white boy ever tried," she replied. "They all knew
Daddy."

"Woo-wee! Them cowboys must be real men." He laughed.

"You hush up! They respect their women down South."
Then she laughed. "Sure is boring for the women."

76

"So I see."

Miss Lee took an ebony ear and pinched it.

"Ouch."

"Those boys, you wouldn't believe. Why they turn red in the face if you admit you have to go to the ladies' room."

"Fine. I'll remember that. Next time in Texas I won't say I'm going to the ladies' room."

"Honey," she drawled obscenely, "in Texas you'll cause trouble just going to the men's room." She grabbed for his smooth shoulders and they wrestled into a loggy embrace. Katie Lee was happy. "Chuzz Jackson without his shades," she sang. "I like that."

"You like it," he said, "because you know they're the last thing I take off."

"You ain't wrong," she agreed. Suddenly, she found herself hugging him desperately. Tears welled in her belly. Chuzz was startled, and touched.

"Chick? You all right?"

"Chuzz?"

"Yeah, babe?"

"It's not just a race thing, is it? I mean, between us. You don't think we're just acting out some kind of silly rebellion, or something? I don't want to believe that."

"Baby, where do you get ideas like that?"

"Now that, Chuzz Jackson, is one hell of a silly question."

"Yeah."

"Ideas like that, they're all around us. What else would anybody think? They're not going to let us have any kind of life together, Chuzz. I'm not strong enough; I shouldn't have to be." She took his head in her hands and pulled his eyes up to hers; they lay as close as nature would allow. "You know that, don't you? You knew that all the time."

"I live in the present, Katie. I might be shot in the streets tomorrow."

"Don't say it."

"You know it's true. You might be there one day, teaching

your honky history to the little brothers and sisters, and you'll hear it. Just another campus rumor. And you'll tell them to shut up and get back to work. You'll have better things to talk about."

"That's the role."

"Ain't nothing more important than the role. Mine, or yours."

"We could live until then."

"That's what I mean."

"No. I mean, we could forget Daddy. We could come out in the open. We could have a son."

"Baby, your Daddy is just one little problem. He's yours. I got my own. You forgetting? How're you gonna look at a meeting of the Panthers? It may get cold in Texas, but that ain't nothing next to the bloods and their chicks when a honky girl comes on board. You're the enemy; you know that. First lesson, curriculum of the Los Angeles ghetto. They'll freeze your balls off."

"Then I'm safe. I don't have that infirmity."

"Yeah, thank God for—infirmity, huh? Wait a minute."

"Besides, you won't be the first brother with a white chick on his chain. That's a big status symbol; everybody knows that, too. I'll be proof of your big black virility."

"Yeah, sure, sometimes it's like that. But you don't want to string along on that ride, do you?"

"No." She was very quiet.

"Right on. That's just smearing your face in the dirt. That ain't gonna happen to you, babe. I'm your lover, not your sexy black serviceman. And, by the way, you're my lover, or you better be, not my badge of honor."

"Thanks, Chuzz. Thank you for being so decent that . . . I want to cry." And she did.

"Lawd Gahd!" he said. "Ain't them white women something else? Just sweet-talk 'em a little, uh-huh, and they be ready to die for you." He kissed the tips of her mussed hair. "Or maybe even cook for you."

"You bastard!" she screamed happily. "I'll fix you. I'm going to get up and cook you the finest, richest white man's food you ever ate." She made a face. "I hope it gives you acid indigestion."

"No chitlins? What kind of place is this? I'm starvin' for soul food."

"Chitlins? You big fake. You never had them in your life. I bet you don't even know what they look like." She stood up and looked down at her naked lover. His dark body lay across the pale-green sheets which matched the painted stucco walls of her Beverly Hills apartment. Hills of Beverly, the nacreous dream of a little girl reading fan mags in an East Texas beauty parlor. An expensive address, but not that expensive. Some enterprising developer had built long rows of cramped little cottage apartments for all the young immigrants bent on Beulah Land. And they were never empty, not with that address; the rent was always paid, for their tenants could not afford to do otherwise. Beverly had her backside, too.

She listened . . .

She listened to the melodious twitter of Hollywood fags passing down the tree-lined lane outside. *Strange,* she thought, *and I thought I was coming out to California to meet movie stars. I did much better than that.*

"Music?" she asked.

"Just you walk naked," he said huskily. "That's music enough for me." She smiled with delight and slapped his buttocks.

"More, more," he pleaded. "Harder, Miz Lee. You the mistress now."

"Mistress? I wonder. That can mean a kind of master. Or a kind of slave."

"Don't you worry about that. Just get your pretty self over to the woodstove and fix me up a passel of hot victuals. I need me some motor fuel. I been working hard."

"Goodness," she said. "You ain't half-finished your job. I

just better do that. I'll cook something to charge up your weary batteries."

And she would have, if the phone had not rung at that moment. "Damn," the lovers said together. "Leave it," said the tenor. "Can't," rejoined his soprano. "Might be one of my students. Forgot a page number." "I'll bet."

"Miz Lee?" came the mechanical sneer. Katie shivered. At current prices, she thought, this phone could include a hate filter.

"Hello, Beverly," she sighed. Chuzz jumped.

The harsh voice at the other end became warm and sticky, like margarine left on a sunny table. "I'm terribly sorry to bother you at home like this. I know you don't like to take school problems home to Beverly Hills." Katie winced. "But I have to speak to lover-boy."

"Why . . . who do—"

The voice lashed out. "Tell Chuzz to put on his shades, miss. He's had his fun. We need him back where he belongs." Beverly was enjoying herself. "Or, uh, shall I send the Defense Squad over there to make things more convenient?"

"Hold on, honey," said Katie Lee in her sweetest tones. "You just hold your horses, now." She turned to an angry Chuzz. "It's the Queen of the Nile," she said. "Must be looking for a eunuch."

"Cool it, babe," he answered tersely. "I didn't tell her."

"Yeah, I know," said Miss Lee. "Looks like somebody got to Benedict too late to do us any good. Here."

Chuzz took the receiver, puzzled now on two counts.

"You ain't playin' fair, black woman." He tried to sound friendly. "Don't you know you don't interrupt a man at his work?"

"Well, don't we sound cute? You trying to sweeten me up? Isn't your juicy little white piece satisfying enough for you, honey?"

"Cut the shit, bitch."

Beverly Minere laughed. "That's better. That's a black man talking."

"You call just to give me lessons in blackness? Forget it. I don't need conversion."

"Don't I know it. Look brother, get me straight. I don't care about you or your honky-licking prick. That clear?"

"Sure."

"But this is something big. I have a feeling, brother, that you're going to need all the help you're going to get. You're going to be glad your brothers and sisters stick together. You see, the pigs are on to something."

"What are you talking about?"

"Murder, man. Murder. They been talking to one clever white man."

"Finch?"

"The same. And they figured out how it was done. Smart. Just a little pinch of something called nerve gas."

"Nerve gas?"

"Nerve gas?" She laughed again. "Uh-huh."

"God damn."

"Yeah."

"Hey, now, wait a minute. What's that to me?"

"Maybe nothing. Maybe something. I don't know." She paused. "But I've been thinking, boy, and I remember how you and your woman came by my room yesterday afternoon."

"At different times."

"At different times. Right on. And I didn't notice anything funny until today."

"Go on. Tell me about it. I'm all ears."

"I bet you are, honey. Well, it's like this. After lunch today I felt a little . . . tired. So I opened my purse to get one of my joy capsules, you know? And the funniest thing — two of those big mothers were missing. I know they were. I can count real good."

"So what?"

"That's what I'm wondering. You just think about it a while, honey, and then you might just come up with something."

"Tell you what . . . I don't see what they have to do with anything, but I didn't pop those things." Miss Lee looked at him, suddenly worried. "What?" she mouthed, but he waved off the query. "Everybody knows you take them."

"Yeah," said Beverly Minere. "Real convenient, that. I just want to make one thing clear, Jackson, in case anyone's playing games—you, or anyone you . . . know. I'm not having the finger put on me. Let's get that clear right now. I ain't taking the rap for nobody, as they say in Texas. You all start playing fancy, and some fine and fancy people gonna get they throats slit."

She hung up.

"Chuzz, what is it?" Katie knelt by him and held his arm. "What's going on?"

"I don't know," he said. His head hurt. He looked at her with feelings he had never had before. She tried to smile, but she was too worried. He watched the struggle.

"I don't know," he said again.

CHAPTER X

EMORY Finch woke to the smell of jasmine incense in a velvet-draped room. He lay on zebra-hide cushions. An ancient wooden fertility god loomed over him on the wall above; a candle burned where its penis should have been.

"Ooooooh," said Finch.

"Of course," agreed the solicitous Sugawee. "You know, friend, that I am most avariciously sorry for that unfortunate ambush. It is," he sighed deeply, "one of the precipitous adumbrations of our pendulous condition."

I'm injured for life, thought Finch. *I don't even understand English any more.*

He spoke slowly. "I'm trying not to say it."

"What?"

"Where am I?"

Sugawee roared. "Great Spirit of the Night," he chuckled, "Ulabenzi was preeminently correct in his judgments."

"Ula . . ."

"My trusted messenger. He said that you were, in the dialect of this colonial people, one cool dude."

"Yeah. Same to him." He remembered. "Ouch. You won't believe this. But it really does hurt to laugh."

"I am in sympathetic accordance, friend. These are the indubitable consequences of violence in an immoral, guilt-ridden, dying society."

"How nice," Finch mumbled inanely, "to find someone who understands."

Sugawee's bulk had overpowered a huge golden stool, a massive item, delicately carved, with muscular golden elephants that symbolically held up the world. It was the ancient seat of West African kings, and yet it seemed molded, like the room itself, to fit no one but Sugawee.

This was the headquarters of BAM, the secret organization known as Back to Africa, Mothers. But Finch felt as if he were in a shrine somewhere between the religions of the Far and Middle East. By the light of the one coughing candle (a so-called strobe candle purchased at a hippie store), he caught glimpses, or hallucinations, of flaked gold and hanging crystals. A dark smog of incense smoke curled about the room and made ominous apparitions against the slow flashes on the ceiling.

"No music?" asked Finch.

Sugawee smiled. He had a few hours in the night to play. It was all the time in the world.

Finch drew his weak resources together. Maybe it was, after all, a very straightforward and sensible office with fluorescent lighting and potted palms in the corner. Without his glasses, it was hard to tell.

He sat up and tried to shake the cobwebs from his brain. He felt showers of sparks as his nerve endings short-circuited. Amused, horrified, he watched bright green spots race through the puzzling maze of black and white zebra stripes.

"I suppose," he said finally, "I know something you want to know."

"You know something I want to know." It was a response as low and tuneless as a ritual litany. Sugawee let his head loll, like an old man after a boring dinner. He was thirty-four.

Finch giggled. "I know one thing you do know." He felt slightly drunk. He tried to send down warnings to his loosened tongue, but the tongue rebelled unconscionably. "It's your deep, dark secret."

Sugawee's right eyebrow quivered slightly; his needle-sharp eyes were closed.

"You aren't bald." Finch laughed out loud; he slapped his knee.

His strange host blinked; the bright eyes pierced the incense haze.

"I mean, you aren't naturally bald. You just shaved your head because . . ."

"Because it gives identity to the movement," rumbled the bass chords.

"Oh, no. Because . . . because your grandparents were both . . . uh, white imperialists . . . and, by some perverse law of nature, you've got a genetically assimilated head. And everybody knows that you can't have a Back-to-Africa leader with naturally straight hair. That would cut the rug out from under, as it were." Finch arched his neck back and fairly whinnied. "Like, you can't have a Back-to-Africa leader named Cato Murphy."

Cato Murphy blinked again. "You know a lot," he said evenly.

"Too much?" Finch asked hopefully.

"Could be."

"Goddamn, this is fun." The little journalism teacher turned happily toward Sugawee. "I like this game."

"Do you?"

"So far."

"You'll love the next hand." The great folds of flesh around Sugawee's mouth twitched convulsively, as if a small insect were trying to get out. "Beats grading papers."

"Yeah. Matter of fact, Sugawee, or, uh, Great Chief. Which do you prefer?"

"Sugawee will do fine," Murphy answered wryly.

"Sugawee, I should be grateful for this little adventure. It was beginning to look like a boring evening. Can't stand many more of those."

"Indubitably, then, you will feel obligated to repay this debt by mesmerizing your humble host with some tantalizing tale of urban life."

"Gannett's not on your tail, if that's what you mean."

The fat man spoke with extreme slowness, as if tiptoeing in the dark. "Should he be?"

"Who knows?"

"Consider me, friend, just another curious bystander."

"Curious, all right." Finch smiled shyly; he liked puns. "I also consider," he continued, "the charisma of Benedict Williams. And I consider that he scorned you and your pseudo-African cult, and I consider the difficulties of recruiting young brothers and sisters to the cause when a natural leader like Benedict told them to stay clear."

Sugawee nodded. "He was incurably belligerent. His was nevertheless the colonial mind, processed by long years of oppression and cultural disintegration."

"In addition, his grandmother makes fifty dollars a week sweeping up at the Crocadillo Club, and he couldn't help noticing that you drive a shiny black Cadillac."

Sugawee shrugged. "Black is beautiful," he said.

"In further addition, he couldn't help wondering just how so many dead young bodies began washing up in the streets, all wearing Panther jackets."

"Lie!" shouted Sugawee. His voice tromboned, forceful as any shock wave, but his body had scarcely moved. His eyes burned hotly. "Lie of the white imperialist press. All black men are brothers; we do not kill each other. They want to divide us asunder; we will not be splayed."

"If not your warriors, then—"

Did Sugawee wink? Perhaps it was a trick of the mystic lighting. In any case, his voice calmed suddenly. "However," he said, "uh, constructive strife need not be dysfunctional to, ah, the movement." He smiled. "The Panthers are fascistic, and consequently reactionary. They stand for black hoods, not for blackhood. Understand? From time to time, down the long annals of struggles to make men free, some must fall."

"And some must push?"

"Mr. Finch, I am first and foremost a black man. Naturally,

I regret the demise, even when functionally necessary, of a brother and comrade. Life is hard, as the jungle has taught us." He coughed. "And may I interject that I also regret, even at the risk of extreme discourtesy, the loss of valuable time."

"Dig."

"Ah, Mr. Finch, if this were another time and another place, yea, my ancestral home in the village of my lost past, then we could chat idly of manly things. Alas, it is not to be."

"You want to know what I know about the investigation."

"I want to know how it was done. Irrevocably, I am concerned about certain implications."

"There's no need for secrets, Sugawee. All you had to do was ask. Gannett's so pleased that he's given the story to the world; you can read it all in your morning newspaper."

Sugawee's voice resembled a low hum. It droned, "Let's just say, I don't like surprises." The muscles of his face relaxed so completely that huge slabs of fat seemed on the point of dropping off. "Besides, my subscription has been canceled; I forgot to give them a change of address."

"I'll make it short and simple."

"I am obsessed with gratitude. Here," he said, as he passed Emory Finch a basket carved from bleached elephant tusk. "Eat, and be filled."

"Fried grasshoppers?"

"Please," answered the pained voice. "You must learn, the great civilizations of Africa flourished when your Anglo-Saxon forebears ran naked through the forests of England and tried to frighten Caesar's legions by painting themselves blue."

"Celts, I think."

"Nonetheless, these are exquisite fruits, steeped in lovely sauces whose secrets were found in the vaults of man's first moments of awakening." He took one himself and warmly caressed it in the large cave of his mouth.

"Thanks," said Finch. The exotic taste was undeniably exhilarating. "Shall I?"

"Inexorably," answered the wise Sugawee, and Finch took that as a signal to begin and get done with it.

"No one beat Benedict to death; no second or third parties pushed him through the window." A furry eyebrow, like a fat caterpillar, was roused. "He was alone in that room, from first to last."

"Black men don't succumb to suicide. That's a weakness of the white man's dying civilization."

"Maybe. In any case, Benedict didn't commit suicide. But he did kill himself."

Sugawee heaved a billowing sigh. "It is no longer time to play," he said. "We drift into the dead hours of the night, when things must be done."

"Nobody's playing, Sugawee. Benedict found that out. Somebody very clever, somebody who knew a lot or read a lot, devised a little scheme. It took little more than logic, and left little evidence; therefore, it only took a little logic to discover it. That's irony for you."

"Go on."

"Someone read the *New Republic,* or an anti-US speech written for the 'third world,' or a congressional report, or a journal of chemical developments. Someone learned about a useful substance known as Theldhron 12."

If Finch had expected some upheaval in the mound seated before him, he was disappointed. Not even a twitch.

"Okay. Have it your way," he continued. "You never heard of it. It's nerve gas. Nerve gas so concentrated that a capful might contaminate a small city. A capful," he said meaningfully, "or a capsule full." Still no response from the fleshy heap. "It has the usual effects—choking, vomiting, uncontrolled weeping. But there's a special bonus. In every experiment, volunteers have instantly gone mad and tried to kill themselves."

One eye flared, then was extinguished.

"Tantalizing," commented Finch, but did not explain himself. "A philosopher might suppose that some higher center of the brain is affected, an area that controls the instinct for survival, the will to live. More likely, the gas is so excruciatingly painful to the lungs and abdominal area that death seems the only way out."

"Black people love life," chanted Sugawee.

"In this instance, the observation seems irrelevant," answered Finch. "On the other hand, the broken window can be taken either way—a jagged edge to bleed on, or an escape to the open air. We'll never know. There was not enough time."

"Smart, Finch. If you're right, but . . ."

"But how was it done? We didn't know until late this afternoon. If Gannett could keep a secret, I still wouldn't know. First of all, a medical report confirmed the first suspicion; there were signs of violent deterioration in Benedict's one lung and—"

"One lung? Yeah, I forgot that."

"Yeah? Well, the murderer didn't; it helped things along."

"Of course."

"Of course. After the report, Gannett was willing to listen to reason."

"Yours, you mean. Finch, you're dangerous to somebody."

The teacher ignored him. "So he agreed, as if he were giving blood to the Viet Cong, to check over the ditto machine." Again, his interlocutor looked sound asleep. "As you can guess, he found something. You might even guess what it was."

"No," came the unruffled reply.

"A faint trace, actually no more than a smudge, of gelatin." He no longer waited for his effects to sink in; Sugawee had won on that score. "The kind used to make the little capsules we all depend on nowadays."

There was a scented pause, and Finch began to fear that he sniffed more than jasmine in the heavy air.

"It has been many years," moaned Sugawee, "since it has been my lot to operate a ditto machine. Perhaps, if you will be so kind, you will enlighten me as to its construction."

"Simple."

"Have mercy, O white man; don't rub it in."

"Sorry." Finch cleared his throat; he was lost without a chalkboard. His awkward hands built strange geometries as he explained. "A ditto machine, as the name might imply, does not use ink; at least, not in the usual sense of the term. Impressions are made by means of a clear fluid; this stuff soaks down into a felt brushlike affair, smears the paper and prepares it to receive the message."

Sugawee snorted. "As it were."

"As it were. Now, the container for the fluid might be a plastic case (a rectangular solid) or a metal cylinder; our machine had the latter. In either case, you upend the container when the machine is, as they say, not in use; otherwise, the fluid seeps out the little nozzle and . . . ."

"Yes?"

"Well," Finch laughed. "I never have known why you're supposed to do that; maybe it gets the felt thing too wet." He shrugged. "I'm not, so to speak, mechanically inclined . . . all I know is that the head of the English department screams when you . . . ." He stopped; he seemed to be retracing the path of some stray memory.

Sugawee did not notice; his voice slightly trembled. "You mean, of course, that someone could plant a capsule in the upended container. Then Benedict, when he turned it over, would splash fluid down into the nozzle. The gelatin would dissolve, the nerve gas would dissipate, and that was that." His smile was open admiration. "Finch," he said, "you were disingenuously clever to discover that." He stood up. "I wonder," he said slowly, "how much else you've—"

"Listen," interrupted the excited Finch. "That tells us almost exactly when—for the love of . . . Now why did it take me so long to see it? That's it! Why am I so slow?"

"I beg your pardon?" Sugawee's great weight slid noiselessly off into the black velvet draperies of a far corner.

"Didn't I tell you? The container. You're supposed to turn it over when you finish with the machine."

"So you said," answered the muffled voice.

"But I never do."

"What?" The voice was cold.

"I never turn it over." He chuckled apologetically. "I mean, I always forget. Otherwise, the head of the department would never have cause to scream, would he?"

"And that means . . ."

"And that means," Finch frowned, "that the capsule was placed in the machine between four o'clock, when I left the room, and, at the latest, four twenty-five, if Montana Neversmith's memory can be depended upon."

"And that means . . ."

"I don't know. I suppose Gannett could . . . ." Finch suddenly came out of himself and looked up. The *soi-disant* chief of enslaved tribes had disappeared. The draperies moved, like shadows made by clouds across the full moon, and he saw a silvery-blue glint. The sight was becoming as familiar as a faithful dog.

"Is that in character?" Finch asked. He waved idly at the exotic room. "I would expect a spear."

Sugawee smiled.

CHAPTER XI

SUGAWEE flowed back into full view. His flesh rolled and billowed; the pistol was steady.

"You are one cold white man," he said, without irony.

"Maybe," said Finch, who still squatted on the zebra cushions, "maybe I don't have much to live for. And maybe my death wouldn't mean much to anyone else, either way." For once, he did not feel sorry for himself; he seemed to be talking about someone else. But he heard loud knockings in his breast. "And maybe," he smiled wanly, "I'm good at faking."

"We'll see."

Finch shuddered. "Torture? Uh-uh. I'll tell anything. I don't faint at the sight of blood, unless it's my own, and I wouldn't harm a fly. But physical pain? Uh-uh. Come at me with something sharp or burning, and I'll turn in my own mother."

"Maybe." Sugawee standing was an ominous bulk. Finch thought of Wordsworth's terrifying mountain and almost giggled. "And maybe you're stalling, as I'm supposed to say, for time." Sugawee let his tiny left hand flutter out from beneath the huge dashiki; it held something. In the other hand, the pistol remained steady. "Nonetheless, you need not worry about excruciating tribulations; it will be simpler. We are going to play a little game. The stakes are simple, and immutable. Life, or death."

"Can we have a practice run?" There was no mistaking the tremor in Finch's facetiousness.

"It is, no doubt, most unfortunate for you, but that will not

92

be possible. One hand only." Sugawee almost moaned, as was
his wont; again, he seemed to doze, although his right hand
held firm. "Let me wish you, with unbounded cordiality and
implicit goodwill, the best."

Finch started as the three stiff pieces of paper scattered
down into his lap. His host's left hand vanished into the
recesses of the violent African print; Sugawee appeared on the
point of snoring. The little teacher took his cue and held the
pictures under the weak light of the dying candle.

"Oh, God," he said.

Sugawee did not move.

"Oh, God, God," said Finch. "You sick, sadistic bastard.
You deserve to die."

Finch lunged, but the great form, with a quick chop, shoved
him back down on the floor.

"I'm going to be sick," said Finch. The three pictures had
fallen beside him on the floor. The one he had seen lay face
up; he would never have the stomach to look at the other two.

"Good." Sugawee smiled. The shiny pistol disappeared and
Sugawee sat down again on his elephant stool. "Congratulations," he said. "You win. Let me wish you a long and happy
life, Emory Finch." He gazed calmly at what had once been a
brightly foiled sale-special TV dinner. "Ulabenzi can clean that
up."

His great foot kicked at something. Ulabenzi materialized
silently and did as he was told.

And while he did, Finch huddled away from the picture he
would never forget. No one moved it. Its ugly colors writhed
with the sputtering of the candle.

"Recognize him?" asked Sugawee quietly.

Finch nodded. It had seemed years, or just an instant, but
Ulabenzi was gone. The floor was only slightly stained; the
smell of jasmine was only slightly fouled.

"One of the Panthers," Finch muttered. "Smoky or something."

"Close enough," agreed Sugawee.

"But why?"

"Law of the jungle," snapped the lazy chief. "Kill, or be killed. Some must die, and some must die horribly. His like are traitors, endemic to the false movements of our colonized peoples." He sighed. "It could have been me, or one of my followers."

"Yeah," said Finch. "But it wasn't."

He made himself look at the photograph again. He would learn to bear it.

Smoky's young brown body, or what was left of it, hung from a steel hook in the ceiling of this very room. Finch looked up; a faint scar marked the black plaster surface. He closed his eyes involuntarily. When he opened them, the picture remained.

He tried to steady himself by placing, in characteristic fashion, the photograph in historical perspective. Yes, he thought, it's like those photos smuggled out of Algiers — French soldiers grinning, mutilated Arabs strung up like prize marlin on a line. Yes, yes, these things happen in the world.

Smoky's dead body was skillfully lighted; it shone in burnished copper against the inky drapes. Of course, decided Finch, those drapes are more than decor for all this mumbo jumbo; it I were to scream . . . Muffled in the cold belly of this angry city.

"Did he . . . talk?" asked Finch.

"Talk?" Sugawee seemed amused. "He knew nothing we did not already know." He paused. "On the other hand, he did . . . well, scream things. I found that highly unpleasant. He stopped after a while."

Finch nodded stupidly, automatically. Where Smoky's mouth had been, the picture showed a gaping black wound, hanging flesh, burned and sliced; lower, much lower, yawned another chilling wound. Bits of flesh, diced, minced — slender rivulets of blood and urine frozen by the fast shutter of the camera. The chest, which had once been human, was now a soggy mat of crimson and deep-brown, crisscrossed with the stripes made by sharp leather or slender wires.

"The color," said Finch bravely, "is rather good."

"Polaroid," said Sugawee. "Amazingly simple to operate; even a child could do it."

"I hope," Finch smiled, "you didn't let a child take it."

"No," frowned Sugawee. "I am not without morals."

"Thank God."

"Would you not like to see the side view? Or the back?"

"You're too kind. But I won't impose."

"Pity. The rear view is extremely interesting. An ancient African practice, enshrined in the annals of our race." He smiled at the pun. "Made modern, in a curious example of cross-cultural fertilization. Coke bottles. Fitting, you know, since the kola nut, on which the secret soda formulas are based, was brought over by East African slaves. Yes, a coke bottle does very well; slides easily into the—"

"For God's sake, Sugawee. Shut up."

"Strange," mused the bald man. "The white imperialist can look without terror or pity on the emasculation of a whole race, and yet . . ."

"Okay, okay." Finch suddenly remembered an important point. "By the way, I gather I just passed some kind of test."

"You did."

"You needed proof that I was . . . squeamish?"

"Hardly." Sugawee laughed.

"Well, then?"

"Simple, if I may quote your previous remark."

"Feel free."

"Difficult, since I have not been free in your country for over four hundred years. But that is another matter."

"I wonder."

"Your reaction proved, unless you are a very clever and daring actor, that you didn't know about those pictures."

"You can take that for granted."

"Now. But not before." Sugawee shifted his mass forward; his eyes drilled into Finch. "Fundamentally, of course, you could never have seen those little works of art, but if you knew about Smoky and so forth . . . ."

"You have a way with words," said Finch.

"Please. I'm quite serious. If you had known about that, you would be an enemy. Your every gesture, every expression, would have been the penultimate lie. As it is, you didn't know. I can trust you."

"It might be unwise of me to point this out, Sugawee, but I can't control myself."

"Yes?"

"Well, now I do know. I mean, doesn't that put me in the position you were trying to find out whether I was in?" Finch shook his head. "Did that make sense?"

"After a fashion." Sugawee bore down on the teacher. "But you can do nothing. The Panthers, irretrievably, already know; the minions of the state will be powerless. The pictures will not leave this room. Nonetheless, I am content. You were not deceiving me. You did not know."

"Your reasoning, Sugawee, eludes my constricted Western mind. Is this the barrier between cultures that you talk about? It must be."

"Perhaps. It is the blindness of the cultivated eye."

"Nice. I like that."

"Please." Sugawee was evidently used to praise. "In the jungle, a man makes himself known for what he is. The tests are simple. If he runs from the wounded leopard that threatens his family, he is a coward. If he swears falsely, the gods strike him dead."

Finch, with some amusement, watched closely for signs that the leader was putting him on. He found none.

"But your poisonous civilization obscures these simple rules; it devises hiding places for the unclean man. One dark act can be hidden beneath a thousand layers of subterfuge and artifice. Now here we are, Emory Finch, you and I, two men alone at midnight—"

Finch wanted to interject something about henchmen in the wings, but Sugawee waved him silent.

"—with but one object: to judge one another as men before we give over our trust, one to the other. You have passed. I brought you here so that I might learn the truth, as you know it, of that poor child Benedict's death. If you are a man who lies, you are of no use to me. That you have seen those pictures tonight means nothing. Know, or not know; it is of no moment to me. What matters is that you saw them, and did not hide your disgust, or an unfortunate wave of contempt for your humble host. That was not politic. But it was honest, and that is a thing of great consequence. Yes, now I know you will not deceive me. You may keep silent, but you will not lie." Sugawee beamed with pleasure in his own reasoning. "Is that too simple, my friend, this ancient tribal thinking?"

"Or is it, instead, a simpler Western trick? You show me your motive for murdering Benedict . . ." Dark eyes flashed, but Finch went on, ". . . and therefore, since you showed your hand, I'm to think you had nothing to do with it. Right?" There was a monumental shrug from the great heap across from him. "Benedict knew, didn't he?"

"Benedict, to use the name fortuitously slapped on him by his white masters, knew."

"And that was reason enough to kill him."

"It was."

"It might be naïve of me, but I can't resist the next question."

"Go ahead, friend." The voice had changed color again.

"Did you?"

Both men jumped as the door burst open. Sugawee, with the instincts of a mongoose, flicked out his pistol; hot flashlights stabbed at him and at the hapless Finch.

"Drop it, Sugawee," ordered the familiar voice.

The black man, whose face had briefly reflected a secret alarm, relaxed when he caught a swift movement of Finch's. His pistol clattered to the floor; he faced a bright sheaf of glittering weapons. The pictures had slipped into the journalism teacher's coat pocket.

"So. This is the new hiding place."

"Shouldn't someone say, 'Aha!' or something?" asked Sugawee.

"Good God, Gannett, am I glad to see you." Finch smiled. The detective did not notice any irony.

"Just in time, I'll bet," he replied with self-assured briskness. His four men, in response to an old-fashioned gesture, rushed upon the unarmed Sugawee, pushed him against the velvet drapes and tackled the awesome task of frisking his huge person. Their victim submitted with dignified hauteur; he had become placid and silent.

"You see what happens, Finch, when you start playing around. This is no picnic, but I guess you learned." The Barge was helping the teacher, who had a sudden attack of hysterical giggles, to his feet.

"Gannett, won't you ever say something unpredictable?" The detective didn't understand, but he was obviously hurt. "Forget it. Ask me if I'm all right."

"You all right?"

"Never better. And, if you won't take offense, I just thought of something that—"

"Sorry, Finch; we don't need it." He turned to his men. "Find anything?" They hadn't.

"What do you mean?"

"While you were playing cloak-and-dagger games with our African friend here, we arrested the murderer."

"What?" Finch suppressed a violent urge to kick the grinning Gannett in the mouth. "How could you possibly . . . ?"

"Police work, Finch. Good solid police work." The Barge beamed like a kindly scoutmaster. "Don't take it so hard. You helped us a lot; you really did." Finch cringed; Sugawee smiled sympathetically. "But we know how to operate these things. You read the *New Republic,* but you haven't been watching your local newspaper."

"Meaning?"

A patrolman spoke up. "It was in all the papers two weeks—"

"All right, Manning, all right." Gannett was annoyed. "What do you want, a medal?" Manning did not answer. "Here," continued the detective, "read this." Finch did.

FREIGHT THEFT
ARMY WORRIED

> Yeggs broke into a local military supply depot and made off with an undisclosed amount of ammunition and advanced weaponry last night, according to informed sources.
> Army spokesmen expressed concern but vehemently denied as false and "alarmist" the rumors that the stolen items included cannisters of a new, experimental nerve gas.

"So?" said Finch.

"So tonight we found the stuff in the basement of the Black Panther headquarters downtown," answered the Barge proudly.

"All of it?"

"All of it," said Gannett, "except for one little cannister which nobody knew anything about. And that, I guess, just about wraps it up. There'll be no demonstration tomorrow. Coming with us, Finch?"

"Wait a minute. Who did you arrest?"

"Oh, didn't I say? Jackson. Chuzz Jackson." He broke off. Sugawee's loud laugh made him strangely uncomfortable.

"And Sugawee?" Finch could not think clearly.

"This bird?"

"They've got nothing on me, friend. They weren't even trying hard." The black man's voice rumbled with hate. "Don't you see? They didn't even bring one of their Toms with them tonight." It was true; all of the policemen were white. "I might put the finger on someone. No, this is just time-honored harassment, friend. Sugawee will have to go underground again, and it gets a little more difficult each time. That's how they get their fun." The Barge smiled coolly. "Let them. Let them jive around until the dawn breaks, friend. Be on the mountaintop, then, and you will see them swept away like so many maggots and turds."

"You got nice friends, Finch," said Gannett. "You coming or not?"

"Sure," mumbled Finch. "I'll be right with you."

"Come on," said the Barge, and his men filed out dutifully in front of him. "Some other time, Sugawee."

Sugawee nodded.

And then he looked deeply worried as the little journalism teacher turned to leave with the detective.

"Aren't you . . . forgetting something?" he asked. He knew that Finch must still have the pictures. Gannett paused in the doorway.

"Am I?" replied Finch. The detective stared at him suspiciously.

"Friend," began Sugawee, who had regained most of his impressive calm, "wisdom would dictate against unnecessary playing of games." His slight frown was lost in the hillocks of his face. "Or do you think you need some kind of insurance?"

"There are many stains on this floor, Sugawee. I did not make the first."

"Be careful, friend."

"Much has been destroyed." He adopted the stony cadences of his interlocutor. "It would be well, I think, if other things were destroyed."

Sugawee raised both eyebrows. "Ah," he said. "If I could only be sure of that."

"Trust me," answered Finch.

"Alas," moaned Sugawee. "I wish I could, but all white men speak with the tongue of a snake. I sincerely wish, friend, that it were otherwise."

"Of course," smiled Finch. He left, or so it comically seemed, in the mothering arms of Gannett. The detective said nothing until they reached the police car. It was oddly rich and shiny in the weak moonlight of that shabby street. The radio talked to itself in the sad silence of early morning; for moments, no one else said a word.

"I bet you're sleepy," said the cheerful Barge at last. "It's after one."

"Yeah," said Finch. "Sleepy. And tired."

"And no wonder." Gannett was as solicitous as a governess. To Finch, he was cloying. "You've had yourself an exciting night."

Finch mumbled something and got into the car.

"By the way," the detective went on, as he sat down beside Finch in the back seat, "what was all that about? You and Sugawee?"

"Nothing," answered Finch, who suddenly did feel very, very tired. "Just talk."

"Uh-huh." Gannett ordered the driver to head for Finch's apartment; they streaked off through the funereal silence of the ghetto plains. "Something about stains?"

"Oh, that," laughed Finch. "Just me, the amateur. I got so scared that I . . . vomited. One of the tribesmen cleaned it up before you came."

"I see." The Barge took out a packet of small Swedish cigars; they had been advertised in *Playboy*. "Want one?" Finch shook his head. "I'm just wondering, Finch, what you and Sugawee had in common."

"Come off it, Gannett. Okay? He wanted to know exactly what you wanted to know; he wanted to know how Benedict was murdered. I told him. Is that all right?"

Gannett inhaled with satisfaction. "In the circumstances, sure. We've got the murderer; no harm in spreading the story around. Matter of fact, when you think about it, you've helped us out."

"How?"

"Well, Sugawee and his boys will be just tickled pink . . ." He chuckled. "Anyway, they'll be happy to hear the news that we nailed on a Panther this time; boost their own membership.

They and the Panthers, you know, aren't exactly friendly with each other."

Finch shrank down into his seat, and into himself. He did not want inadvertently to touch Gannett, or the quiet policeman on the other side, or, in fact, any other human being. He was beginning to feel sick again.

"They sure aren't," he said. Streetlamps, as the car sped toward his home, flashed daylight into the car with a sputtering rhythm that suggested . . . Finch leaned his little head back and laughed. Hysterical tears fell down his cheeks.

Gannett gazed down at him through the haze of his Scandinavian cigar.

The other policeman did not move. He kept staring out the bulletproof pane of the window.

CHAPTER XII

"THANK you," said Principal Orson. "You've done a splendid job."

He hung up the bedside phone and looked across the pale sheets at his wife, who snored lightly. Orson frowned, a reflex reaction. It is scarcely past one, he thought, but she lost consciousness hours ago. No, she was not a helpmeet to watch with him through the tense hours of his long fight upward. Not that one. She was her mother's daughter, who was herself the daughter of another like her, and they would all, the whole line of them, be just as happy washing white lady's clothes in Mississippi as she was in this brick house in the suburbs.

So what, he reflected; I didn't do any of it for her.

And now, in this hour of victory, she slept. There was no one there to share his triumph—a powerful enemy arrested, a dangerous demonstration averted, a murder in his school quickly solved. And before all these victories, a greater still; the white cop had called him "sir."

He could not sleep. He wanted to sing, to shout; but he had long ago trained himself to do none of these things. One incautious moment, one slip, and he would fall down the long shaft to that dirt farm in Alabama. He looked black; there was nothing to be done about that. But he knew he could never think or talk black—not in the wrong place, at the wrong time. He must use the right fork and smile the right smile, or his white superiors would become uncomfortable and suspicious. He had to be "one of them" and "not at all like the others."

103

And that is why disgust and contempt choked his nostrils when he looked at the sleeping body that was his wife's. She would never learn to hide it; through cracks and splinters in the layer of appearances she failed to maintain, the curse showed glaringly. Again, as so often before, she had let her hair go too long; tight curls frizzed at the base of her neck, each of them as tough and sticky as his own. He was a man; it was different. You field nigger, he silently cursed, you god-damned semiliterate field nigger. He thought of the difficulties of reining in her outgoing nature at important parties, of how he must hover near to shut her off if she got on the subject of her country upbringing and her degenerate family. He hated her. And he thought of Beverly.

Somewhere in the far and soundless reaches of his rambling house, a water tap dripped insistently. He sighed. Would his children become impossible, too?

Somewhere in that house a lock rattled, and suddenly gave. Principal Orson jumped to his feet.

Barefoot in white silk pajamas, he slid quietly down the hall toward the living room. He stopped only to snatch a bright new forty-five automatic from an imitation Early American cabinet. Cheap varnish, he reflected foolishly.

"My, my," said the cool young voice. "This be some fine house, uh-huh!"

Orson scowled; the gun lay heavy in his hand. *I could kill him,* he thought: *I have every right.* He sighed wearily. He could remember no clause in the principal's handbook that covered the killing of students. He lowered the weapon.

Orson tried to smile; he failed miserably. "Thanks," he said. "Looks even better in daylight. You should come over some time."

"Well, well, ain't he slick?" said Scrounge Roberson. "Ain't that colored man just *too* slick?"

"All right, Roberson," snapped his principal. "If that's the way you want it. You better be ready to back up the tough talk. I'm tired of playing with you. What do you want? Or has the revolution turned to breaking and entering?"

"You making threats?" Roberson sauntered into the middle of the room. It was hard. The floor was choked with fuzzy chairs and little end tables, tall lamps with brass eagles atop the shades, walnut magazine racks with copies of *Ebony* and the *Saturday Review,* well-fed ferns and huge lacquered cabinets that held marvels of electronic entertainment. "Man, have you dropped so low? You'd turn a brother over to the pigs, just to protect this honky-flavored shithouse? You got to be kidding."

"Shut up, Roberson."

"Woo-wee!"

"Shut up!" Orson felt hot blood in his eyeballs; he let fury run wild with him. "Brotherhood," he sneered, "has nothing to do with this. You've broken into my house, or am I talking over your head?"

Roberson laughed easily. "Calm yourself, man; lighten up on me." The last remnants of his laughter flicked away with the traces of a frozen smile. "I know white man's talk, brother; I've had it shoved down my throat all my life. And Uncle Toms like you have been right there, all along, yelling, 'Faster, faster, Master; sock it to 'em.' Dig? I know white man's words; I know big words. Words like . . . assimilation, slave mentality, collaboration, treachery. Ever hear those? They ever fall on your little black ears when you're down on your knees licking whitey's ass?"

Orson slowly laid the gun down on a walnut side table that held nothing but a lighted aquarium. The automatic, he had suddenly decided, was too insistent a temptation; the dazed fish, startled by the impact of the heavy weapon, scattered sharply, without a sound. Orson drew a deep breath and tried to blow the anger from his bloodstream. He looked up, as if for the first time, and noticed that the cold glow of the little aquarium was the only light in the room; he and Scrounge seemed to be floating in a deep-green sea. He shook his head and turned on a floor lamp.

"You needn't bother," commented Roberson. "Black people are happy in the dark; that's our natural home. We just close our little eyeballs and button up our shiny teeth, and you would never guess we was even there."

Orson felt very, very tired. He slipped down into the warm folds of an overstuffed period chair. Its name had always amused him; it meant, he told his shocked wife, that it should be sat in only once a month. He had laughed when she looked as if she believed him. He was not even smiling now.

"May I?" said Scrounge, as he sat down on a loudly flowered sofa. "Or do you want to drag out the plastic covers?" He grinned. "Don't want my poor black butt to contaminate your fine belongings."

Orson waved his hand idly. "Don't worry," he said automatically. "That little thing can't do much harm."

Scrounge laughed joyfully. "Now that," he said, "is the way I like to hear a black man talk. That sounds fine."

The principal was not listening. He asked, without caring, "You have a key?"

"No." Roberson answered grimly. "Just my brains, and little piece of wire." He sang, slapping cool palms against his thighs. "That's what they teach us, down in the ghet-to."

Orson took another long, painful breath. *Yes,* he thought, *I am so tired, so damned tired of the whole business.*

He sighed. "Where are your friends?"

"Outside, in the car, waiting."

"With their rifles?"

"Maybe." Scrounge stared at his listless adversary.

"And your sponsor, Miss Minere?" He did not sound as casual as he would have liked; he shrugged.

Scrounge, who did not understand the shrug, answered flippantly. "Home, I suppose. Reading."

"Her little red book?"

"Maybe."

"Yeah." Orson closed his eyes, hoping to rest; but it did not help. Unwelcome memories flew onto the dark screen of the mind he tried to wipe blank; he saw scenes that he did not want to see again. The insular darkness could not muffle those wailing voices. He snapped himself alert and looked at Roberson. *Let us,* thought the principal, *get this over with.*

He said, "It's been a long day, dig?"

"Dig."

"So what do you want?" Another dialogue ran counterpoint to the one with Scrounge. In the cloudy back alleys of Orson's brain, a deep voice asked petulantly, *Why?,* and another answered, *Because this is the way the game must be played to the very end, because this is the very reason they gave a black man the job.* Orson hated both of the voices; he wished Roberson would speak louder and drown them both out. Roberson did.

"This time it's war!" the young man shouted. "All-out, bloody war!" Diminuendo. He whispered. "Is that clear, Mr. Tom? Either you come across and show yourself a black man, or the people will rise up and smash down your stack of cards." He snorted, in a curious imitation of Beverly Minere. "If there was ever a paper tiger . . . ."

Orson started. He realized he had not been listening. It was the old rhetoric, but he had not caught the new threat.

"And what am I—"

"Man, are you going to sit there and pretend you didn't set the pigs on our brother?" Roberson spat a vicious staccato. "You tell them to lay off. Brother Jackson did not kill Benedict; this is a frame." He watched the principal's eyes grow cold. "This is a political arrest, like Huey Newton, or Brother Bobby Seale. So be it. You talk to them; you talk to your nice white friends. You tell them this little concentration camp they politely call the inner city will blow up in their fat greasy faces tomorrow night. The lines are drawn, brother. Traitors like Sugawee, like you, will not see another day dawn."

"Scrounge, I had nothing to do with this. The police have evidence. They know Jackson did it."

"And I know he didn't!" Orson frowned. "In my blood. And in the blood of my dead brother. But I won't waste time with you. Our demands are simple. I repeat: Release Brother Jackson, stop this harassment of the Panthers, let the people investigate the murder. That's justice." He smiled sadly. "Otherwise, as a great man said, *Cry, 'Havoc!' and let slip the dogs of war,* or something like that."

"You read Shakespeare? Isn't that counterrevolutionary?"

"Ain't I the smart nigger, though?" jeered Roberson. He paused. "A great man. If you forget *Othello.* And Caliban. He was the victim of a repressive, militaristic, bourgeois society— like all of us. But something shines through in Caliban, and I think Shakespeare knew, and hoped, that someday that little rebellious spark would catch fire in the dry bones of the oppressed man's murdered soul, and that fire would sweep through the foul stench of this corrupt world. Caliban is me; Caliban is every black man, brother. Don't you know that yet? Don't you writhe in your bed, Orson, when you remember how you've groveled on your belly to get this . . . ofay house and your house-nigger job? How do you forget?"

Orson wanted to shout. Instead, he said quietly, "You are a brilliant young man, Scrounge. Why do you—"

"Let myself be used? Forget it, man. We both know that old song and dance. Who's being used, anyway?" He gestured toward the large imitation oil portrait which was hung over the large imitation fireplace; the dead Rev. King seemed to be praying to someone with a very long attention span. "You string along with De Lawd there; listen to his gentle voice. Uh-huh. And where is he now? White man killed him. And the white man is going to kill me, shoot me in the back, but I will die fighting. He won't kill me before I die, if you know what I mean."

Orson stood up. For a horrifying moment, his head swam drunkenly, as if he had not eaten in days. "I'll talk to Gannett in the morning," he said. "I'll see what I can do."

Roberson stood up, too. "Don't con me, man. Just play it straight."

"I really wish," said Orson, "I wish I had as much influence as you seem to think. Things would be simpler." He was playing a role he especially liked, the lonely king whose subjects misunderstood him. His student was not impressed.

"Yeah," said Scrounge. "That would be nice. Then you could do away with smart-ass niggers like me." At the door, he relented; he was too young to hold a grudge. "Mr. Orson," he said, "twenty years ago, maybe, I can understand you. Maybe your way was the only way. I don't know. My mother says it was. But not now." He smiled shyly. "It's not too late, you know."

"What do you mean?"

"You could still join us, brother."

Orson conquered a hysterical urge to laugh. *What naive little fools,* he thought, *when all is said and done.* And he also conquered the fainter urge to clap the young man in a warm bear hug. It would have been awkward; they still stood too far apart. Smooth yards of the thick carpeting lay between them.

"No," he said. "The lines are drawn."

Adolescent anger churned in Roberson's stomach; he felt rejected.

"You said it," he answered bitterly. The older man instantly responded in kind.

"One other thing or two," said Orson. He bit down on the words. "About Shakespeare."

"Yeah? Make it good, Tom. The brothers are waiting."

"Uh-huh. First thing I'm reminded of is a city-wide intelligence test."

"What about it?"

"Well, I shuffled around beforehand, explaining how it was geared to middle-class white standards. Told the board my black students wouldn't relate, and it wouldn't be a fair test of their reading ability, and so on. But we took it, anyway."

"So?"

"And a young man named Scrounge Roberson got a perfect score."

That young man shrugged and opened the front door. A hushed conversation somewhere in the street suddenly lowered, then died out. Stars slowly appeared in the clear sky as Orson's eyes adjusted to the dark night.

"What that means," said the student, "is that I've been listening to whitey all my life, and I've never forgotten a thing."

"It also means," said a vengeful Orson, "that you remember everything you read, that you put two and two together. You're the top student in school, and . . . you've taken chemistry."

Scrounge stiffened. "Go on, brother," he said, and there was a warning growl somewhere deep beneath his changing voice. "Say it out."

"I remember a young man who reads Shakespeare, and I wonder if maybe he ever read *Coriolanus.*"

"He did." Scrounge was stony as an ancient idol.

"Coriolanus, as I remember, was everything a man could be, a man chose of the gods who do not often choose men. He was handsome, brave and intelligent." Orson frowned. "But he was too handsome to see beauty in other faces around him, too brave to fear other men, and too intelligent to believe, as they would have him believe, that he was their equal. He was too proud, or too good, depending on your point of view, and the rabble turned on him."

"Say it." The young voice shook slightly.

"I think," said Orson, "that I just did."

Scrounge stepped back into the room; he left the door open. "Benedict loved the people," the voice throbbed. "The people loved Benedict."

"But you did not agree on what the people needed."

"Benedict . . . forgave too easily."

"Uh-huh." Orson sounded assured, self-satisfied. But he was quick enough to dodge the boy's hot and angry fist. Scrounge jumped at him, then slumped to the soft floor as the heavy hand chopped savagely into his shoulder. He groaned as Orson fell on him.

"You little black bastard!" the big man roared. "Don't touch me. Nobody touches me." His powerful thick fingers tightened into a tight vise around Roberson's slender neck. His wide knee dug into the gasping boy's choking belly. "Just . . . you . . . remember . . that," Orson puffed hoarsely. He twisted at the helpless neck like a madman pulling weeds.

And then something—maybe it was the light trail of spit that trickled down the boy's chin, or the feel of the expensive carpet that had been charged at Bullock's, or the tentative click of a metal door opening somewhere in the street outside—something slapped him in the face and he jumped back, shocked at what he had almost done. A brawl. A street-nigger brawl. He watched Roberson stumble onto shaky feet; Orson could not deny the crude pleasure of seeing terror stretched across that crumbled face.

"Get out," he whispered. "Get out, boy." He started to laugh. Quietly. With a lunatic regularity.

Scrounge stared. He felt he had passed a boundary, like his first night with a woman, that could not be passed over again. He had seen what he did not want to see.

"Get out," said Orson, who was laughing freely now. Light footsteps could be heard on the flags of the walk outside, but neither cared. Something had ended. Something had been forever lost.

Scrounge could say nothing. He walked out. Orson closed the door behind him.

The first black principal in the district returned to his chair and sat down beneath the lamp his wife had chosen. Grinning, he regarded the closed door. He heard low voices. His gun was not far away.

The low voices faded out into the silence of early morning. Orson heard the car doors gently closing with metallic coughs. He smiled.

He did not flinch when he heard the crack of the Army's newest rifle. He did not flinch when the high window burst and showered in bright jewels on the polished walnut table below.

He laughed out loud.

CHAPTER XIII

FLOYD Hockby, who had a BA from Howard University and a master's degree in classical literature from the University of Wisconsin, wiped the thick sweat from his horn-rimmed spectacles. He gradually stopped panting; the pleasurable madness in his jaded pulse subsided slowly.

It had been a masterful performance, well worth Snatch's ten-dollar fee. McAdoo's most competent Latin teacher turned, content, from his observation post in the dim hallway of The Palace of Mirrors. He did not glance back through the one-way mirror; he knew that Montana Neversmith and her unknown lover, who thought themselves secret in the lascivious opulence of a bare little room walled with cheap, gold-streaked mirrors, were struggling out of their satiated torpor and into clothes. The five-minute warning buzzer had sounded.

Hockby smirked. Did any of these couples ever find out? It pleased him to imagine their shock and horror. A sucker born every minute. He slipped out the back entrance past a bulb which would never burn again. He was alone in an alley; he, and the gray moon, and a scrawny kitten that wailed hopelessly in a sparkling undergrowth of broken bottles and smashed metal cans.

The crumbling motel was the only live thing in that desolate neighborhood of fire-gutted storefronts and blasted lots. Mechanical artifacts, monstrous beneath the spectral stars, lay as sad reminders of a civilization which had camped there, and starved on barren ground. Strong weeds, Alabama and Georgia

113

weeds, burst up through gashes in the splintered cement surface of what had once been a parking lot; diamonds, rubies,
emeralds, golden topaz lay like mounds of bright sequins,
some set in fragments of cheap whiskey labels.

Hockby, in that wasteland, wanted to throw off his three-
piece tweed and bay at the moon.

"Currite, currite, nocti equi," he sang softly. The horses of
that still night paid him no mind; they grazed on the cool air
which drifted into his expanding lungs.

Far off, six feet away, behind the peeling stucco of the old
motel, The Palace of Mirrors, strange cries were born and
quickly died. Bumps, slaps, groans; the unheard *basso pro-
fundo* of money changing greasy hands. Floyd Hockby smirked again. It all reminded him, by some curious indirection, of
hidden torture chambers he had seen in Europe; of men
screaming, gone mad with torment, to stone walls that would
not hear; of poor Edward II skewered with a hot poker in the
seat of his unnatural delight, while terrified peasants huddled
in their marriage beds and shuddered at those miserable howls
in the midnight dark.

Sensual pleasures at this establishment, however, were none
so violent. Young couples in the ghetto who could find no
private room at home paid ten dollars an hour for the magic
trysting places. Each bedroom was lavishly mirrored, for added
delight; each had an old brass bed with one sheet, and a small
refrigerator with two diet colas, and that was all. And no
customers were supposed to know that the motel, through the
capable services of one Obadiah Snatch, actually made twenty
dollars an hour. Bad for business. Voyeurs could get beat up.

Hockby wandered off toward his aged Italian roadster. It
was an affectation he had picked up from a rich white kid in
Boston. He had other pleasures, but the motel management
drew the line at black punks, even if Snatch didn't. They had a
reputation to uphold.

Hockby jumped at the roar made by his finely tuned engine.
He had forgotten the pale silence of the deserted street. A

window of the motel yelled down an ancient obscenity. The Latin teacher wondered what Juvenal would have made of all this, then eased his sleek car off toward more respectable parts of the city.

He had things to worry about.

But they had not hindered his usual interlude at The Palace of Mirrors. Life is short, his Roman studies had taught him, and each thing has its place.

He thought of Benedict Williams, and of what the boy had known about him, and of what Emory Finch might know.

Hockby drove toward Santa Monica, where bachelor apartments cost sixty-five dollars a month and offered access to a crowded pool. He smiled. He could not imagine the Bookworm in a lounge chair beside that.

Finch was annoyed that Gannett had followed him up the walk to his apartment building. The trotting Barge, as if giving off unwholesome effluvia, somehow blotted out the regal palm trees that lined the street and made the sweet ocean air rancid.

"Thanks," Finch said politely. "I'm glad it's over." He did not believe it was. "I'll see you." He paused. "Or will I? Now that it's solved, I mean."

The detective shrugged. "I'll be around."

Finch frowned. There seemed to be something else.

"By the way," said Gannett, "there is one thing."

Finch leaned wearily against the cold metal mail lockers in the entrance archway. "Shoot," he said.

"A little thing. But you were wrong about the capsule in the ditto machine." The teacher was taken aback. Wrong? But that ... "It wasn't in the container of fluid. As anyone with scientific knowledge would know, the gas, in that case, would have soaked into the liquid, or through it, and gone to the top of the container. It wouldn't have leaked out into the room."

"Oh?" That made sense, but—

"But the capsule was placed in the slot beneath the container. It was punctured, when the fluid was turned over, by the point of the dispenser cap. The nerve gas shot up into the Williams boy's nostrils."

"So?" Finch didn't see the point; it seemed a minor quibble.

The Barge was disappointed. "Oh, nothing," he said. "Just something I figured out. I wanted to tell you."

Poor Gannett, thought Finch; *me and my fat lip.* "That's good," he said. "I would never have seen that." It didn't sound sincere.

"Yeah." The detective spoke grudgingly; he was watching his own feet kick stray pebbles from the walkway. They bounced through the blue and orange and green floodlights that are only seen outside living quarters in southern California. "You know . . . you've helped us a lot on this thing. You might make a good . . . cop." He laughed curtly. Even in the pastel half-light cast by Finch's apartment house, the crimson glow of his embarrassment shone brightly.

Finch smiled. "Thanks," he said. "I think."

"Yeah," said the Barge. "Nobody likes a cop."

No, thought Finch; *no one I know, anyway.* He waved and turned to go inside. And then he heard the other man's voice again — something pitiable, almost a sheep bleating. What was it? What was it, this time, that he had trampled over in his headlong rush after logical answers? He did not know the man before him.

"It's out of my hands, Finch," said the Barge quietly. For a moment, he looked ready to cry.

"What is?"

"Goddamn, Finch, do I have to write it in bloody letters across your door? You figured out so much; can't you figure this out?" Gannett sighed. "I'm not able to say it right out, you know. I'd lose my job." He cleared his throat, and looked away. "Not . . . when you think of it . . . that the job means so much, considering."

The journalism teacher bit his lip. He was uneasy in emo-

tional scenes, especially when he had no idea what the
emotions were all about.

"I must not . . . have been listening very well," he said
awkwardly.

"I guess not," Gannett answered bitterly.

"Sorry. Give me a second chance." He did not sound flip.

"The man upstairs, and I don't mean the Holy Father, has
taken it out of my hands. Is that clear enough?" Finch shook
his head stupidly. "Man, what world are you living in? The
lid's been shut by the politicos. They've got an answer; it's an
answer that pleases the generals, the Pasadena bigwigs, and the
voters who believe anything they're told. Even if they don't
have enough evidence to convict Jackson . . ." He stopped
talking and kicked viciously at a particularly offensive pebble.
He missed. "Damn," he said.

"And they won't," Finch said absently. "He didn't do it."

"That," Gannett whispered, "is something only you could
find out. I've been switched to a case of grand larceny.
Second-hand television sets," He laughed. To Finch, it was a
sad sound.

"How can this happen?" he said. "It doesn't seem, if you'll
forgive the phrase, in the public interest."

"The public interest?" The Barge was incredulous. "Yeah. I
believed in that, too. Don't laugh, but that's why I'm a
third-rate dick in this fucking . . . Yeah. I believed, oh, I
believed. Until that phone call tonight." He shrugged. "You
can't fight the . . . whatever it is. Call it the establishment, the
power structure, something like that."

"The rich old bastards who sire rich little babies who
become rich old bastards because their grandfathers plundered,
and got away with it," Finch mumbled.

"What?"

"Nothing. Something I heard once." For the first time in
that early morning, he remembered Benedict.

"Something else you might think about." Gannett glanced
back toward the car; punchy laughter, light and jocular, fil-
tered back from the tired policemen. He lowered his voice, just

in case. "The lab went over the machine again." He paused melodramatically. "They found smudges."

"Smudges?"

"On the fluid container. Not prints, not recognizable; just little blotches that might be made by the fingertips."

"Oh."

"Wait." Gannett was strangely persistent. "Think a minute. If Benedict's were the only prints, what would you expect to find?"

"Do I get a prize?"

"Please."

"Well . . ." Finch tried to follow the obvious possibilities, to brush away extravagant decorations. "Benedict was right-handed. I'd expect to find a thumb smudge on the top. And . . . unless he performed some unusual contortions, four finger smudges, fairly close together, on the side . . . ." He tried to picture the little machine concretely. "On the side facing the roller."

"That's what we found."

"Fine. Do I win a trip to Disneyland?"

Gannett grinned. "Why does a nice guy like you have to talk smart to cops?" Finch grinned back. "You just might win that trip," the Barge continued, "if you can explain the others."

"The other . . . smudges?"

"On the other side. Made by a left hand—because of the placement, because of another thumblike smudge on the top."

"Groovy," Finch laughed. "A left-handed murderer!"

Gannett was not amused. He said dryly, "Yeah. A left-handed murderer with a finger missing. Narrows it down a lot."

"What?"

"Didn't I tell you? There are only three of our little smudges on the other side of the container. And before you say that one finger just got crowded out in the rush, get this· the marks are spaced widely apart. Even a presti—"

"Prestidigitator," Finch snapped. "I read books."

"Yeah. Even he wouldn't do that naturally. Try it. Besides, there is a very large gap between the second and third . . . uh, smudges." The detective spoke with dry humor. "So that's what I'm leaving you with, Finch. A left-handed murderer with a missing finger. That's one for your books, isn't it?"

"Or a paralyzed finger."

Something in his tone worried the detective. "Mean anything?"

"Yes." Finch frowned. "But it doesn't make sense. You see—"

"Hold it, Finch. I'm off it, remember? If you want to get involved, that's your lookout; you're on your own. You call for help, and I never heard of you. Got it?" The teacher nodded, thinking of several things at once. "No theories. No guesses. No wild leads. But when you find him, if you do, then call me. It's not much, but it's all I can do. Then I can nail him. Not before."

"Justice in the City of the Angels," said Finch.

Gannett was already lumbering down the walk toward his car. He turned back briefly. "I hope," he said, "you'll be careful. I don't like sweeping up the remains of aging idealists." He didn't wait for an answer; he expected none. He liked to be able to deliver the punchline. Even at two in the morning.

Finch, rusting in the heavy dew, heaved himself manfully out of stupor and rolled his sagging body, like so much dirty laundry, toward his apartment—first floor, in the back. He passed the pool, which seemed to be filled with Prell concentrate; angry insects debated around a dim safety bulb, and did not pause to take note of him. Idiotically, because it was something to read, he perused the huge signboard with its list of ten warnings. "Warning: No loud talk or card-playing or butter-and-eggs rackets. Warning: No use of intoxicants or stimulants or mutilants. Warning: No female swimming (was it a kind of stroke?) without a bathing cap. Warning: Respect the rights of other tenants; ours is a happy community. . . ."

As always, Finch read the words and thought of something else.

He remembered the detective's question, "Man, what world are you living in?" It seemed relevant.

That word. Small change.

He was alerted, outside his door, by the sudden pricking of his thumbs. Cold waters flushed to his rib cage. He stared at what he saw.

The door was ajar.

A light was on.

CHAPTER XIV

"A thousand pardons," said Floyd Hockby, who sat, elegant as a poet, legs crossed in Finch's one chair. "I am not, despite the proud heritage of my race, the outdoor type, and your door was invitingly unlocked." He tightened his lewd smile and sucked at the brandy he had brought.

"Oh, yes," said Finch absently. "Of course it was." He finally remembered why. Ulabenzi. Sugawee. Guns in the night. But that seemed so very long ago.

"I took the liberty of coming in, rather like the protecting god of the hearth and household," Hockby continued, in a rushing stream. "I also took the liberty of making use of one of your glasses." He swirled the golden fluid in a coquettish tease. "Have some. Man is not meant to drink alone."

"I . . . yes, thanks." Finch took another glass from the tiny sink and came to himself. "I hope," he said pleasantly, "you also took the liberty of washing the glass. I forget. Several thriving colonies of bacteria have found shelter here."

The Latin teacher looked apologetic, for some reason. "Not to be mentioned," he said, "between gentlemen of the world. I am the thrall of this century's most efficient anal-compulsive complex; for this relief, my psychiatrist has had ample pecuniary rewards."

Finch, who was indeed up past his bedtime, wondered: Am I just getting punchy with the dawn's early light, or is everyone else really batty? For the moment, the question seemed irresolvable.

121

He made a decision. "Excuse me," he said. He picked up the telephone.

"Far be it from me," commented the mellowing Hockby, "to cast aspersions on the habits of your friends. But will they be awake at this hour? Or does my rude assault necessitate an alarum to the *carabinieri?*"

"Fortunately," Finch answered, "the Los Angeles Board of Education has enough money to keep its little machine running all night. For such emergencies."

"Ah," drooled Hockby. He lapped at the brandy like a contented tabby. "The Mother of Us All."

The machine which answered the phone warned Finch to speak slowly and distinctly when the bell sounded. The machine did not speak slowly and distinctly; it sounded definitely annoyed. It had the weary, martyred tones of a machine which had time and again told Finch to check the number he was dialing and to hold the line because he had foolishly called at just that moment when all the reservations clerks were busy. It sternly reminded him that he must spell his name and the name of his school. The bell rang.

"Emory Finch. F-i-n-c-h. McAdoo High School. M-c-a-d-o-o. Journalism. First class, nine-twenty. One-day absence. O-n-e. Because of—" The cut-off bell made a raspberry; the dial tone stabbed his eardrum. "—sudden illness," he finished ineffectually. The machine had beat him again. He should have practiced beforehand. "Damn," he said.

Hockby was laughing. "I never finish. We are veritable slaves to the mechanical monsters we have created."

"I suppose so," Finch answered politely.

"No one could blame you a bit," needled the other man. "I predict we'll have more than the usual number of substitute teachers tomorrow morning. Our disadvantaged youth, as rumor hath it, intend mischief and mayhem. Discretion, as they say . . . ."

Unaccountably, Finch lashed out at him. "Hell, no! I'm not running out."

Hockby found this vehemence distressing. "My good man, my apologies. I could hardly have meant anything so crude. You merely take the reasonable position. After all, we cannot blink our eyes to the recurring theme of race in these matters, much as we would all like to ignore it."

"Someone will cover my classes," came the cold response. "But I'll be there." He took a melodramatic slug of brandy, and almost choked. "It's my place to be there."

Amused, the Latin teacher shook his head. "No," he said, "the gods have not granted me the wisdom to understand this phenomenon. Here we see, if I may speak so baldly, the white liberal shouldering his unnecessary cross. Our modern-day flagellant."

"Is that what it looks like?" Finch grew belligerent. He did not like the smooth voice, the smooth tailoring, the smooth man.

"Who is to say?" Hockby shrugged. "Nonetheless, the disinterested observer, if he existed, might note from his lofty eminence that some have burdens thrust upon them, some are born with them, some are inclined to snatch them up. What is the fascination of my backward race? Let them rot, Finch. They will continue to breed like vermin, poison themselves with drugs and whiskey, and, in the end, conspire to murder themselves—with, or without, you. And your kind. Let them save themselves, though there's little likelihood of their doing so. Or do you believe these spurious arguments which lay blame on the terrible white man? Come to your senses. They're weak; let them die out. I am, quote, a black man, unquote—and they mean nothing to me. I spit on them. Those who survive, will survive."

"Like you."

"Like me." Hockby frowned slightly. "Yes, I think it's fair to say that I have survived. And by my own wits. Moreover . . . ." He paused. "Moreover, I will continue to survive." It sounded vaguely like a threat. Warned, Finch finally wondered why Hockby had come.

But he had other things to say; tact had walked out on him at midnight.

"A hundred years ago," he said, "it was considered bad form for a host to insult a guest."

"A hundred years ago," Hockby echoed, "this particular problem would not arise; forgive me for bringing it up, but I would be chained in the outhouse." His voice was level. "Besides, you didn't invite me here."

"These are different days," Finch continued, as if he had not heard Hockby's gloss, "and it is considered a virtue to be frank."

"Brutally frank."

"You disgust me." Finch met his visitor's angry eyes. "Maybe, as a white man, I have no right to judge. But there it is. You disgust me."

The Latin teacher held his glass firmly, clasped between both hands; he gazed soberly into the amber film, the sticky patina that was left. "Benedict Williams," he whispered, "said the same thing."

Again, Finch sensed the threat. But he also felt that it was far-off and vague; it was not directed against him. Something more precious, or someone, was at stake. He waited.

"The point, Finch, cries to be made, does it not?" Hockby slowly raised his sleek head, as if he had just been crowned with the gravity of a state. Finch nodded assent. "Then I make it. I have reasons. I do not want to be dragged through the mud and slime of this investigation."

Finch tried to interrupt; he was not interested in further seamy revelations. He tried to tell Hockby that the case was closed; in a sense, in the official sense, it was true.

"No," snapped Hockby, as he saw the words gathering at the white man's lips. "I will finish." Finch shrugged and leaned back in his chair. He was tired. He would let everyone say what they wanted to say. And tomorrow, God willing, he would think.

Hockby stood up. The customary jauntiness, the lightness,

slipped from his frame like a borrowed cloak. He walked the one step to the yellowed porcelain sink and set down his glass; mindlessly, or so it seemed to Finch, he took a decayed sponge and wiped at food stains on the ugly counter. He did not look back at Finch.

"Among other things," he said, "it would kill my mother."

"My God," exclaimed Finch, without thinking. "You mean, she doesn't know?"

"Ah," sighed Hockby. "So you did."

Finch did not consider an evasion. "I knew. I rather think," he continued, without meaning to be unkind, "that practically everyone knew. Or guessed."

"I see." Hockby laughed shortly, bitterly. "Our Great Liberator was right, with his simple country instincts. What is it? Some of the people some of the time, but not all of the people all of the time."

"Something like that."

"But idle whispers, Finch, despite what the great poets say, do little harm. They are entertained, played with, then packed off to rust with all the other discarded accumulations of finite minds. It is the great tyrant, the printed word, that would ruin me." He walked over to a window and watched, without knowing it, the room where the Italian family slept. "In former times, they called it scandal."

"Don't worry," Finch said simply. "It will not come out."

"It may fly out into the light of day," said the black man quietly, "at the light touch of a jesting hand."

"Trust me, Hockby. It doesn't—" A madman's wild laughter cut him short; he stared.

"Trust you?" spluttered Hockby, convulsed by private demons. "Trust you, white man?" He fairly squealed and doubled over in high-pitched giggles.

And then the joke was over.

Hockby's voice bubbled with acid; he grabbed the little man's arm. "Listen," he spat, "and you listen to me good. You think I've fought my way up from ratholes to reach the fine day when I have to be grateful to you, white man, for saving me?"

Finch pushed him away. "I didn't mean that."

"That," growled the furious Hockby, "is how it adds up, boy."

"Not to me."

Something dangerous glinted in the far corners of Hockby's eyes. "It will soon enough."

"You take a cynical view of . . . your fellowman."

"I have one hell of a clear eye for seeing the world and my place in it." He paused, and Finch again remembered something Gannett had said. What kind of world . . . . "But I'm throwing a new element into the equation, Finch." The Latin teacher grinned hideously. "Changes the sum. You won't cover up for me; I won't owe you a thing." He dangled the hook, and Finch bit.

"Because?"

"Because I will give you, in the words of the sage, something to think about." Again, the horrible grin—which seemed to herald a triumph which only Hockby knew about. "Put it another way. You won't be doing me any favors. You won't blow the whistle on me." Hockby leered. "Because I won't blow the whistle on you."

"Me?" Finch stared stupidly. He had never considered himself paranoid, but now, in response to that nameless, unreasonable dread that chills innocent men on the witness stand, his breath caught. And then, like so many others this tense night, he found himself laughing inanely. "That's ironic, Hockby; that really is." Hockby showed no appreciation of the irony. "The tragedy of my life, shall we say, is that there's nothing in my dead dull past that could shock anyone. Or," he said more seriously, "that anyone would envy."

"No?"

"Sorry." Finch gave a wan smile. "I wish there were. Katie sleeps with a black man; Beverly with students; Orson with . . . a statue of Booker T. Washington; you with little boys—you've all got something to hide. Not me." He paused. "More's the pity."

Hockby answered with peculiar calm. "I agree."

"So you were bluffing, after all. Nice try."

"Not exactly." Hockby spoke too softly. "I admit, I was hoping to find something . . . personal. But it doesn't matter. You see, I still have the trump card, Finch. You may not lie to protect yourself; even if you had murdered your own mother with an ax, your perverted sense of justice might dictate that you give yourself up, ecstatically throw yourself into the comforting womb of the law and purge your groveling bowels with confession and self-sacrifice."

Finch wrinkled his pale nose. "You have a way with words."

"You wouldn't lie to save yourself." Hockby clasped his hands together, content as a prosecutor. "But you would lie, you'd cover up for me . . . to save someone else."

"What do you mean?"

"Even if that someone . . . is no longer alive."

Instantly, Finch saw it; he wondered why it had taken so long.

"Oh, no," he began, but words did not come easily. Lewd pictures, half-heard stories, obscene jokes clogged his racked brain; ugly shouts beat through his bloodstream. He felt sick, and helpless, and something small and bright was drowning in the churning confusion. "Not Benedict," he said weakly. "Please, God, not Benedict."

"The same," Hockby answered smartly.

"You sick bastard . . . ."

"There is a letter," said the buttery voice. "What's the surprise? Benedict grew up in the ghetto; he lived by its laws. Show me a black boy who hasn't been some man's punk and—"

"Shut up!" Finch writhed, miserable with the frustration of a small man who wants to smash his tormentor, but has neither the strength nor skill to fight. Even an emotional Finch could not forget his innate rationality. He shook, he quivered;

but he didn't know the first thing about knocking a man out. He gasped, "Show me this letter."

"Saints preserve us," Hockby mocked. "How the innocent do suffer in this cruel and vicious world. Let's hope there's a better life to come."

"You're lying."

"And you know I'm not. I'll mail you a Xerox copy. Feel better? You'll love the part about my strong—"

He stumbled and fell against the wall from the unexpected shove. The last thread had snapped and Finch, who for the first time in his life succumbed to emotion, had exploded. Immediately, he felt foolish. He stepped back apologetically, his face flushed.

And then the gentle whisper of crunched glass froze him.

"Damned fool," said Hockby, getting up. He quickly patted at one of his coat pockets, so quickly that Finch, if he had not been alerted, would never have noticed.

"I think," said the flustered Hockby, "my position has been made clear enough. I think we understand each other. I will leave you now to your own speculations." He headed for the door. "Although I must point out, purely as a personal observation, that your conduct, Mr. Emory Finch, hardly shows the restraint worthy of an educated man."

"You don't wear eyeglasses," said Finch. He sat down in the room's one chair, hunched over, regarding the floor serenely.

"It's late," Hockby said warily. "I will leave you, with further apologies for the unusual hour, and . . . uh, circumstances. No doubt the strain of this wearing day goes far in excusing your—"

"You don't wear shades, either. That would identify you with the sharp ghetto black man. You wouldn't like that."

"Does it please you to be humorous?" asked Hockby sharply. "It does not please me to be the straight man. Good night, Finch." He had swung the door open, and the night air gushed in to clear the choked air between them.

"Pills, these days, usually come in plastic vials."

Hockby gave in. "Okay, Finch, you guessed it. But don't push it. It will get you nowhere. It changes nothing about the letter; that's all that matters."

"Heroin?"

Hockby laughed. "Man, what kind of fool do you take me for? That's shantytown stuff; what's happened to your irreproachable, unprejudiced, fair and honest view of my poor race? Or is it, blood will tell? I would hardly fall into that trap. I'm no junkie."

"Speed?"

"Methedrine."

"My, my," smiled Finch. "Now aren't you the hip and with-it swinger?"

Hockby answered with a nasty smile. "Don't push it, Finch," he said. "It means nothing to you. And I do have, because of the distressing events of my clouded past, some unmentionable and disagreeable acquaintances."

"Of course," said Finch. "It means nothing to me."

"How pleasant," commented Hockby, "when reasonable men can settle their differences amicably, can sit down together and work toward the greatest good. Is it not the love and trust that our martyred leader, the good Dr. King, so often—"

"Get out," said Finch.

Hockby sneered. "Good night, Finch. Sleep well. The morning brings sweet release."

"Get out," said Finch again, but the Latin teacher had already slipped into the floating shadows of the early morning.

A hypodermic, thought Finch. One of hundreds carried in the neighborhood around McAdoo High School. Nothing strange in that.

And yet . . . he had learned something from his visit to the Science wing that day, already become yesterday during the long night. He had learned that it was difficult, but possible—difficult, and dangerous, but possible; it was sometimes done in experiments. A clever man, a cautious man, could, with an extremely fine needle, inject a gas through the gummy wall of a gelatin capsule. The gelatin, if he worked slowly, would draw together over the tiny hole as the needle was drawn out. He would have a margin of safety; it would not take much gas. It would be tricky; it would take a rare combination of nerve and imagination, but it definitely could be done.

It had been done.

Surely, the risks had been great. But if the right precautions had been taken . . . and if the man were desperate enough . . . .

Finch yawned and decided to go to bed. Hockby was right about one thing: it would all look better in the morning. Or something like that. He turned out the light and fell on the bed.

He slept. But not before he remembered the most sensible statement he had ever heard the late John Kennedy make:

"Life isn't fair."

CHAPTER XV

"SOMETIMES I feel like a-a-a motherless child," crooned the mournful baritone.

"Shut that damned thing off, will you, honey?" The woman's voice was cracked and stained with long years of hard use, but it was warm, and still liquid. "We had enough of that stuff in this house for one day, if you ask me."

"Glad to," said Beverly Minere, and did so. She tried to hide a yawn. "I thought they meant to stay all night. I felt like we had taken a trip back a hundred years and I was talking to Sojourner Truth and Harriet Tubman."

The old woman chuckled lightly. Death was no stranger in 1er house; she had not sobbed when the others wailed.

"Maybe they would, if there'd been a body . . . ." She closed her eyes; some hidden force rallied the momentary twitching near her lips. "I say, colored folks love dying something awful; why, Benedict used to laugh and . . . When I was a little girl in Alabama, you had to be one bad business if everybody in town didn't stay up, singing and praying, and drinking, for at least three . . . ." She noticed Beverly's rigid back at the ancient phonograph. "I do go on," she continued cheerfully. "I know you don't like to hear me talk that way, Beverly, but us old folks ain't gonna change. We set in our ways."

Beverly turned and came over to Mrs. Williams' chair. She knelt by the wrinkled grandmother. "I'm sorry," she said quietly. "Don't think I ever—"

"Hush, child. I know what you think." She looked down at the beautiful young face, its harsh pride and anger now softened by something deeper between them. "Who can say?" she laughed. "Why, if I was a young woman today, maybe I wouldn't be satisfied with scrubbing floors neither."

"Mrs. Williams," said Beverly, "you have nothing to be ashamed of."

"Why, honey, I know that." She smiled. "But I guess that's something you young folks won't ever understand. No, times have changed, all right." A tiny hand touched the younger woman's natural. "Everybody else calls me Mama," she whispered. "Mama Williams. Even my proud dead grandson." She paused. "Or is that too much like darky talk for you?"

"No, Mama," said Beverly, and wept helplessly as she dropped her regal head into the cleaning woman's lap. "No, no."

And silent tears finally came to the old woman's eyes. "Oh, honey," she moaned. "Each time seems the last."

"No, Mama, no." Beverly did not move her head. "Never again."

"Over and over again, honey. Till the day you die."

Mrs. Williams looked around the dingy little living room in the heart of Watts. It was clean, it was spotless; but it had the dinginess of poverty, and of age, and of hard use. She smiled. The great crowd of mourners and friends had disarranged her few shards of furniture, crumpled an old rug. But it didn't matter. These few possessions were the trophies of her long life; tomorrow she could dust and put everything back in its place.

In her tidy mind, she had already rearranged things. Yes, the sofa would be Benedict's; he had slept there so many years . . . he had slept there two nights ago. It would always be his, as the brown chair belonged to her dead husband, and the vase to her favorite daughter, and the chipped plastic table to that poor cousin who disappeared, and the broken . . . Yes, they were all there with her, and would not leave again till she died. Years ago, she believed that they would all meet again, as they had in life, on the farther bank of some great river no living man had ever found. Now, she was no longer sure. But it didn't matter. They were with her now.

She saw that Beverly's sobs had died to silence. Mrs. Williams turned to practical matters; she knew the value of routine in times like this.

"Honey," she said, "did you talk to the Reverend? I know Benedict didn't think much of church and all, but I think—"

Beverly lifted her head, smiled and sat back on the floor beside the chair. "Yes," she said. "He's arranging things for Sunday. That's time enough, he thought."

"My, yes. Nobody round here needs practice in getting ready for a funeral."

Beverly frowned to herself. *Nobody,* she thought, *but the Black Panthers and Sugawee's BAM boys.* No doubt the struggle was already on. It was matter of political honor that each take over the preparations, prepare the eulogies which might degenerate into rant. But they would not share the platform. One side must win; the other, suffer defeat. And for once she was not interested. Benedict had belonged to neither of them; in fact, one of them might have . . . .

"Mama," she said with sudden vigor. "Who did Benedict hate?"

Mrs. Williams looked surprised, but she was resilient. "Why, honey, what a . . . Goodness, I don't know." her eyes twinkled. "When you two got together, I would have sworn you hated the whole world."

"Do we . . . did we really sound like that?"

"Well, it wasn't the Women's Missionary Society, that's for sure." She checked herself. Even gentle teasing seemed too cruel now; young people are so sensitive, and take things so hard. She thought a moment. "To hear him talk, and Benedict sure could talk, well, he hated a lot of people. But I'd need a dictionary to remember them all."

"What do you mean?"

"Well, there was capitalists, to begin with. And imperialists. And then entre . . . entr . . . ." She shrugged comically.

"Entrepreneurs." Beverly laughed. "Right on," she sang. "I can hear him now. As the students say, that young man could tell it like it is, lay it on and really teach." The bright memory left her; she shuddered in the sudden cold. "No, I mean, people. Particular people."

"Why, I . . . ." Ever so slightly, Mrs. Williams stiffened; Beverly barely caught it. "No. No one like that."

"You started to—"

"No! No such thing!" Mrs. Williams barked. Beverly felt slapped in the face. "Don't you be playing around with something you don't know nothing about, child."

"You have to tell me," the young woman pleaded. "Don't you see? It might—"

"I see what I see. And I'm older than you, girl. I may look like a used-up old Tom, but I know what life is, honey. And that's all I'm intending to say on that subject."

"Mama, you can't keep quiet." Beverly bit her lip, but the anger rushed out. "You've got to tell me." She stood up. "It's your grandson dead, woman; don't you want his killer found? Don't you want—"

The old woman trembled with fury; her firm voice cracked like summer thunder. "Hush up, Beverly; hush up about things you don't understand. Talk about the revolution, and social progress or whatever, and all the rest of it; talk on until your tongue's hanging out the side of your pretty head. But don't talk about life and death; you know nothing about them." She stopped to catch her breath, and then leaned painfully back into her chair. "I'm sorry, honey," she said, as her eyes closed to rest, "I don't mean to shout at you like that. You're the only one to stand by me, and I ain't meaning to lose you. But I know what I'm talking about." She smiled shyly, and opened her shiny black eyes. "Now, how many times have you had to listen to an old colored woman say something like that?"

Beverly tried to smile in answer, but she was single-minded.

"But why?" she persisted. "If you know something, the smallest thing that might help, why won't you tell it?"

"Can't you get it through your thick little skull that I don't?" She was gentle again. "What I know won't change a thing. The man knows what he's doing."

"The pigs, you mean."

"Call them what you want. They've got their ways. I can't prove a thing, and I really don't know a thing to prove. A wrong word can cause nothing but trouble all around; that's one thing I do know."

"But you might just—"

"Now, honey, don't you know I'm as stubborn as a back-country mule?" Beverly smiled. "All right, then. Just you remember that."

"I will."

"Hey!" Benedict's grandmother sat up straight, a bright change in the corners of her eyes. "Ain't you forgetting my education?"

"Now? At this time of the morning?" Beverly made a face. "That stuff can wait. It's going to take a long time, anyway, to reeducate someone like you."

"That so? Well, I just wonder how good the teacher is, if anyone feels like asking me." She grinned coyly.

"Maybe you're right," Beverly answered, humoring the old lady. "You need all the extra work you can get." And then she wondered if the old lady was humoring her. It didn't matter. Neither of them would sleep that night. It would be better to think of other times and other places. She took a worn paperback from her purse. Her hand brushed against the bottle of sleeping capsules, but she tried to forget. "I hope I don't choose something that puts you to sleep," she said.

"Maybe it ain't the reading matter; maybe it's the way you—"

"Okay, okay." Beverly sat on the sofa, Benedict's sofa. "We were reading tales from Southwest Africa."

"Fine," said Mrs. Williams. "I'm gonna listen real good, and before you know it, I'll be a real, genuine Af-ro-A-merican.

You just watch. No more of this colored folks stuff for me."
Her eyes twinkled mischievously.

"That'll be the day."

"You wait and see."

Beverly read quietly, but with force; she tried to inject
harsh rhythms suggestive of the original into the pale English
translation. The little room in the slums of Los Angeles faded
down the tunnel of her imaginative vision. She was not Beverly
Minere, the imitation white woman; she was the Wise Woman,
the Teller-of-Tales, She-Who-Lies-With-the-Gods. She saw herself, crouched near the flickering stabs of a dying campfire,
and she heard what she read, resonant in the marrow of her
slender bones, as if she had heard it a thousand times in a
thousand generations. No mystery more profound than a simple tale which men remember.

She told of a time when men did not die, but passed their
whole lives as slaves. Finally, they could stand the situation no
longer and sent a messenger to Wuni to request an end to their
bondage. Their friend the dog was selected as messenger. But
he had many friends along the way, including the goat. The
goat, knowing of the dog's leisurely ways, took it upon himself
to deliver the request himself. But the goat had a fault of his
own: He loved to elaborate.

Coming back, the goat met the dog, and told him that it was
no longer necessary to deliver the message since he had done it
already. The dog, worrying about the goat's loquaciousness,
asked him what he had told Wuni. The goat told him that he
said to Wuni that men were tired of being slaves and now
wished to die, a privilege previously given only to their chiefs.
The dog was horrified and rushed to Wuni to correct the
mistake. But Wuni refused his anguished request, for he had
already given the gift of death to men, and would not go back
on it. And because of this, death now comes to all men and
yet they remain slaves.

Beverly closed the book as she closed her eyes. There is
something there, she thought, something more valuable than

all the equivocations and tintinnabulations of the modern industrial state. She wanted to crack kola nuts, to run naked down the windy beach of a subtropical night. She wanted to sing in the language that had been bled from her ancestors' veins. She wanted . . . .

The gentle noise, so much like the fluttering of a small songbird's wing, was nonetheless a snore.

Beverly smiled; she was warm with unaffected compassion. Oh, no, Mama Williams, she thought, I am not ashamed of you. Not of your speech, not of your old-fashioned ideas. Without you, and such as you, we would have all died in the long years of bondage. You are stronger than I have had to be, and you are stronger than he . . . .

She froze in the horror of what she had almost thought.

CHAPTER XVI

KATIE Lee read the principal's note with curious relief. *Thank God,* she breathed to herself, *I could not have faced my classes today.*

Orson's message was peremptory, but polite. A substitute had been assigned to cover her classes; she was to appear at "an urgent meeting" in the school's conference room.

Ordinarily, these summonses sent her into fits. Meetings, conferences, councils—none of them profitable or interesting—were the curse of her teaching life. Let her plan an especially provocative lesson, then the cheerleading committee called an emergency session to consider the case of a candidate with two D's; let her design a particularly effective test, then a vice-principal appeared for a sudden, prolonged discussion of a student who had been absent two months.

There were times when she could spit in Orson's eye as he stood up for one of his lengthy speeches about attendance forms, bell schedules, or waste paper in the halls.

Not today. Chuzz was in jail, and she had nothing left over for her students. She was beaten, for the moment, and could even have faced a day of in-service training. *Let them waste time,* she thought, *let them—until it starts again for me.*

Miss Lee sat wearily at her desk and mechanically wrote out work instructions for the day; each class was on its own level, and it was necessary to set out five different textbooks for the substitute. What nonsense, she thought: he probably won't bother. On the rare days when she was ill, she had discovered that the usual substitute was a young man or woman who wanted to "relate"; consequently, the class was diverted by a "free discussion" of abortion or LSD or free love. The students were always amused by these strange events, and the substitutes always winged homeward with a song in their hearts, convinced that they had brought light into the dark tombs of compulsory education.

She would not have minded; she was too self-confident to feel that she was being undermined. But she wished that these young missionaries would, at least, take roll; she was legally bound to do so. With little hope that they would be filled out properly, she made out five copies of the standard Temporary Roll Sheet.

Still, she admitted, she was glad to escape this one day. News of Jackson's arrest had hit her in the early hours of the morning—a cautious, but friendly call from an anonymous voice. He was being held without bond, the voice had said, but "the brothers" had instantly gone to work. They would spring him soon.

She shuddered. The thought of Orson calling them all together to gloat over this . . . The well-chewed ballpoint pen dropped with a soft plastic clatter. Or was this something else? She was only assuming that everyone had been invited to the meeting. Was the net closing in?

As Miss Lee considered her own place in the rush of events, William McAdoo High School pulled itself together out of the cool gray loneliness of the foggy morning. Montana Neversmith, or Scrounge Roberson, or any other student walking down the shabby streets to school, was forced to pass through the gauntlet of warring political factions.

At strategic points never less than a block away from the school in several directions, short young men garbed in Sugawee's strange robes had uncannily materialized. Wary as jungle cats, brightly colored as birds of paradise, they darted back and forth across the intersections; with Swahili incantations, they quietly slipped their pamphlets to the surprised students. To a man, the subtle followers of BAM looked capable, despite the glorious dyes of their dashikis, of instant disappearance. Their pamphlet was a strange blend of plea and warning: *Brothers! Be on our side in tonight's battle!*

The politic student, however, would surreptitiously crush the BAM material in his fist and, like a hardened litterbug, let it slide down his legs to the sidewalk before reaching the second stage in the Psywar—the tall, leather-jacketed Panthers on the street corners near the school. These warriors, their booted feet set wide apart, stood defiantly in the open. Their rifles were missing, for they wanted no embarrassing scenes with the pigs before school started. To most of the students, they still looked like Death walking. Their black shades were as ominous and cold as the mask of an executioner. Their printed handbill was also clear and simple. *Brothers!* it said, *Be on the right side in the coming war!*

They did not have to push themselves. Arrogantly, they stood, unmoving. No one refused to take their little announcement.

The coolness of the morning was intensified by this other kind of cold. No laughing, joking clusters of students loitered, as was their wont, on the small patch of grass in front of the main building; no one, not even the most bumptious sophomore, lingered outside the front gate for a last cigarette. Usually, a loud game of craps was played on the rotted steps of an abandoned church across the street. This morning, no dice rattled on the hollow boards. The school's two security guards, black policemen in plain clothes, stood by the front entrance; they looked at each other and raised eyebrows. Perhaps it was their ears that felt strangest of all; this morning, portable radios did not blare and shout at them.

The last missive hit students at the very doors of the school. Members of the Black Student Union, who had dittoed their handouts just an hour before, gave out a message which undercut the others: *Brothers! Stick together! Our real enemy is the Pig!*

Some ignored the young men and women in their revolutionary green fatigues and paratrooper boots; some smiled and took the slippery sheets of paper. Usually, there was heckling from other factions within the student body; after all, these brothers and sisters were only students like themselves. This morning, there were only silent stares.

Orson looked out his office window on the quiet spectacle.

"Someone," he joked, "is going to have a lot of cleaning up to do." He pointed to the snowy wads of discarded paper that rolled tediously, like tumbleweed, across the school lawn.

"You could be only too right," answered Finch. He smiled painfully, and both men knew he was not referring to the litter of pamphlets and handbills.

They looked out the window, but did not really see. They listened. And in the silence they heard something. It was the sound of the ghetto holding its breath.

Chuzz Jackson would not relieve himself on the floor.

"Bastards!" he shouted, but the muffled voice bounced limply about the stifled air of the cell. There were no windows, no ventilation—except for an uneven crack under the crudely fashioned metal-plated door. A single plank was fixed into one of the cement walls of the five-by-four room. Too narrow for relaxed sitting; too short to lie on. The damp concrete floor seemed to roll, like disease-ridden layers of gray dough, toward the rusty sunken drain. Atmospheres of vintage urine and stale sweat and gaseous fear pressed thickly against each other. Sounds came from outside, as if beaten down on the way, only in barely distinguishable bumps and knocks and small cries.

Just what the mother-fucking pigs want me to do, thought Chuzz, *is piss on their rotten floor. Then they can run tell Lone Star Reagan that niggers don't know how to act, don't appreciate the fine facilities their democratic government has provided.*

He tried not to laugh at his own ironies. After all, his

bladder was near the bursting point where the gentlest tickle might . . . . He looked at the luminous dial of his wristwatch. Seven-thirty. It was nearly eight hours since the police had blocked his car on Sunset Boulevard, just at the bottom of the winding canyon road where Katie lived. No questions, no struggle; he was used to the game. He had more than the usual reason for playing it cool. If they had found out about Katie . . .

Funny, about the wristwatch. They had left it, and all his other possessions, on his person. Not usual procedure.

Moreover, they had been reasonably polite. None of the accepted heckling and insults; no shoving, or accidental jabs. Maybe it just proved what Brother Rap had written in his autobiography: stand up to the pig, and he moves out of your way. The Paper Tiger. After all, every cop in the town knew Jackson by sight, and every one of them knew that he was backed up by a well-trained and well-armed paramilitary operation. It was an army that moved, not on its stomach, but on seething hate. Hate greased its rifles; hate disciplined its troops. And every cop in town also knew, or entertained the reasonable fear, that he himself had fueled that hate, and that, someday, he himself would lie bleeding in the debris and destruction wreaked by that hate. To many of them, it was simply a question of who made the first move.

Jackson smirked, to avoid outright laughter. This bladder bit, he thought, is the closest they've dared come to police brutality. They're scared shitless; they see the graffiti on the wall. Their capitalist overlords are shaking in their boots, and the lackeys have lost heart. Maybe they're trying to soften me up for some gutless attempts at accommodation. Why this hoked-up charge of grand larceny, or whatever it is, when they know the briefcase will bust me out of here by lunchtime?

He leaned back into the one bearable position he had so far discovered—spine slanting into the corner, shoulders propped up against the intersecting walls, head slumped and feet braced. No sweat. His grandfather, and the grandfathers without number before him, had suffered imprisonment more bitter and final. He could doze, but not so deeply as to grow groggy; he would be alert enough for whitey's next move.

Eyes closed, limbs numb, Jackson thought of the darkness and of nothing and of Katie Lee. A tiny smile jittered about his lips. Yes, he was growing old. Or something. Life didn't seem so full of imperatives anymore; emotions, not so kinetic. He loved Katie, and sought nothing further; but it was not like the first time, not like the bowel-crushing agony of that first hot malady. Never again. And he hated the constriction of this tiny cell, but that was not like the first time, either. Not that young man's electric terror when the door slammed shut, and his heart skulked down to his maw and trembled. He wasn't jaded. Far from it. He had just . . . grown used to things, learned the ropes. And that's what manhood was all about.

Patience. Cool. He would see Katie again; he would walk the free streets again. He would remember that they were not free, and neither was he, and he would plunge again into the work of the revolution. This setback was simply the aimless move of a desperate antagonist; he would counter, and time was on his side.

Fatigue could not dim his smile. Was this all the pigs could come up with? A piddling—

Suddenly, Chuzz Jackson jerked up straight.

They knew.

Theft. And his well-armed troops. And that meddling Finch. They knew.

CHAPTER XVII

AT eight-twenty, the tardy bell trilled down the main hall, and Emory Finch saw that he would be late to the meeting in the conference room.

He continued to argue with, wheedle and threaten the diffident black telephone receiver. At eight twenty-three, he hung up. And breathed what is called a sigh of relief.

He had been forced, for many reasons, to use the students' pay phone, which was set in an alcove across from the school's main office. Apologetically, he had smiled throughout the ten-minute call as several students, burdened with errands of their own, had frowned at this impropriety.

At one point, a wide and towering young lady had moved down upon him with the ominous placidity of a battleship.

"Hey, man," she had growled, raising a hand larger than his head, "that be for students. Ain't you got you own phone?"

"Shhh," whispered Finch, thinking fast. "I don't want the principal to know about my love life." He winked.

With a scream that diminished to desperate chokes and giggles, she had slapped him on the back. "That so?" Her voice had taken on the musical overtones associated with a heavy-duty cement mixer. "You checkin' up on you woman, huh? Got to make sure she stayin' where she belong?" Finch nodded, and she roared again. And then, as if the gods of deceit and trickery were in the ascendant that day, she mounted guard in front of him, like an Amazon before the treasure-house, and kept other interruptions at bay.

144

Finch had not been calling his woman. He had no woman to call.

But he had cut one thread in the Gordian knot tied around him by a certain very clever murderer. Or so he hoped. There was the strong possibility that he had simply followed a subtly constructed decoy down a verdant garden path.

"Well, well, well," Beverly snarled. "Looks like we going to have ourselves a kangaroo court, uh-huh." She closed the door of the conference room. "Excuse me, sir," she said, going out of her way to knock against a tight-lipped Orson, and slouched down toward the end of the long oak table.

Hockby, the only other person yet in the room, was standing by the end seat. The three pieces of gray tweed stretched tight across his rounded surfaces made more than one kind of contrast with the tall young woman's loose-flowing, blue-and-white West African robe. Her smirk was unthinking, a reflex action.

Hockby adopted the drawing-room-comedy manners of men who hate women. He bowed slightly and whisked out the end chair.

"Dear lady," he cooed, "may a gentleman offer his seat without appearing presumptuous?"

Beverly smiled.

"He might," she said. "I wouldn't know." She slipped into the old wooden chair to the right of his. "Would you?" She ran her eyes conspicuously up toward the head of the table, where Orson stood clothed in grim decorum. "Besides," she continued sweetly, "if it's proper that the host be seated at the head . . . is it not equally proper and fitting that, at the opposite end, his consort sit?" Her eyes looked fetchingly innocent.

Orson might have fired back, but Hockby, ever conscious in what quarters his paycheck lay, drew more flak toward himself.

"I'm flattered," he said as he sat down, "that a black

women deigns to sit down next to a Negro. Perhaps integration is on its way, after all."

"Oh, baby," hooted Beverly. "That word, black. You been hearing it, too? My, my. You sure you can spell it?"

"Better than that, dear. I can give you its etymological origin, its Latin equivalent, its sociohistorical—"

"Never mind all that, honey. I just wonder if you can spell it. I mean, that's 'B' as in black, not 'P' as in—"

"Jesus!" exclaimed Miss Lee as she swept into the little conference room. "I don't mean to gross everybody out, but I dropped one of these eyelashes into the john and I've had the damnedest time getting the other one off and then making my face look like something someone would want to come home to." She giggled nervously at the three stone-faced black colleagues and suppressed the obvious jokes. "Anyway," she went on, "I guess that doesn't sound very teacherlike; hope no one here is on the Professional Committee. With all that's going on, I don't honestly feel very professional this morning."

"Really?" chirped Beverly. "That's a surprise." She grinned broadly. "You certainly look like a professional, honey."

Katie Lee smiled back with the intoxication of a woman given reason to unsheathe claws.

"Why, thank you," she said. "In that outfit, you don't look much like an amateur yourself." Beverly nodded in appreciation. "It must be very comfortable," continued Katie. "Loose-fitting like that, it gives you plenty of room to move around; easy to put on . . . or take off. It's just the thing for you. Did you make it yourself?"

"No," answered Beverly, and her voice sounded slightly stiffer. "I'm not very . . . uh, domestic; like all the black women in Texas. And I don't have natural rhythm, either."

"Why, Beverly, honey," said the pained Katie. "You know I didn't mean—"

The sharp thud surprised both contestants.

Orson, who never thought patience a virtue if practiced to excess, had struck the table with his fist. He had tired of the pretense that he was an administrative official meeting with

nameless, mechanical functionaries of the educational bureau-
cracy. He was Orson, and they were Katie and Beverly and
Floyd, and they all knew enough about each other to pull
down the walls of the school. No strangers were watching; he
did not see the point in playing sadistic little games.

"Girls," he said, "cut it."

Miss Lee flinched, but Beverly Minere laughed loudly.

"Now that," she said, "is a breath of nice fresh air in this
stuffy room."

"Thanks," the principal wryly replied. "And now, at the
risk of sounding pompous, let me apologize for keeping you
waiting. Despite what you probably suspect, Beverly, this is
not one of my tricks. Finch has—"

"Finch!" Beverly snorted.

"Oh, Christ!" Hockby chimed in.

"The two are not connected, I think," Miss Lee said coolly.
"Nevertheless, the former appears to be assuming some of the
prerogatives of the latter." She sat down wearily in the middle
chair on the left of the table—across, but not quite across,
from Beverly. Katie laughed softly.

"You are amused, Miss Lee?" Hockby kindly wrinkled the
smooth flesh around his eyes—a fatherly touch.

"Oh, hell, Floyd. Drop the funny stuff, okay? I'm tired, and
I'm confused, and I want this foolishness to end. I don't mean
just the investigation and the (quote) campus unrest (unquote); no, I mean the whole business. The way we live here,
the way we get along and don't get along, the way we hate
each other. . . ."

"Welcome to the ghetto."

"Beverly, that's not it. Not really it." Miss Lee sighed and
pushed back her coiffure. "I was laughing because I keep
thinking the that old saying . . . about strange bedfellows. . . ."

"You've got reason, of course."

"Damn it, Beverly, come off it!"

"Hey, girl, you watch—"

"Drop that crap!" Katie almost screamed. "Drop it! You

think I'm ashamed of sleeping with Chuzz Jackson? You think you can get your jollies needling me because I'm hiding a black man under the sheets?"

In that dead-silent room, Beverly did not answer. No one answered. Hockby froze, and Orson looked at the young white woman with something that resembled admiration. Miss Minere gazed stolidly at her own tight fist.

Katie's voice dropped to a kind of gentle, mindless chant.

"I'm sorry," she said, "I'm sorry for the whole mess, and for the way you feel, and for my being so damned white, and for the hurt to a black woman when a black man sneaks off with any pale-faced broad. I'm sorry. But I love him, Beverly. His blackness may be part of that; I suspect it is. But blackness is a part of him, and so I'm loving the man he is. That's what I think. That's what he thinks. That's what I wish you could think."

When Beverly's reply finally came, it was almost inaudible. Katie could not tell whether it was muffled by embarrassment, or by hate.

"And what do you care what a little nigger girl thinks?"

"Oh, Beverly," cried Miss Lee, and looked the other woman in the face. "Please don't keep that up. I can't take it. I'm a woman and you're a woman. We need each other. You loved a man who was killed; I love a man who's been jailed, who might be beaten or killed without—"

"And so now," said Beverly, "now you see what it is to be black in the white man's world."

"No." Katie Lee shook her head slowly. "No. I see what it is to love a man so much that I am hurt when he is hurt, and I will be unable to live, I will die if he. . . ."

"Sounds like vintage soap opera to me," said Hockby, who had kept quiet long enough and enjoyed making light of feminine hysteria. He hated women for being allowed to show feelings he wanted to express.

"Shut up," said Beverly.

"Help me." Katie almost whispered; she could no longer look up. "Please help me."

And Beverly Minere rose to her feet heavily, and walked to the room's one window, and looked out into the gray street below. She stared for several moments, and saw nothing; her thoughts lay in a great void as she drifted back across the wounded past which had made her what she was this morning. She did not smile. She did not turn.

The dirty pane of the window gave off ghostly reflections —her own proud face, and pale shadows in the distance that were all she now remembered of Orson, and of Floyd Hockby, and of Miss Katie Lee, the white girl from Texas. She was alone. And that was nice in its familiarity. It was a station she had stopped in often; it was home.

Her voice splintered into little chips that fell awkwardly to the floor.

"Interesting," she said. "But I can't. I can't." She turned around and looked sadly at the frightened Miss Lee. "Uh . . . Katie?" The other woman did not move. "Maybe . . . I would like to. Maybe I would be more of a woman if I could. Old habits are hard to break." Instinctively, Beverly shrugged her shoulders, as if brushing away an unpleasant thought. "I just can't."

"Good morning, everybody!" said Finch, casting unwanted sunshine into the gloom he had not yet noticed. "Have I missed anything?"

"Finch," laughed Orson, "your timing is—"

But Beverly interrupted savagely. "Nothing," she said, "that you can't dredge up later." Angry, or so it would appear, she sat down.

"Now, now," Finch said. "Cooperation is the word of the hour." He scurried to the chair at Orson's left, seated himself and looked gaily across the one empty seat at the scowling Beverly. A grimy little notebook slipped magically onto the table. "Everyone's not here yet, but when they are, one person in this room will be a very, very bad person."

He smiled. But the others frowned.

"But," he continued, "What's a little murder among friends?"

CHAPTER XVIII

"THIS is presumptuous," glared Hockby.

"No doubt," agreed the journalism teacher.

"I don't have to stay for this," said Beverly.

"You do," said Orson.

"Begging your pardon," rejoined Finch, "she doesn't." He looked around the room from one suspicious face to another. "No one does. I have no right, I have no authority." He paused. "I do not even have . . . the answer."

"Then why," said Katie very quietly, "drag us through all this when the school's about to blow up outside?"

"A good question." Finch gazed at his little notebook. "It's my belief, or my intuition, that, when our other three friends arrive, there will be only one person in this room who will not be looking for the truth. And that person, I would think, will be—"

"The murderer," Beverly interjected.

"It would seem so."

"Beautiful," sneered Hockby. "The man or, if the ladies present will excuse me for saying so, the woman in question will inadvertently reveal himself, Gannett will leap out of the closet, and Finch will return home with a warm heart."

"I doubt it," said Orson.

"And so do I, of course." Finch spoke calmly. He flipped open the cover of the little notebook; his right thumb moved down the first page lazily.

"Well, then," said Miss Lee, who for some private reason

had reverted to a long-lost drawl, "we are wasting time. And I reckon there are better things to be doing."

"Maybe." Finch leaned over the table; his thin form dwindled beneath hunched shoulders. His irony came gently. "But I'm a-thinking, Miz Lee, that we shore nuff ought to get ourselves together right now." The contrived dialect failed, and so he dropped it quickly. Finch was too gentle, too forgiving, to develop the cruel perceptions that make a clever mimic. He flushed slightly, winced, fell back on his own flat vowels and accurate consonants. "In a manner of speaking, we are all in this thing. We hate each other, or distrust each other—which is much the same thing at bottom. And I don't mean to change that. Let it lie. But we've got two common enemies: the threat of violence here—"

"That frighten you, huh?"

"Frightens you, Beverly. We all know that. You didn't want it this way; neither did Benedict. Oh, you wouldn't mind flag burning and explosions and a few knocked heads, but this is something else. And you're scared, damned scared."

Miss Minere did not deign to reply. Nor, this once, did she deign to shrug her shoulders. She did not even snort. Finch went on, his voice colorless.

"Anyway, as I see it, that's one enemy. The other is the murderer himself. Now, I don't think he's a maniac out to kill off the rest of us. Far from it. But his very success exacerbates the hostilities of our precarious world here at McAdoo. It could be any one of us, and so we all fear each other the more." He frowned slightly. "Naturally, I do not expect human beings to become concerned about such an abstract danger. There is another, more practical danger. Until he is found, we are all suspect."

"And what's the harm? The innocent," Hockby sententiously intoned, "have nothing to fear."

"Nothing," Finch shot back, "but an unrelenting scrutiny into the secret nooks and dark crannies of our private lives. Is that, all things considered, a pleasant prospect?"

The cold silence, which began as a sharp gasp, finally became so oppressive that only Orson had the nerve to make cracks in it.

"Strange," he ventured, "that no one here concurs with the analysis of the police."

"Yeah, you'd think so," snapped Beverly. "That's a Tom talking." Katie fought back tears, and Hockby fought back a fit of laughter. Finch just rolled inexorably on.

"Their analysis is, in the truest use of the word I've heard lately, irrelevant. Neither true, nor false. They had their reasons, as the saying goes, and their reasons have little to do with us, or with the facts."

"He's been implicated," said Hockby.

"So have we all," rejoined Finch. "And that's exactly why I, uh, suggested to Mr. Orson that we have this meeting."

"I still don't get it," murmured Katie. "Please. I just want to go home."

No one knew just what Beverly almost retorted, but they were all surprised that she didn't say it aloud. Katie, who was not unaware or ungrateful, breathed a sigh of relief.

"As usual," said Finch, "I probably haven't made myself clear—"

"No matter," grumbled Beverly. "If this is the kind of hokum I think it is, we're just passing the time of day. Another thing . . . ." She glared directly at Orson. "All this honesty and laying of cards on the table might thrill some people to the marrow, but not this sister. I don't forget where I stand. This business affects the school; it affects the students—"

"Beverly's got her wind back."

"Shut up, Hockby. By the way . . . some white man actually give you that sanctified name, or did you peel it off the back of some cereal box?"

"I never nay-say a lady." He grinned.

"No. And you won't touch them, either; you're one fine dude. As I was saying, the one principle I've fought for around this honky-run institution is student involvement. I'll sit still for your parlor games, Finch. What's the harm? I'll just play-act that I'm dozing in the back of the bus, you know? But I'm not getting tricked into backstage maneuvers where the students are concerned. No matter what happens here, I'm not the girl who's going out to the BSU with the word: Lay off now, boys; trust the great white fathers and their ass-licking Toms. No, sir. Doesn't work that way with old Beverly. You want the boys called off, then you bring them in here and let them listen for themselves. That is . . . if you think you can come up with some reason why they shouldn't burn the place down."

Hockby fairly sputtered. "Students, Beverly, have no place in the councils of—"

"Shut up, Hockby," came the familiar refrain, but the voice was Orson's. Hockby shut up.

"As our President would say," smiled Finch, "I'm glad you brought that one up."

"I just bet you are."

"Coincidentally, one of our missing three guests is Scrounge Roberson."

"My God!" choked Hockby. "Why? Because he's the leader of that illiterate rabble that calls itself the Black Student Union? I see again," he said, looking angrily at Beverly, "where the power lies in this uppity shantytown. You let him into an adult deliberation because he's got half the faculty here scared white?"

"Partly, I guess," answered Finch. "And partly because he, like all of us, is a pretty hot suspect."

"You are more addled than you look."

"Beverly, I'd be the last to disagree on that point. But before we get into that scene, there's one important point which, surprisingly, no one has yet brought up. And the very fact that no one has proves that it is important; I mean, it (that is, the absence of its discussion) implies an incredible but

significant assumption which, if we were to take its reverse
implications, might just—"

Miss Lee laughed aloud. "Good old Finch! I do declare, you
can make simple things confusing."

"Right on," agreed Beverly. "You can't be for real."

"Maybe I can explain," Orson said. "Finch and I discussed
this earlier."

"I yield to the uh . . . clearer man," Finch laughed.

"What he means is, there's a question no one has asked,
because we all think we know the answer. Now, if we know
the answer to that one in some mysterious, subconscious
manner, we might know the answer to some others."

"Oh," said Hockby with his characteristic sneer.

Beverly threw off another of her famous smirks. "Thanks a
lot, old man."

"Just what," Miss Lee asked levelly, "is the question?"

Finch lit up boyishly.

"How do you all know," he asked in answer, "that I didn't
kill Benedict?"

Once again, that little room fell suddenly still.

Katie Lee saw her decision first.

"I wish you-all would stop dropping bombs," she said. "I'm
getting shell-shocked."

"Right on," agreed Beverly, as the few voices stirred into a
small hubbub and the lungs relaxed with air that seemed
suddenly fresher.

Hockby appeared much more cautious. "Smart," he mused
aloud. "Damned smart, Finch. My congratulations."

"I beg your pardon?" Finch caught on, but smiled.

"Well, it's obvious, isn't it? Take the bull by the horns, that
is, before you get gored from behind. Or, if you prefer, you
offer to drink from the poisoned cup, and we are diverted
from suspecting that you might be the poisoner. Or, to take
our imagery from the era of—"

"You're a trip, Brother Floyd," said Beverly at this junc-
ture. "Please shut up."

Finch laughed amicably. "Logically, Hockby, you're on

target." He paused. "My point, though, is that we should, as a kind of experiment, throw logic out the window. You see—"

"But you couldn't have," interrupted the upset Miss Lee. "This is silly; we all know—"

"On the contrary," answered Finch. "Logically, I'm in the best, or, depending on your point of view, the worst position for committing the crime. It was in my room, after all, and occurred at a time which was most convenient for me. Further—"

"But why should—?" Katie could not contain herself.

"Further, I might have more reason than anybody. Everyone knows that Benedict and I shared the secrets of the school. It is not unlikely, nor would it be unreasonable to assume, that I might have spilled too much, or that Benedict inadvertently let something slip that I wanted to use for myself."

"But," Katie stepped on the word, then backed off and spoke more slowly. "If . . . if you could do that, Emory . . . if you really did . . . murder Benedict, then . . . ."

"Go on," snapped Beverly, who seemed suddenly impatient for some reason of her own.

"Well . . . then everything we've believed about . . . everything . . . about . . ." She turned distractedly from Beverly's clouding brow to Orson's fixed mask. " . . . Finch, and about Finch and Benedict . . . . The whole feel of the thing has been a lie." She frowned. "Know what I mean? Nothing specific, nothing definite . . . just the feel of the thing . . . just everything we took for granted."

"Thanks," Finch said with quiet sincerity.

"What do you mean? For what?"

"Dear little Katie," came Hockby's characteristic smirk. "He pretends gratitude for your faith, trust and charity; he's actually grateful, I should think, that you jumped so eagerly into the breach."

Miss Lee let her impatience show. "Shoot it straight," she said, with unaccustomed venom.

IT NEVER RAINS IN LOS ANGELES   157

Hockby faked a courtly inclination of the head. "A pleasure," he said. Orson winced and Beverly mumbled an oath. Hockby silently forgave these plebeians. "Your touching confusion, your despair at the prospect of seeing old gods topple, suggests that you accept the man's logic, which runs something like this: we must throw logic over the sill and accept illogic as our credo. We must, as it has been phrased, listen to the gentle murmurings of the heartstrings. Finch, to the casual observer, is a prime suspect. And yet, as even the cynic in me must cringingly admit, none of us thinks . . . my mistake. I should say, for it is more to the point, none of us *feels* that Finch is the one. Correct, worthy Finch?"

"On the head," agreed Finch.

"And so we have here," Hockby continued, "a fine jewel of a paradox. Emory Finch, the cold and logical one, now lowers himself to the greasy pools of sentiment; he asks that we feel around for the murderer. And why not? We have nothing better to do this morning. I, for one, am not inspired to lead my first period class through further repetition of *America est patria mea;* it would seem, as Beverly puts it . . ."

"Irrelevant?" She obliged him.

The door burst open and Scrounge Roberson shot into the room, breathless and sweaty at the seams.

"Miss Minere," he gasped, as he ran toward her chair. "Come quick!" The teachers, instantly alert, now heard low squeals and muted tread beyond the green plaster walls. "The Panthers are here, and they've got their guns—"

"Typical," sniffed the imperturbable Hockby.

Roberson ignored him. "They've come in by the main gate," he rushed on, "and they've taken up defensive positions down the hall. And Jackson is—"

"Oh," Katie bleated, and gripped tightly the seat of her chair. Beverly waved her silent.

But Roberson was not to be stopped.

"—is marching this way straight into—"

"Into the hearty welcome of loving arms," Hockby sang.

"Into a group of the BAM boys. That cat who calls himself Ulabenzi and preaches about how he's going to kill all the—"

"Finch," barked a tense Orson, who was already on his feet and headed toward his inner office, "you didn't tell me that—"

"Finch?" an amazed Beverly almost shouted. "Finch? You mean you know about this?"

"Fools run in . . ." murmured Hockby.

Finch still sat calmly and caressed his little notebook. "Well, well," he said happily, "it looks as if I'm a fairly successful host. No one declined the invitation. The party can begin."

Someone groaned softly, and it might have been Hockby. He wasn't smirking.

CHAPTER XIX

MURDERER LOOSE;
GHETTO TREMBLES
by Herman Steidman

Terror stalks the streets of the black ghetto this morning. A vicious murderer lurks while mothers and their babes shudder behind closed doors.

Even to this seasoned reporter, tensions seem strung to an unbelievable pitch. The lone white journalist, although escorted by police officers, meets with naught but fear, suspicion and hate. Friendly questions are shoved aside rudely; well-meaning comments are met by baleful stares.

Yes, today's terror springs from deeper roots than the isolated murder of a student at McAdoo High School. Area residents well know that fighting, knifing and even shooting are often the order of the day at that institution. Ghetto children and their parents are not surprised by violence; they feed on it.

And that is the real tragedy today.

For the sages of history have been proved right: violence breeds violence, and those who live by the sword . . . . Well, the reader knows the rest.

It is time that the right-thinking citizens of the black community take heart and stand up to let themselves be counted on the side of human decency. So long as they remain silent, the banner will continue to be carried by dissidents, paramilitary revolutionaries and other self-styled spokesmen for the people.

This paper operates under the firm conviction that all men can be persuaded to reasonable behavior. We urge that rewards be consequent with the deeds. Those who mislead their followers into the paths of irresponsible action should be dealt with accordingly; on the other hand, those who subscribe to the principles which have made this society great should be given their just due.

It is time our black people realized that publicity-seeking, so-called charismatic leaders are in fact a pack of modern-day Judases, twisted by ambition and impudence.

Chuzz Jackson, the Panther leader charged with Williams' murder, has openly advocated overthrow of the government and mass executions of those who disagree with his totalitarian methods. Today, he is loose on bond.

In this instance, we agree with that police official who says, "We need a reexamination of the system which allows obviously dangerous men to roam the streets at will. What about the constitutional rights of the general citizenry?" We can only echo his question.

Commendation is due the fine investigative work of Detective Sgt. Gannett and his capable staff. Within twenty-four hours, despite a prevailing lack of cooperation from recalcitrant black leaders and frightened white faculty members, he wrapped up the case. Now his work may be nullified by the slow processes necessary on the way to conviction.

Meanwhile, other elements in the ghetto divide the people and sow distrust of the honesty and competence of the city's duly elected officials.

BAM, an alleged Afro-cultural organization headed by a shady figure who calls himself Sugawee, is no doubt delighted by the prospects of today's tense situation. They do not love the men and women who are the lifeblood of the ghetto. Their only interest is the extinction of those who would oppose them.

Sadly, the students of McAdoo and other black schools in the area are caught in the vise of these warring factions.

We have it on good authority that the Black Student Union at McAdoo, which switches ideologically from one militant stance to another, is at present dominated by young firebrands who sympathize with the Panthers. One wonders at a principal who would cloister such extracurricular clubs on his campus. The downtown Board of Education might take note. The overburdened middle-class taxpayer might well ponder how his monies are being used.

The BSU, further, is under the guidance of a young radical of dubious qualifications, a certain Miss Beverly Minere. Popular with students because she concurs with their every move, Miss Minere has a background of questionable activities which stretches from her own school days at McAdoo through police confrontations at Berkeley. She is often photographed with nationally known black demagogues; she rarely misses a violent demonstration or an anarchists' conference.

We cannot, therefore, place full blame upon the backs of the unsophisticated albeit idealistic students.

No crime is more heinous than the subversion of our young people. Let the cynical manipulators who masquerade as their friends take warning. Society is growing impatient with reckless adventurers; the ax will fall.

Sane counselors will entreat our city's black folk to adopt a course of calm deliberation. No lasting reform will result from chaos. Patience should be the watchword today.

This is not Mississippi in 1830.

Who can doubt that the black man in Los Angeles has good friends in high places? In government, business and educational circles, there are sincere men at work; they must have time to find answers which will be fair to all. The world cannot be changed overnight. Already, many influential leaders of the community have met with advisory groups from all races; hard-hitting questions have been entertained with an open mind.

The city watches with bated breath as the day dawns in the ghetto.

Will it be truly a New Day for our black citizens? Or will it be another dark day? Will violence erupt so viciously that the guardians of the law will be forced to take a firm hand?

Make no mistake about it.

Our public servants have promised, above all, to protect the lives and property of all Angelenos. Those who use the death of Benedict Williams as excuse for their looting and anarchy will be paid in kind. They will be paid in full.

Tighter methods of control are already mapped out. The extent of repression will depend entirely on the extent of the rebellion. Wisdom will prevail.

CHAPTER XX

"Goodness," Miss Lee giggled with a strange new giddiness, "this makes the United Nations look like a down-home reunion." For that unspoken reason which everyone in the room well knew, she let her words reel out in a tipsy stagger.

It looked, indeed, as if everyone was there.

The major philosophies which clashed daily behind the doors and on the street corners around William McAdoo High School were represented. For the first time, these leaders sat around a common table. After so many months of seclusion within dark shadows, they made a shocking conjunction beneath the school's cheap fluorescent lighting. Some had sworn death to others. Now they were arranged neatly, as if awaiting a prospective buyer.

At the head of the table, Orson sat again. His functional respectability made him seem the strangest of them all; it did nothing to allay his loneliness. He, least of all, could see a friendly face within the room. In one opinion, the other seven undeniably concurred; Orson was a Tom. The term meant different things to these differing people, but they all felt it fit Orson like a handcuff.

Finch sat to the principal's left. He waved no banners, but he was seen as the library-reared intellectual, another do-gooder white fed on unrealistic theories. His kind was not often seen on faculties in the ghetto; they did not last. They quickly moved to "advisory" positions downtown, or they published a mournful book and made their names familiar on the pages of liberal magazines.

Next to Finch sat Chuzz Jackson. He was a Panther, and no one needed further explanation. There was no mistake in the meaning of his black leather jacket, dark shades, shoulder holster and shiny-smacked boots; they spoke for him. He was solid and formidable as any statue; he had not even looked toward Katie Lee, who sat directly across from him.

Beverly, who now proved she could be equally cool, sat next to Jackson. She was the campus-bred revolutionary; her idealism could not yet stomach the fascist tendencies of the Panthers nor yet the cynical manipulations of the BAM leaders. She did not trust their answers to the questions she thought important; she was still asking. And this trait kept her still younger than the others. In another time, she would have been happiest as sponsor of the senior class, or of the cheering squad. But those things had been drowned beneath the babble of revolutionary voices. She trusted no one in the room.

Hockby still sat at the end of the table. He wondered, although his imperious stare did not appear reflective, how these insignificant people could consider their actions important. *So,* he thought to himself, *I am the only white Negro here. So be it. I have taken the only honorable position.* He was confident that he had remained above the filth of involvement; he had avoided the extremes represented by Orson, the ass licker, and Jackson, the ass kicker. He smiled secretly. What he did to that forbidden altar of the body was purely for sensual pleasure. No, he was the only one who had steered his path in the direction of history; of that, he was sure. He had not detoured into the inconsequential bickerings peculiar to this part of the twentieth century.

Between him and Miss Lee squirmed the only person in that room who showed emotion. Scrounge Roberson was too young, or too sensitive, to play it cool. He felt deeply; he worried hard. Unlike the others, he thought something might be solved by one speech, or one right decision, or one meeting.

Even this one. Now he was confused by the ideological jumble around him. It could not be graphed.

Miss Lee smiled. If they thought she was the bleeding-heart missionary trying to assuage shameful guilt feelings, that was just fine and dandy. She didn't mind being put in her place, if it was a safe place. She could think of worse.

Ulabenzi sat stiffly between her and Principal Orson. He was, in effect, Sugawee's ambassador on earth; he was the prophet, and no one would question his authority. The great man himself, no doubt, had already found a new lair and might even now be feasting on mystic thoughts so that his followers could scramble for crumbs. Ulabenzi could handle these temporal affairs; he was a useful machine. Swathed in violent hues, he tried for his master's air of judicious solemnity. He just looked empty.

The eight people seated around the table looked, in their jarring variety, like guests assembled for a provocative panel show. Curiously, however, they remained silent. Because they hated each other passionately, and for no other reason apparent to an outsider, seven of these vocal people sat back and let Finch and his little notebook speak.

"Curiously enough," began Finch, "each clue in this case points to a different suspect." He spoke without preamble, as if they had come near the climax of a prolonged discussion. In a sense, they had. No one had spoken since the entrance of the last three participants; Katie's slight remark had lain unnoticed on the table. But the preliminaries had been taken care of long before. They all knew why they were there. They all wanted to get to the point.

"I have been talking to several people since yesterday morning," Finch continued. "I have made guesses and assumptions. Let me make one thing clear." He opened his notebook again and held up the first page. "To save time, this is a list of our names and our . . . uh, incriminating circumstances. This is not an accusation; few things written here can be proved. After I read it, I will . . . uh, as if it were a flag, burn it." He smiled at his little joke.

No one laughed.

Finch cleared his throat. "To the point, then. As you like. I will, to be fair, start with myself; I head the list. If you doubt my intentions, they are simple. I want to show how the murderer, whoever he is, has taken care to implicate each one of us." He paused. "And then we will deliberate. Agreed?"

A head or two nodded. Most did not move.

"Well. After me, we'll go around the table, to the dealer's left. Benedict was killed in my room at a time most convenient for me. He was killed by means of a machine I had given him permission to use . . . had, in fact, taught him how to use."

"But why would you—?" Scrounge bit his lip.

"Sorry, Scrounge, but motives need not come into this discussion. Not yet. No one needs to protest innocence, as I go down the list; again, this is no proof." He turned toward Chuzz Jackson, who stared at the wall behind Miss Lee. "Mr. Jackson here—"

"Call me Chuzz." The Panther leader laughed in a brief burst of life. *"Mr. Jackson* sounds like a pallbearer at some dirt-farmer's wake."

Beverly snickered, but Finch warmed up to the stiffer man beside him. Jackson's remark had been an encouraging sally from the potential enemy—wary, poised for self-defense, but not yet edged with hostility. Here is a fair man, thought Finch. Or maybe he has nothing to hide.

"Chuzz, as we all know, is a competent leader. He's a tough disciplinarian, and his men don't move without his orders, or at least his foreknowledge." The Panther leader raised an eyebrow. It was not idle flattery; Finch was leading somewhere. He waited him out. "Therefore," continued the journalism teacher, "it is safe to assume that he knew of the arsenal thefts—"

"Reappropriation," corrected Jackson coldly.

"The reappropriation of certain weapons and supplies. In short, he had principal access to the cannister of Theldhron."

Even Finch faltered. Chuzz Jackson was a terrifying figure, even to his own men. The room thrilled with the anticipation of some retaliatory move. A denial, or a counterattack. Or something more violent.

Jackson slowly turned his full gaze toward Emory Finch. No expression softened his proud and lonely face. Katie's heart went out to him.

"Well?" he said simply. "If I understand the rules of the game, we're just running down the list. Without comment. Please continue."

Scrounge Roberson sat up straighter. He had found a new idol.

"Thanks," smiled Finch. "Those are the rules." He glanced at his scrawled notes, then indicated Beverly with a slight wave of the left hand. "In some instances," he went on, "I transgress into private affairs. Under ordinary circumstances, my . . . uh, snooping would be inexcusable. Even now, it is difficult to—"

"Ain't foolin' nobody," Beverly drawled. Her pulse raced, but she looked calm as any judge. "No secrets, right?" Her grin was defiant, but her hands met nervously beneath the table. "Or are your middle-class morals sizzling with shame? Want to bring up my little jazz with the dear departed?" She seemed contemptuously amused, but the effort cost her plenty. And Finch knew it.

"No," he answered quietly. His next words came in a whisper. "The sleeping capsules."

Everyone stared at Beverly, who had suddenly looked away. Only Katie Lee did not seem to grasp the significance of Emory's information. "What capsules?" she blurted out, then foolishly covered her gaping mouth.

"What capsules?" echoed Beverly. In the moment, she had regained her fighting stance. "Don't play dumb-eyes with me, girl. You and your boy both knew; don't try sucking me under, sweetheart." Her eyes flashed and her voice trembled in the lower ranges of its rich alto. "And two were missing right after—"

A firm hand grasped her elbow.

"Cool it, Beverly." Chuzz did not raise his strong voice. He did not even look at her. But the hand stayed; its grip was sure. "Nobody's pointing at nobody."

"Shit they ain't!" Beverly shouted, but the Panther had won the round. Breathing heavily, she subsided into a petulant heap. It was a posture that never failed to amuse Orson and he grinned, knowing he would not be noticed.

Miss Lee, however, was not satisfied. "Nobody believes me, apparently, but I'm still confused. Suppose I took the capsules. What was I supposed to have done with them? With my Southern background, I need uppers just to keep up with the rest of you—not downers." She laughed, but it was a tired sound. "You see what kind of language I'm learning from the students."

Finch ignored her last remark. "The nerve gas was . . . uh, transferred to a gelatin capsule that would fit into the duplicating machine."

Katie seemed fascinated, or very cautious. For a moment, Finch could not decide which. "I'm no scientist," she unnecessarily began, "but just how—"

"That," Hockby boldly interjected, "is where I come in." He had decided there was an advantage to jumping in before he was pushed. There was no avoiding the confession, but at least he might select the words. He knew the dangerous suggestiveness of language. With a grimace of condescension, he met the puzzled faces which beamed toward him. "I am a sensualist," he said. "I am in love with life. I groove, as it were, on fine foods and rare wines and choice poetry. Nevertheless, it must be admitted, there are occasions on which, in my pursuit of pleasure, I experiment in ways that might be somewhat offensive to delicate sensibilities. The world offers—"

"In short," sneered Beverly, "you like—"

"No," Finch mouthed at her.

"In short," continued Hockby, stamping on them both, "the nerve gas was, as Finch so elegantly phrased it, transferred to the gelatin capsule through the agency of a device known as a hypodermic." He paused briefly. "I have such a device."

"Jesus!" laughed Scrounge Roberson. "So old dictie Hockby's a junkie. Well, well."

"Young man," came the hate-soaked response, "I trust you understand and subscribe to the rules of this affair. This is private business. It does not leave this room. That was the agreement. I trust you understand."

"He does," Finch said mildly.

"He hasn't said so," Hockby countered. "I want his word."

"He agreed," said Beverly, "when he walked into this room. We all did. Even you."

"But he's just a kid!"

"And what has that to do with it?" Beverly's fury rose to match Hockby's. "He is a responsible human being; he has a stake in all this, just like all the other students. Besides," she cooed suddenly, "I hear you usually like kids like him."

"That's enough, Miss Minere." Orson, the silent commander, stood up at the head of the table. "I fully appreciate the contempt in which you hold my superiors downtown. But, as they would say, this petty bickering is counterproductive. Four people have now been tenuously linked with Benedict's death. We are all, I expect, eager to hear how the rest of us may be implicated. We are all suffering from the strains and tensions of accusation, suspicion and, to some extent, a nonparticularized fear. We have little time to play." He sat down. "Mr. Finch, I trust you can speed us to some useful conclusion."

"I'm sorry," said Katie with determination, "but I have to say something—even after that nice speech, Mr. Orson." The principal merely shrugged his shoulders; he wasn't entirely certain that her naivete ran that deep. "I think it's terrible to make Scrounge go through this. I mean, he's just a student." She realized her mistake. "Now don't get me wrong, it's just—"

"I know what you mean," the boy said, as if to save her further embarrassment. For him, this was an unusual gesture. "But I could have done it, you know."

"Why, you were —"

"Fair enough," said Hockby. "He wants the privileges of adulthood; let him share the burdens, too. And don't bother to shut me up, Beverly. That's all I have to say."

"Now ain't that cold?" Beverly was clowning again. "You spoiled my fun for me."

Finch stepped in quickly. "Since we're all friends again, let's get back to the main subject," he said. "Scrounge, after all, comes next. I had the machine; Chuzz, the gas; Beverly, the capsule; Hockby, the needle. From here on, connections are more suggestive than specific. Scrounge, for example, is the only one here who would be in close touch with the necessary scientific know-how."

Hockby snorted. "I don't believe it. That would take a young genius."

"And that," replied Finch, "is exactly what you have sitting next to you, Hockby. Scrounge Roberson is not so articulate as Benedict was; he's not so original as some of the young poets in your Latin III class. However, if you ever bothered to read the little newspaper my students put out every now and then, you would notice that he has copped every city-wide math and science prize offered during the last year."

"I warned you that all that apple-polishing would get you in trouble," said Beverly kindly. But young Roberson still frowned. He took himself, and Benedict's death, too seriously to entertain these speculations lightly.

Finch saw the boy's difficulty, but it was too late to be kind. He made his point.

"Moreover, according to Roberson's teachers, he has a particular affinity for chemistry. He reads widely on his own; in fact, he subscribes to a scientific journal which, during the last year, has twice discussed the nature and possibilities of Theldhron 12."

"That's n-not proof," Scrounge stammered.

"It's all right, son," said Orson with fatherly warmth. The principal's pose galled the young man; he could not bear being in the position of seeming to need comfort from the man he loathed. He struggled for speech.

"I-it's not . . . it's not all right." he looked Finch square in the eye. "I'm interested in . . . genetics; I want to prove—"

Jackson caught it first.

"Yeah, man," he said, and the rumble of the deep voice somehow clasped the nervous boy in its warmth. "Dig." This tough leader of militants smiled; his stern lips relaxed gently into soft promises, like the petal of a rose. "That's cool. I dig you."

The moment was quickly over, and Finch moved on. He, like every other person seated around the table, sensed that something precious had passed between the boy and the man. It was something no one else could share. It resembled the love between brothers, or the love a good officer gives his wounded soldiers. And yet it was really neither of these things and would not be easily understood. It was real; it was embarrassing. And so attention shifted hastily to Katie Lee. She was next on Emory's little list.

"Miss Lee," said Finch, "is no better off than I."

"Gracious," she laughed. "How did I fall so low?"

"You just walked into my room that afternoon," he replied seriously, "and we talked a little while about the South, and about your Mama, and about domesticity, and—"

"Oh my God," Katie breathed.

Jackson started, Orson smiled and Hockby beat Beverly to the obvious question.

"Come now," he whined, "are the rest of us not to be allowed—?"

Katie interrupted him. "But I was just playing, Emory; you know that. I was just trying to cheer—"

"She came into my room" Finch told the others, "and we kidded around for a few minutes. She said I was sloppy and careless and needed a woman to straighten me out." He slipped a hand automatically through his thinning hair. "I suspect she's right. Jokingly, or so it might appear, Katie offered to show me what I was missing—"

"Hey," said Beverly. "Let's keep it clean."

Finch begrudged her a wan smile. "What I should have said, is that she offered to clean up my room. I accepted and, because it seemed to be the spirit of the thing, she actually did go around the room and bring it to order."

"Chuzz, honey, I swear—"

"And that means," Finch went on, "that Katie Lee is the last person I saw go near the ditto machine. We left the room together."

To her credit, Miss Lee had not enjoyed seeing the others put on the stand; she relished her own position even less. Her mouth twitched strangely; her eyes darted nervously about the room. It was her natural impulse, in times of stress, to lean on a man; but this was definitely not the time and place. She was on her own. In a moment, she would have started to babble nonsense, but Orson unwittingly saved her.

To lighten the silence, he asked, "But are you sure she actually went to the machine?"

"No," Finch admitted. "She had time. She could have. She might not have. But the point, as with all the others, is that—"

"The point," sobbed Katie, who had finally broken down, "is that this whole thing is turning us into monsters." On her right, the embarrassed Scrounge shrank into his seat; Ulabenzi, on her left, remained as impassive as he had been throughout the entire meeting. "We aren't human any more."

"That," mumbled Hockby, "was the implication of the term, monsters."

"Mr. Hockby," began an annoyed Orson, but Katie cut him off.

"Finch is right," she said. There was a gasp that ran around the table; Jackson tensed. "No, no," she continued with a grimace of impatience. "I mean, what he said earlier; before everyone got here. About how we've all been shut off by this thing. No one trusts anybody." She was steadier now, but she could not yet look at Jackson; the undeniable impulse was still too strong. "If Finch can't tell, just because of the trust that exists between decent human beings, whether I was sincere that afternoon . . . then what does it matter if we find the murderer? It's all over for us." Now her voice was firm, and tinged with anger. "If you don't know, Finch, then we never knew each other."

"Granted." Finch had not paused; his reply had been sure. Now he let an idle smile wander across his slender features. "I keep having to remind you," he said, "that I'm just going down the list . . . without fear or favor. You could have done it, Katie; you could have." He turned the page of his notebook, almost as if dismissing the subject entirely. "Whether or not you did, of course, is matter for conjecture. Or intuition."

"And what's your . . . intuition?" asked Katie, still angry.

"First things first," was her colleague's businesslike response.

"I think old Finch be like an alley cat playin' round with Brother Rat," crooned Beverly. Scrounge Roberson laughed curtly. "I b'lieve he enjoyin' hisself."

"We have," said the journalism teacher, "another suspect." He was gazing curiously at the immobile representative from BAM.

"Two more," corrected Orson. He seemed as hearty as any good sport at a fraternity initiation. "Don't forget me."

"I hadn't," replied Finch. "It was you I meant."

If Orson had been ten years older, he would have developed into the kind of pompous Rotarian who actually splutters. He wasn't; he didn't. But he wasn't quite so hale as he had been the moment before. Defensive, but cool.

"Fill me in," he said. He leaned back in his chair and looked down at the smaller man beside him. It was a posture fit to intimidate suspended students and their shamed parents, but Finch was looking elsewhere.

"Wait your turn," Ulabenzi intoned. He had met the white teacher's gaze without rancor. He had nodded slightly, as if to an old friend. "Mr. Finch likes to do things his own way."

"You have met?" asked Orson. He was the congenial host once again. "I wouldn't have thought it."

"We have met."

"We have met," echoed Finch. "I carry the memory with me."

"Sorry," said Sugawee's minister. "Nothing personal. We were pawns of fate, the leader says." Jackson coughed. "I was very careful. It was a clean hit. There should be no serious damage."

"Only to my self-respect."

"Hey, man," came the sincere response, "don't feel that way. You were straight; you took my word. You just didn't know the game, you know? That jive don't mean nothing. Just alley tricks."

"Maybe. But that's not what I meant." Finch frowned slightly and pawed over his next words. "I've always thought myself a nonviolent man. With my . . . uh, physique, there's not much choice. But I was proud, or self-righteous, and thought I was a little better than the barbarian in the street. I was civilized. I was a man of peace. I was not prey to the baser pleasures, like revenge and sadistic cruelty. My life could be lived according to principles of reason . . . and compassion."

"Nothing wrong with that." The words were Jackson's, but the voice was hard to place.

"Yeah," laughed Finch. "So I thought. That was the keystone of my self-respect. But when Benedict was murdered, I wanted to tear his killer in pieces. And that's natural enough. Then Ulabenzi here knocked me up side of the head last night. When I returned to consciousness, I wanted to beat him to death. Slowly. And that's natural, too." Finch looked slowly around the table, his face darkened with confusion and shame. "The thing is, I thought I was better than that. I thought—"

Quickly as he had fallen into these reflections, he gave them up. The others did not understand, or did not sympathize. Either way, he must return to business.

"Well," he said; his tongue brushed out to moisten dry lips. "Number seven, chief minister to the great and terrible Sugawee. Shall we go on?"

No one made comment. Finch strode onward.

"Ulabenzi, of course, is here as a kind of representative. His organization works as a highly disciplined group; if there is guilt, it is likely to be group guilt." Finch did not tarry for correction. "In a sense, BAM is the least suspect."

"Shit," muttered Chuzz Jackson.

"Agreed. One has a feeling, but there are no obvious traces."

The Black Panther was strung on wires. "Man, they've got the motive. Those punks hate anybody who—"

"Ah," whispered Ulabenzi tersely, "we are not here to discuss motives. My leader says—"

"Fuck that shit, punk! Any time you want—"

"Boys, boys!" Beverly laughed out loud. "You want whitey to think you a bunch of street niggers? We on Sunday best here. Look at old Hockby, and fine-man Orson up there. Look, and repent. We got to keep our dirty washing at home, you know? I mean, that's one thing we damned good at—doing washing."

The two enemies were not amused, but they were calmed. That was Beverly's aim. Jackson shrugged his shoulders, hunched slightly forward and studied the surface of the table in front of him. Ulabenzi, detached as any aristocrat, wore the mantle of superiority well. He looked back at Finch, as if pleased to hear a story that would be mere entertainment on an idle morning. If he saw nets closing in, he did not flinch. He was ready.

"Motives, of course, are not our business this morning," said Finch, "but we're forced into a realm of conjecture which is just as insubstantial."

"Goodness," Miss Lee breathed. Chuzz nearly smiled.

"So far, something concrete points to each of us; there are links that can be seen and touched. My thesis, obviously, is that a clever killer wants to clear himself by spreading the blame around. Now the question: Is BAM guilty because no finger points at them? The evidence against them, it seems to me, is the lack of evidence. Put another way—"

"Please," Miss Lee sighed, "don't bother to put it another way, Emory. I'm still working on that one."

"Contrived," commented Hockby. "But possible. Eminently possible, Finch. My congratulations."

"But . . ." Scrounge began hesitantly, then stopped.

"Yes?" Ulabenzi was not as unconcerned as he might appear.

"Well . . . that's a clever killer who . . . isn't clever enough."

Finch smiled. "Go on," he encouraged him.

"He goes to all that trouble to design a murder that might implicate any of the rest of us, but he leaves himself in the clear. In the open. And the open, when somebody's shooting—"

"Is one hell of a place to be," Beverly said. "Well, Mr. Investigator, you've taken us around the circle. We're back where we started. With nothing."

"In a sense." Finch closed his notebook. "It all hinges on how smart Sugawee really is, or on how astute he thinks us. I agree with Scrounge in principle. But it's the kind of logic that might reverse itself indefinitely. You see, it would be smart to leave himself in the clear, if he knew that we would assume that a really clever murderer would be too cagey to leave himself in the clear. And so on, and so on."

"Well," said Miss Lee, "that makes everything simple."

"Oh?" Finch was amused.

"We just have to test Sugawee and figure out his IQ."

"My leader," said Ulabenzi without emotion, "is damned smart."

"That," replied Finch, "is something he has in common

with our murderer. Obvious. But, at this point, we can use the obvious."

"If one of us had noticed the obvious," Orson said sententiously, "this whole thing might never have happened."

"Strange you should say that," Finch mused.

"Why, Mr. Finch?"

"Because the clue which implicates you, Mr. Orson, is an obvious one." The principal started, but said nothing. Finch raised his thin eyebrows. "We see it every day, and none of us noticed. No one but you, and the murderer. It gives us," he lightly went on, "an interesting lesson in human psychology."

"I see," said Orson quietly. "It has something to do with my little secret." He smiled sadly to himself. "Well, perhaps I am a vain man. I had hoped it would never come up."

Finch almost whispered. "May I?" he asked.

"Of course." Orson's response was vigorous; he seemed self-assured again. "That was the arrangement this morning; no secrets left sacred in the pursuit of justice. I just don't see, on the face of it, how this came up."

"Police lab," Finch answered tonelessly. "Checking the ditto machine for prints. Missed them the first time, but they are very clear now. Perhaps too clear."

"Yes," said Orson, "but the damage is done. Tell them."

Finch faltered. "We only see," he began, "what we look for. Basic human nature, or something. I would never have seen it if Gannett's boys hadn't gone over the duplicating machine again. Last night, after he was taken off the case, the Barge couldn't sleep—"

Ulabenzi made a noise that might have been a laugh.

"—and so he gave me a little present. The police lab found no real fingerprints; the murderer was cautious enough, as you would expect, to wear gloves. But they did find a pattern of smudges that resembled a handprint."

"Big deal," hissed Beverly. "Them pigs be right smart, huh? Now we know the killer had a hand."

"Not quite," said Finch, with a frown.

"Meaning?"

"Meaning that they only found four smudges—spread out evenly with a space between the middle and fourth fingers."

"But who—oh, dear!" Katie gasped. She stared in horror at Orson; like the others, she could not pry her eyes from what he was doing. Without a word or expression, he had raised his hand, palm outward, as if ready to take an oath. Slowly, horribly, he folded in his thumb, and then his index finger. It was like some child's game played in reverse; in sequence, each digit came down to build a fist.

She had gasped as the third finger remained rigid, while the little finger bowed gracefully down beside it.

"How awful!" she said, and then tried to stammer an apology. "Oh . . . I'm so sorry. I really didn't—"

Orson was benign. "I quite understand," he said in his most effective fatherly tones. "It is an ugly sight. With a normal hand, you can almost duplicate it—but not quite. There is an extra touch of horror in those last few degrees of unnatural rigidity; it is like a dead thing." He smiled toward the others, but he was not himself. "That was my little secret," he said, "or so I thought. Someone else noticed. Someone else used it. He is a cruel being."

"We already knew that; after all, he did murder Benedict." Beverly did not sound as flip as she had wanted to. Despite her creed, she felt sorry for this man; she knew he had lived his life by appearances. Such a little thing, that crippled finger. But it was a crack across the smooth surface of his well-wrought armor.

Orson became Spartan again.

"Cut muscles," he said tersely. "They do not grow back." He extended the other fingers, stretched his palm flat upon the table and regarded the hand coldly, as if it were an interesting artifact displayed in a dusty museum.

"Man is circumscribed," Hockby intoned, "by inevitability and the processes of decay. A limb destroyed, or the mind poisoned, or a moral violated—regeneration made impossible. Up against the wall."

"Dead end," interposed Beverly. She turned toward the others. "We've reached another dead end. Correct me if I'm wrong, but it seems we've spent this hour showing that everyone's on the hook . . . and no one's on the hook. It's been fun," she smiled wryly, "but we've come full circle."

Finch met her challenge. "Not quite, Beverly. Something has been accomplished."

"What?"

"For one thing," Katie Lee interrupted, "we aren't screaming at one another. That's a start."

"Beautiful," Hockby snorted. "The days of peace. Now that we all love with such fervor, we can just overlook this nasty business and march off singing. Let us clasp our sweaty palms in brotherhood; the Day has come."

"A little too much technicolor, Floyd, but not so far from the truth." Finch stood up and stretched his arms awkwardly; he yawned. "It's still early in the morning; it could be a nice day. BAM and the Panthers have taken up their positions in the halls outside, but we haven't heard gunfire. Not yet. Roberson's BSU members are still in class, waiting for the signal. The LAPD tactical squad is on the alert; they read the papers, too. Orson isn't ten feet away from his hot line, in case reinforcements are needed." He yawned again, a monstrous cavern. "Excuse me."

Jackson laughed heartily. "Don't overdo it, Finch. What you're trying to say, or act out, is that we all need a good rest."

Finch stared down at his own feet. "Anyone agree with me?" he asked simply. The room was quiet, and he listened for a telling undercurrent. Nothing. It was impossible to discern which way the wind lay; it was impossible, for that moment, to judge whether the morning had indeed been wasted. It was the shyest who spoke first.

Scrounge Roberson stood up. He nodded toward his principal.

"If you will excuse me," he began. "If there is nothing else here, I . . . have things to do." A warm grin bounced across his young features. "I have a physics test tomorrow. If I don't get to class, I might flunk. And then how would I get a scholarship to Harvard? They need some revolutionaries, I hear."

"Out of the mouths of babes," said Hockby. He stood up and cuffed the boy playfully on the shoulder; Scrounge was not offended. Chairs scraped and the room filled with the cheerful noise of a meeting breaking up.

Only Beverly remained in her chair.

"Meeting adjourned," Katie fairly shouted. She went out into the hall, followed by the silent Jackson. Orson shook hands with Finch, then disappeared into his inner office. Hockby and Roberson, somewhat intoxicated by the brief truce, enveloped themselves in mild banter and vanished with the others.

Three were left behind by the swift exits.

"Everybody's pretty eager to leave your little party," said Beverly. She still sat, as if strapped with thongs to her chair.

Ulabenzi, who had spoken to no one, stood ominously in one corner. He seemed lost in meditation.

Finch regarded them both. "It's almost over," he said.

"Yeah. Yeah, sure." Beverly did not look at him. "Twenty-four hours, boy; that's all you get. You can start counting right now. You lowered the pressure, but you didn't put out the fire; that's one trick nobody knows—not in this man's world. Tomorrow, the lid blows off."

"Tomorrow," answered Finch, "is not a school day."

"You bastard!" Beverly shouted. She jumped to her feet and slammed the heavy chair against the wall; her slender arms tensed hideously. "So that's it! Of all the—you won't get away with it, Finch! Ten minutes out there in the hall—no, five minutes—and little Beverly can undo all your clever machinations. Want to try me?"

"No." Finch smiled grimly. "I believe you."

"All right, then. What the hell do you mean by that snide remark? You think one more day, or even three, is going to

make any difference? We can wait until Monday. Take all the
time you want; I give it to you. If you think a weekend's going
to—"

"I don't." The journalism teacher still spoke softly, but an
icy strength cut through. "I don't. Anyway, I'm playing
straight with you. Twenty-four hours is more than enough.
Twelve or fourteen will do. You see . . . I was more correct
than I hoped—about this morning."

Ulabenzi jumped. He was not so articulate as his leader, but
he was no dunce. He had caught the man's meaning.

And so had Beverly. "You mean . . ."

"I do."

She laughed harshly. "Still playing games, Finch? Give it to
us. Who tripped himself up? Who is it? Or do you want to run
and snitch to your little friend in the pig department? He
promise you something nice from downtown?"

"Gannett's out of it." Finch chewed foolishly on a broken
fingernail; he seemed to forget the other two. "We," he em-
phasized the pronoun, "we may be on our own."

"Christ!" Beverly breathed, suddenly awestruck by the full
implication of his remark. She had thought herself tough, but
the reality stopped her heart. Theories were one thing, but
this . . . "No," she faltered, "we . . . you can't."

"Due process of law?" Finch enjoyed his advantage. "An
old friend in a strange country."

"That's horrible." She shuddered. "What if you're wrong?"

"I'm bringing in experts," he said flatly. He turned toward
Ulabenzi and bowed slightly. "I made a phone call this morning," he announced. "Would you convey that information to
your leader, with my regards? And would you ask him to call
me at home this evening? I think he will understand. I think he
will agree that he owes me a small favor . . . for last night's
inconvenience."

Ulabenzi nodded without expression. He did not stop to
make polite farewells to the lady present. Without a sound, he
slipped out the door and left Finch alone with Beverly Minere.

"Finch," she said, and her voice broke. "You can't. Or did I get you wrong?"

"You got me right."

"That's . . . that's murder."

"Those who live by the sword . . ."

CHAPTER XXI

THE English Conference Room was ill-fitted for a secret rendezvous. Originally designed as a fair-sized broom closet for the convenience of the school's custodial staff, it had been pressed into more academic service when the war babies clogged the straining halls of McAdoo High. It was a cubicle without comfort; young teachers dubbed it The Pit, and the name, although never printed in the annual report of the Los Angeles Board of Education, stuck.

There was no window, there were no ventilation ducts—and that is partly why the airless room was hot and stuffy. The other reason was that half the English faculty resorted there between classes for a clandestine smoke. The relative pollution, in fact, made a reliable gauge for tension at the school; on calm days, a visitor could breathe with only minor discomfort, but during a violent week, a dense fog choked the room as the teachers chain-smoked to suffocate their riddled nerves.

It was kept locked, but not private. Every teacher had a key, as did some enterprising students. But Katie did not care. She only cared that Chuzz was back and that she could throw herself into his powerful arms. And this she did.

"Hey, hey, babe," he comforted her. "It's all right."

"Oh, Chuzz," she sobbed. "I'm not strong enough."

"You're doing fine."

"No." She sank back from him a little; she tried to stand on her own, but failed. She feared he might push her away when she made her confession, and that would be the worst blow of all. "This morning . . . I . . . Oh, Chuzz, I let them see it. They know." She raced ahead over her words, stumbling toward a reasonable explanation. "You were in jail, and I didn't know what—"

Her breath caught as he shook her hard. It was over.

"Cut it," he hissed. "Pull yourself together, Katie." His smooth voice became jagged and sharp; she couldn't move in his viselike grip. She was afraid, and very lonely. "Forget it, you understand. Forget the whole thing!"

So, she thought, *that's how it ends. And what am I to do now? I've made a fool of myself over this man, and now I'm dropped, like so much litter. The refuse of the revolution, that's me. So what? I'm a liberated woman and these are the days of the New Freedom. I can swap stories around the bar, compare the size of—God! It wasn't like that; I may be old-fashioned, but it wasn't like that at all. But I'm not broken; he won't get that pleasure.*

Katie Lee arched her eyebrows and inadvertently looked very foolish. She was Innocence trying to appear Worldly-Wise, a grotesque miscasting.

"Okay," she said weakly. "Okay. It's been fun. Shall we shake hands and part like two sensible—"

"You little fool."

"That's not necessary."

"You dear little fool," said Chuzz, laughing. He expertly slid one hand to the nape of her neck and kissed her with a frank hunger he had not felt in years. *This is it,* he thought, as her heart and body passionately answered his. *I love this crazy woman.*

It should have been a long and sacred moment. But neither could ignore the dangerous turmoil around them. Their joy could not thrive in that hostile atmosphere; it was a hot spark that would be rekindled later, when there would be time to bask and drowse in its steady flame. Other matters had to be settled now.

"I didn't mean to forget us, birdbrain," he whispered.

"So I see," she smiled. No man could have faked that kiss. And if he could—it wouldn't matter, anyway. She was hooked.

"I meant, forget all those prying clowns. We're all right, nothing to hide."

"Finch made us promise to keep the whole meeting confidential," she replied. "I suppose we can trust th—"

Jackson's laughter was immediate and delighted. "You sweet little old trusting thing," he said as he hugged her playfully. "Finch is no fool, as we've all found out. Those people aren't going to keep their lips sealed because of a pledge. Honor is dead in the modern world, or haven't you heard the news? He planned that beautifully, honey. Nobody's blowing the whistle on nobody, because everybody can blow the whistle on everybody else."

"That's funny," she mused.

"You see anybody laughing?"

"No, I mean . . . well, I thought Emory was pretty indecent, exposing everybody like that. It seemed cruel." her dark eyes brightened with a new emotion. "But it turns out to be the best way. I mean, everybody's safer than they were before. We're all forced to respect the other man's privacy. Funny. Finch cares about human feelings, after all; he's really protecting us, after his own fashion."

"Maybe that's what I love about you, Katie," Chuzz said quite seriously. "The rose-colored glasses. You have to believe the best of people. Even when—"

"Even when some cat's out to steal my virginity?" She blinked her lids outrageously and wriggled coquettishly in his grasp.

He tried to remain serious. He started to say, "You are too innocent and need to be protected," but decided against it. She was worn out and needed to relax, so he caught up her mood. "Steal? Steal? When it's free for the asking?"

She giggled happily. "Just a little charity for our underprivileged brothers in the miserable ghetto," she said.

"That kind of charity," countered Chuzz, "is going to bring the poor black man to his knees."

"If that's the way you like it, boy. Actually, I thought you preferred the Greek—"

"Hush your mouth," he gasped in mock horror. "What if someone were to overhear?"

"You don't like my privately endowed Peace Corps?"

"Jesus," he groaned. "Tell me I didn't hear a nice girl make such a dirty, filthy, disgusting remark. Where hath virtue fled; where doth purity hide her shamed head?"

"And who had the gall to say I was a nice girl? Let me at him; I'll damage his seed for him. Anyway, if you're so disgusted, how come you ain't making for that door? It's unlocked from the inside."

"I ain't that disgusted." He leered comically. "Know what I mean?"

"Reckon I do."

The therapy had worked, and Chuzz was relieved to see how quickly Katie had bounced back from the rigors of the last few hours. She was tough; maybe not as tough as she was trying to sound now, but much tougher than she realized. She wasn't going to be crushed, not that one. Their little game had helped, his love had helped, but she could have pulled through without them. No, the danger was not that she was too weak; it was, as he was often reminded, that she believed so naively in the basic goodness of other human beings. She had believed in him; she had trusted him. Of one thing he was sure. He would never prove her wrong. Above all others, that was one vow he meant to keep.

Beverly was exhausted. Her emotions had run the gauntlet from hysteria to frozen terror, but Finch would not be moved. He had listened, politely, and then he had turned to go. He was one stubborn white man; once he got an idea into his head . . .

Finally she had resorted to a desperate threat.

"I'll stop you," she warned.

"How?"

Her cockiness raised its head briefly, gratefully. "We have our ways, you know."

"Not this time." He was dead serious. "I'm not alone this time; there will be others. It will be a kind of . . . community effort."

"But," she faltered, "are you certain that . . . you know who—"

"I will be. In a few hours."

Beverly made a lame joke, but her rising fear smothered its punch. "Is it I, Lord?" She had tried to sound mocking, but her apprehension was too great; her voice had the toneless fall of a serious question.

"That's nice," he said without irony. "You try so hard to throw everything away—the old morality, the old-fashioned beliefs, the fundamental concepts of right and wrong—but you fail. The childhood phrases return."

"It was a literary reference, Finch."

"I don't think so. I think you have been able to dump Christianity, but you still have faith in a godless covenant between human beings. You aren't amoral. You believe in love and peace and brotherhood, and that's why you can hate so much. You hate the world for not living up to those ideals. And that's nice . . . but it must be very hard on you."

"Thanks ever so," Beverly cooed mawkishly. She performed a slight curtsy and gravely dipped her natural.

"Believe me, Beverly. We're on the same train, you and I, and we'll get there. Peace, okay?" He held out his right hand.

Beverly smiled warmly and walked over to him.

"Peace, and love, and brotherhood, right?" He nodded. "You forgot one important thing, you know?"

Curious, he raised his eyebrows in silent query, and that proved to be a tactical mistake. It made a better target when she spit in his eye.

The dull thud of a sleepy oath was nothing new to the old walls of the rented room. They could take it. It was not blasphemy which had cracked the weary plaster and flayed bare spots in the pale brown wallpaper. It was another kind of curse, and the words poverty and despair were too good for it. It left its mark on the broken radiator that hissed ineffectually, unable even to dry the shapeless and dingy underwear that lay across the pipes. It left further marks in the cracked panes of the one window; it moaned with the gurgling dirge of the little toilet that stood in the corner and crooned interminably.

But it was ten o'clock in the morning and Obadiah Snatch, as he fell back on the unhappy bed with its moaning springs, did not contemplate his position in the socioeconomic structure of Los Angeles, the USA and the world. It would have been a bummer, and he was already overstocked on that item. His head pounded at him in reprisal for last night's cheap sherry. The memory of his landlady's violent knocking an hour before was not pleasant, nor was the recollection of the turgid phone call, taken in her junky bedroom, with that nutty white man. And then Snatch, ever the gentleman, had stayed to comfort the poor old fool of a woman who owned this dump. He did his deed; he convinced her that somewhere in those three hundred pounds of sweating fat was still a woman that a man might want. Against the sane objections of his own stomach.

He lay still, and the old springs trembled finally to silence. He closed his eyes and begged his body for mercy, but the damage had been done. He could not rest.

"Ooooooh," he managed to comment, then loosed a shower of four-letter words that was a masterpiece of its kind. It was beautiful; it could have stopped the hearts of veteran car-thieves and rapists. But it did something worse than that. It woke the young boy sleeping on Obadiah's floor.

"Sorry, kid," Snatch was able to whisper; his voice was nearly spent from the last noble effort. "The old man's cracking up."

The boy did not answer. He sat up painfully, for the floor

had not been kind during the night, and stared around sleepily. He could not yet remember where he was, or why he was there. But he did not seem too concerned. He did not often sleep in the same place twice. He was curious, but not worried.

"Get back to sleep," mumbled Snatch. "Fridays be damned quiet around here. Cats already geezin' stuff; they faded out for the weekend. Be nice and restful 'til the sweet chicks come home from they school." *Hell,* he thought; *nice and restful for who? I be too old for this shit . . . all tied up like a whiney hog, my head 'bout to bust wide open. And on Friday, too. Just when I got to be in on the action.*

"What's the time?" the boy asked, without much interest.

"Don't you be worryin' about that. You lie back down and think on your sins, you hear?" Obadiah cackled, but a sharp pain cut his amusement mercilessly short.

"Fuck that jive." The remark was automatic, not angry.

"I ain't jivin', son. Somewhere you got a mama; yeah, even gutter wash like you and I don't want her findin' out that ol' Snatch didn't take care of you. You need ol' brother Sleep; ain't nobody that young in this world."

"Yeah, sure, old man." The boy stood up. He was very thin and fairly tall, almost six feet. But he could have been no more than fourteen years old. He still wore paint-spotted blue denims and a pale green T-shirt made from open webbing, like a clinging fishnet. His hair was long and stiff; it would have made an impressive natural, except for the curious part which gouged one side like a shortcut through a hedge. The new scars across his upper arms were all the more visible, because his skin was pale and golden, not dark. In come countries, on some islands, he would have been called "copper man"; he was called other things in the ghetto of Los Angeles.

Some words he found hard to say. He struggled with one, then let it casually drop.

"Thanks." He spotted his torn tennis shoes near the old coffee can that was Obadiah's spittoon; he squatted to put them on. "I got to be goin'," he said, over the shoulder. He didn't look at the old man on the bed; some things are best ignored, and left unspoken.

But Snatch did not agree.

"Boy," he said. "You aimin' to go back?"

"Back? Where you mean?" One shoe was tied; he worked on the other. He did not turn toward Obadiah Snatch.

"Where you mean?" the old pimp mocked. He swore, but it was melodic and gentle, like an old-time spiritual. He looked out the miserable window and sighed. "Not where. What? What you goin' back to? Back on the job you was makin' last night? That you style, boy?"

Ordinarily, the kid would have shouted something like, "Fuck off, you old fart! Ain't you concern!" But he didn't. Snatch meant well; moreover, Snatch was right. The boy shrugged his shoulders and stood up. As he turned toward the door, he put on, like a helmet, the sightless and unexpressive death mask of the ghetto gut dweller; his smooth features sagged limply, the dark jewels of his eyes became dull as pebbles and a kind of slouch made soft putty of the muscles in his slender shoulders and thighs. He was ready for the streets; he had his armor on. His coat of arms was a cringing, fawning puppy on a field of dazed blue; only the sharpest-eyed observer saw that from behind the mongrel obtruded the tail of a rattler. The boy suddenly looked lazy, listless, a bit stupid. These were his surest defenses. They were the legacy of his family, and they worked, like seasoned weaponry, as they had for his father, and for the father before him, and for the father before him ... back until the first of his blood who had walked into an alley and come out the far end alive.

Snatch only sighed, but it sounded deep as a moan. Yeah, man, the kid was tough, and smart. Good enough to survive. Like the hundreds and thousands and millions of others. Some of them survived; most didn't. So what? *Obadiah,* he lectured himself, *you mind you own business; ain't no future in up-settin' youself about each and every pointy-headed little street nigger. Right on,* Obadiah answered, *I got better things on my mind . . . like a ton of bricks, to start with.*

When the boy reached for the rusty doorknob, Snatch had decided to let him go without further comment. It was a firm vow, gravely taken. All the more easily, then, it went the way of so many others.

"Boy," Obadiah snapped. "Ain't no punk ever be a man."

"What?" The boy whirled, then caught himself. No point in fighting with an old man. "Ain't got time for playin' around," he said. "See you."

But Snatch was an avalanche that could not be stopped. He swept down, thundering in cascades of moral indignation. The old sinner made a strange evangelist, and yet the sincerity of his outrage saved him from being ludicrous. It was an impressive sermon. Snatch did not take his text from the Holy Bible; he did not base his morality on the teachings of Christ, though he knew them all by heart, or on the Code of Justinian, of which he had once heard a learned man speak. He had appreciated that speech as well as the seventy-three dollars he had gleaned from the loose pockets of eager students; to be fair, he had silently thanked the professor for both benefits. And so Snatch wandered off the subject . . .

The young boy loosened his mask and smiled. What was all this to him?

Snatch saw and jumped back into the saddle. No, he lamented, in this world there are no laws, and there is no good and evil. Let there be law, let there be order, and still the old devil's going to get his due. It's the jungle, it's the snakepit, and the lion will not lie down with the lamb. And so on and so on.

"But," whispered Snatch, shaking his ragged finger, "there is one sin. Yeah, Lawd, there be one commandment, that's sure." The boy, who had been laughing openly at Obadiah's enthusiastic performance, frowned uneasily. He had enjoyed the show, but now something dangerous was sneaking up behind him; he was about to be shanghaied. "Know what it is?" Snatch grinned.

"I be too ignorant," the boy answered quickly. He had tried to sound casual, but had failed.

"Yeah. So I figured. Las' night I figured to myself, uh-huh . . . that be the one commandment this boy gonna break to his dyin' day. Seems like he don't mind stoopin' down low enough to be any man's punk. Yeah, when he—"

"Shut up!"

"Don't be tellin' me to shut up, boy. I ain't that old I can't bend you body some, you hear? What you so hot about, anyways? Huh? Did ol' Snatch cut into your business las' night? He keep you from turnin' over another couple quarters?"

The boy tried a diversionary tactic. "What you care? You 'fraid I gonna take the business away from you holes? I be too heavy for you fuckin' chicks. Them big bucks want me 'stead of them little pieces, uh-huh."

"God Almighty," Snatch intoned. "You ain't shamed to say it right out loud."

"And why not, Mister Right? You so proud of pimpin' down Rawmeat Avenue for a dollar an hour? I see now. That be why you carry you head so high and proud. You be the action; yeah, you the big man, all right."

Obadiah cut the slang; he was another man, but he was no caricature.

"At least," he said quietly, "I am a man. No one has to ask. I am outside the law, but I am a man. Can you say the same?"

"Go to hell," the boy hissed. He shook with something that could have been either rage, or shame. "I got to eat," he stammered. "I ain't livin' off no chicks. I be on my own."

"A punk's way to live," answered Snatch.

"Yeah, what do you want? Today I clean myself up and put on some sweet smells, for real. Then I saunter on down to the Security First National Bank, and I smile real big and show off my nice white teeth. They say, *You look fine, mister, but we need your papers.* And I say, *That's all right; I understand how it is, sir. You can't allow just any of these colored brethren to come in here.* They smile, and they say, *Well, you are an intelligent young man; we can see that.* So we go back and forth, and everybody smile, and maybe drink some tea or Fresca. At the right time, I pull out a college paper, and letters from the richest honky dudes in this town. And they all jump up and say, *Yes sir, right this way. Which office would you like, sir? Would you like to be vice-president or treasurer?* I wave my hand and say, *My good man, whichever you prefer; the money really doesn't matter, don't you know?"*

"Lovely," Snatch giggled. "And you gonna do all that today, this afternoon?"

"Right now," the boy replied. "Can't take no more of this street life. Time I went back to where I belong."

Obadiah Snatch laughed happily, but cut it short. Poor black man, he thought, like to laugh at trouble and slick hisself up in funny stories. Then walk right out, and forget the whole thing. Yeah, laugh if off. Ain't no future in that.

"Hey, now," he said. "There be other jobs beside punkin' and bankin'; there be a mighty lot of people who ain't either one. Now you just let me—"

"No. I on my own." He started again to leave.

"Sure," rasped Snatch. His anger flared again. "You on you own las' night when the pig come, ain't that right?" The boy did not answer. "Something happen to you tongue, big man? Huh? Where you be right now if ol' Snatch didn't step in and talk to that pig. And you, shakin' and mumblin' something fierce and promisin' never to do nasty things any more. That you, weren't it, not somebody else who looks a damn sight like you? Weren't that you?"

"You know it was."

"All right, then. I also know this . . . you ain't bad yet. Oh, yeah," he lifted his hand to forestall argument, "you actin' up a storm, but you just a beginner. I don't know why, and I don't care why, but you ain't been out there long, that's for sure. You go with that schoolteacher for three dollars, eh?"

"Hell, no!" the boy said with new confidence. "I ain't that low. He pay five."

"Damned bastard." Snatch shook his head sadly. "Not you, boy; I mean that punk, Hockby. Somebody gonna cut his gourds off one of these days. He a bastard, but you a fool. A wet-eared, baby-assed, dyed and made-to-order fool, I swear. This be Big City, boy, not some holler-and-crick in the piney woods. You don't do nothing for under ten dollars; believe it brother. That Hockby know that; he done taken you for a sucker."

"He say—"

"He say lies, boy. Look round for yourself." Obadiah cursed his irksome instincts for meddling and looked back out the window. He saw nothing. Perhaps there was nothing to see. Something familiar caught his eye, but he had sunk into a fog of half-conscious meditation; when he roused himself and focused his failing vision, the thing, whatever it was, had disappeared. He didn't really care. And, now that his early-morning weakness surged back over him, he cared less about the boy. Let him go. Let him choose his own poison. Way of the world.

"I be one tired pimp," he groaned. "Boy, you do what you—" But he stopped. One more try. "Hey, you see that burger stand down at the corner last night? Called Sam and Terry's?"

"Yeah, I seen it." It was a noncommittal answer to the questions Snatch was about to ask; it gave a yes, and several maybe's.

"Over there . . ." The old man pointed to a cardboard box in the corner. "Those raggedy black pants got some money, just a little change. Nothing worth cuttin' me for," he smiled wearily, "but enough to buy some doughnuts and some coffee."

"I ain't on welfare," the boy snapped.

"And I ain't givin' it out," Snatch countered. "I be a sick and tired old man who needs hisself a little nuuutrition. Now, if a good brother, somebody like you, goes out to get me something nice and hot, then that good brother deserve something nice and hot for hisself. That be how I work it out. Don't that make sense?"

The kid shrugged. He walked to the box and rummaged through the mess until he found the change. Painfully, he counted the tarnished bits of metal; second time around, he was sure.

"Sixty-three cents," he said.

"Should be," said Snatch. He lay back slowly on the bed, closing his eyes. Neither man nor boy moved for a long moment. At last, the boy spoke; Snatch did not open his eyes.

"I could just fade."

"You won't."

"Because you . . ."

"Because I might trust you?" Obadiah sneered. "Lawd, no. This ain't no soap opera, son; this be the lair of the champion pimp. No, you come back. Not because you be good and honest, but because you ain't stupid."

"I want to live."

"That's right." Snatch giggled at the catechism.

"You got friends."

"You know it."

"All over."

"Round the world."

The boy, who seemed almost handsome when he smiled easily, relaxed and threw open the door. "Be right back." He laughed. "Since you put it that way." Something passed over his face briefly, and he paused in the doorway. "If you got so many friends . . ."

"Yeah?"

"Maybe they need . . . maybe they got a job." His words dwindled to a shy whisper, but Snatch heard them clearly. He smiled broadly, uncontrollably, but lay still upon the bed.

"Maybe," he said.

"You let me know . . . when I get back."

"I could call the bank," the old man teased.

"Yeah," the boy replied. He wasn't offended. "And if they ain't in, try the grocery store." He laughed.

"If you don't get on, I gonna die from starvation."

"For real." The boy, with a look that might have been taken for affection, looked closely at the dry and thin old form. For a moment, he thought of his family . . . and then he laughed. He hadn't seen any of them in eight or nine years, and, anyway, he had hated them all. Yes, he had hated them all. Yes, he had hated . . .

Without another word, he slipped out and closed the door behind him. He would come back. But he wouldn't be trapped.

As the boy went out, he found much to think about. He noticed nothing around him. He saw nothing strange on the staircase; for all he knew, he was alone on the sidewalk. He did not see the face he should recognize when the time came.

Miss Lee felt stranded.

Aimlessly one moment, playfully the next, she wove complex patterns down the long, empty hallways of the school. Her movements made a graph of her thoughts. She thought of her professional responsibilities and would take a straight line toward the classroom; but cold fear, like death in a nightmare, stepped out and she veered back toward the principal's office until the memory of Chuzz, like a warm smell called back from the summer, brushed against her cheek and sent her skipping foolishly.

"Miss Lee!" giggled a student. "You trippin' out?"

"Watch your tongue, Cleotis." Momentarily startled, Katie had gasped in embarrassment. But recovery was quick; she smiled, more impudent than any student. "Hey, why aren't you in class?"

"You ever see a class without the teacher?"

"Your class has a teacher."

"Yeah, but she's out playing in—"

"That may be. But she's excused. You have a substitute."

"You jivin'."

"Bet."

"You got to be jivin'."

"Just you go look and see for yourself. Your teacher's excused, but you aren't. And the substitute's taking roll."

"But you see that I—"

"I don't see nothing. I ain't working. I ain't no English teacher today. You better go and explain to your teacher why you're late."

"Ain't that cold?"

"That's me, man. Cold Katie Lee." Realizing what she had said, Miss Lee bit her lip to keep from laughing out loud. Cleotis, pretending to take her threat seriously, scurried off to the classroom. Had he caught the pun? She thought not. Not because he was pure and innocent, of course, but because he wouldn't be on guard for suggestive remarks from his young, but respectable teacher. She was a paragon of virtue in the students' eyes. They protected her; they even refused to curse within her hearing. At McAdoo High, that was a very special compliment, indeed.

Yet Katie had lost interest in the honor and glory of a good name. *Some paragon,* she thought; *I just want to shack up with Chuzz.*

A hand tickled her waist and she whirled around to see, of all people, Emory Finch. She stared stupidly; no one, so far as she knew, had ever seen him so playful. He was exhilarated.

"Emory! You been popping uppers?"

"Nothing like." He grinned foolishly. "It's the joy," he said, "the joy of living. Don't you feel it?"

"Oh, sure. This is an earthly paradise. Whoopee."

"Arcadia. And thou, gentle maid—"

"Nut." It sounded like a mild oath. "Hey, where has everybody run off to? Beverly and Hockby aren't in class; Scrounge is—"

"Don't know." He clucked his tongue suggestively. "But I got to run off myself. TCB, you know . . . taking care of business."

He started off, but Katie restrained him. His unwonted hilarity made her uneasy, as if there were an obscene joke she hadn't understood. Moreover, she was conscious of dangling useless in a vacuum, no longer privy to the machinations taking place around her. The others, she knew, were plotting, or keying their organizations to the alert. Even Chuzz had—

"What's wrong?" Finch asked.

"I don't know," said Katie. "But I'm worried again." She smiled wryly. "I guess that's my part to play."

"The clinging vine?"

She did not smile. "Something like that."

"Hold on a few hours longer." His face worked strangely. "Or even less. Nobody believes me, but it's all going to be over soon."

Her laughter startled him, but he humored her.

"No pun intended," he said. "By the way, how did Chuzz think—?" He paused, then mentally kicked himself for being thickheaded. "That's it, I suppose. They called him?"

"Wrong, for once," she said brightly. "They sent a messenger."

"Is he . . ." It was hard to ask the question. If a stronger Panther had been angered, if Chuzz had misstepped, it would not be a simple dismissal with a slap on the wrists. Jackson would more likely collect his severance pay at the city morgue. "Has he been called on the carpet?"

"I don't know. As usual, I'm not supposed to know anything."

"That's for your own good, as the saying goes."

"Oh, sure. What I don't know can't hurt me, and so on. But how do I handle the worry? Every time might be the last. Somebody puts out a contract, or there's a fight with the police, or the other Panthers, or Sugawee's boys." She stopped herself. The old hysteria was lurking nearby, and it had already won too many rounds this morning. "Like my speech?" He nodded. "I wish," she continued, "that I actually had taken some of Beverly's pretty little capsules. I could use some."

He patted her arm, like an old monk giving blessing to a little girl. "You're right about one thing, anyway. Keep it flippant. Best way to get through it."

"I wonder. I wonder if I should come out of my hole and face it squarely." She smiled halfheartedly. "Like a Rotarian."

Finch, who liked his little joke as much as anyone, became grim. Some paths, he felt, were safer than others.

"No," he said seriously. "No."

"Because the little Texas belle can't?" She was almost defiant; at least, there was a new glint in her eye.

"Because she shouldn't," he replied. "The Panthers are not your local boys' club, you know. Read the newspapers. People get killed in those pretty leather jackets. And they kill. Belle or no, that isn't easy to face; even for a tough girl like Beverly. Your man seems to handle it pretty well, straddling the gap between the true revolutionaries and the thugs. Maybe he can keep it up, but who knows? Seale, Cleaver, Newton, that guy in Chicago—they lie with the snows of yesteryear."

"You're cold, Mr. Finch." She wasn't trying to be funny.

"You know it. These days, it's dangerous to be anything but. Chuzz wants to keep you warm and happy in a well-hidden nest. Luck to him. But they may be out to get him if they feel he's played them false in this little murder business. They don't like mistakes that show; they don't like getting their names in the papers. It took courage for him to join us this morning. And that's why I've got to keep the wheels in motion. They may not be so willing to wait for the answer; they may think they have it already." He frowned, but let the subject drop. "Sorry," he said. "No time for the amenities. I've really got to get busy."

He was ten feet away before she grasped it.

"You mean, they might think he did it?" She blurted it out.

Finch turned slightly and shrugged, but kept moving.

"But they have a committee. They'll decide to . . . They'll kill him!"

Katie Lee was talking to an empty hall. Finch had vanished around a corner. She was alone.

Obadiah Snatch was almost asleep when he heard the whispered rattle of the doorknob.

That boy sure must be scared, he thought, or move like greased lightning. The old man had had barely enough time to discover a position which did not anger his insistent hangover. He had settled, cautiously, into a fetal crouch; he had waited as the crashing in his brain had dwindled to a far-off roar. Day thoughts tired of their jabbering; he crawled painfully to the quiet rooms of his familiar dreams. Old friends appeared, and they were young again, and that made sense. After all, he had never seen himself grow old.

But he would not be selfish. The boy had kept a promise, and deserved attention. Snatch turned slowly to greet him, but suddenly froze, propped awkwardly on one elbow.

"Hey, man," he whined in his peddler's singsong. "What you doin' with that thing?" His smile guttered like a dying candle. "You tryin' to look bad?"

And those words, on that quiet morning, were his valedictory to this world.

He felt, but did not hear, the three gunshots that killed him. He said nothing. In his eyes, as he fell to the grimy floor, lay no terror or pain. He was confused, simply confused, to see his little room from this unfamiliar angle. It was the last thing he ever saw, it was his home. And yet he scarcely recognized it.

Minutes later, the boy rushed in. The killer had gone. There was nothing new in the room but the sharp smell of gunpowder and the bright swatches of the old man's scarlet blood.

The boy set down the steaming cups of coffee and took in the scene. Old stuff. He had seen it happen before. He did not weep or shake with fright; this was nothing to him. All he did was take a dirty pillow and place it behind the dead man's head, and then laugh at himself for doing so.

Before he slipped out of the room, he remembered the doughnuts. Six of them, still warm. Warmer, now, than the old man. He put them in the pocket of his torn denim jacket, for he would need them. He had made a decision down at the hamburger stand, and it was a long and hungry road back to Arkansas.

He left.

And that, in a way, was the one legacy Obadiah Snatch left behind.

CHAPTER XXII

No single chant could be distinguished yet among the thousand shouts and curses which pummeled Orson's office. McAdoo High was back to normal. More than three hundred students, mostly boys, choked the hallway and pounded the walls with tight fists; some swore hoarsely, others giggled and some manfully struggled to keep their dignity as every little push and shove rippled like seasickness through the packed crowd.

Most of the girls were terrified in the press. They were tough, they were wilier than their boyfriends; they had learned to protect themselves in the dark alleys of the ghetto. But they had lost none of their female instincts, and they were growing into women. For them, the smell of danger lay heavier than the scent of fun. They knew how panic could explode through a mob and leave horror in its wake.

So the girls did not laugh when a young prankster threw a lighted firecracker among the tangle of milling legs. They kicked him hard and threw him against the wall, and he was too canny to fight back. When a school security guard opened Orson's door slightly and someone threw an empty beer bottle at his head, the girls did not laugh. They would not be reminded of Newton, but they knew in their bones about action and reaction.

And so they were the most relieved when the principal finally came to the door himself and asked five of the most vociferous leaders to come in for a few hands of confrontation. He invited five; he got fifteen. Once that door was open, students involuntarily fell in like gumballs from a smashed vending machine. Orson and a security guard fought hard to staunch the flow; they succeeded and locked the door.

With this objective gained, chaos subsided to mild pandemonium, and the students spread out down the long hallway, talking easily and joking. Some few, nervous and watchful, ringed the door, as if expecting a trick. A couple of sophomores were sent out to act as lookouts for police cars or plain-clothes infiltrators. But most of the young students leaned against the wall or stood casually, jerking half-consciously to the soul strains of a hundred hidden transistor radios; most took a few deep breaths and turned from shouted demands to the traditional forms of school gossip. Rumors of pregnancy flew gaily around and softened the angry air.

"Who broke the noble truce?" wondered Floyd Hockby. He and Miss Lee were standing in the afternoon sun just outside the glass double doors that led to the packed hallway. They were alone on the cracked cement of the old walk. The other teachers, or so it seemed, had all scurried underground with a quick fillip of their tails, like so many prairie dogs before the oncoming hurricane.

"Looks like Beverly's work to me," Katie answered. She tried to sound light, but her voice had the unmistakable quality of frightened sparrows chained in the bowels of a deep cistern. She was only conscious, again, of a painless exhaustion that had turned her limbs to balsa wood; she was stiff, but light.

"The Queen? Go back on her royal word? Impossible!"

Katie, who was usually revulsed by the characteristic humor of effeminate men, nonetheless played along. She was determined to float with the tide and give up on thought and debates of the conscience; yes, she meant to float, unthinking, on pink, naughty clouds of criminal negligence and irresponsibility.

"Maybe," Katie smiled, "she had to. In the interests of the state. Or on behalf of her subjects."

"They do come first," leered Hockby.

Odd, thought Katie, *if Chuzz had said that, I would have broken up in hysterics, but when Hockby . . . I'm grossed out. Maybe it's his sex thing, because that's enough to send my flesh crawling anyway. Or maybe . . . The awful thing is, my first reaction was pure Texas; I felt like a lily-pure white woman insulted by a . . . Damn! Damn, damn, damn. Just goes to show . . . you think a thing's lying dead and buried, and then it pops right up, reeking of filth, at your best dinner party.*

She managed a lame smile, and Hockby chose another tack. He was nothing if not sensitive.

"You're probably most correct," he said, returning to the original question. "Not the style, the elan of a BAM demonstration. And it lacks the primal force, the . . . well, the urge and the tightly controlled ferocity of the Panthers. Yes, it's hers; we can be sure of that. Not quite ragged and rough-hewn enough to be Roberson on his own."

"I concur in your analysis," said Katie, imitating the lilt of his peculiar sententiousness, "and in your captious criticisms. However, despite the reservations of experts, it worked."

He bowed. "I am flattered at the implication; I hardly considered myself an expert in these matters."

"The most amazing thing," she went on, although not quite ignoring him, "is that she managed to move so quickly. In the first place, school had been dismissed half an hour before she started to round anyone up. Most of our students skedaddle on home; I don't know how she got them to come back."

"As her work goes," Hockby commented, "this isn't one of the largest and best-organized performances."

"It'll do," Katie laughed.

"Besides," Hockby continued, "it will be over soon."

"You playing on the inside now?"

"No chance, as my people say. But I well know the quaint cultural habits of this area. It is almost four-thirty now, and

most of these young ruffians live at least a fifteen-minute walk
away. Now, the natives here do tend to adopt strange customs
with the changing times, but some taboos are sacred. One of
them involves the ritual of feeding. Like pigs at a trough, these
noble people line up to feed their faces at five or five-thirty.
No revolution is going to keep them here when it gets too near
dinnertime." Hockby crooned suddenly, "Ol' Br'er Stomach,
he come de fustest."

The Latin teacher had, as usual, succeeded in making Katie
edgy and uncomfortable. Her own strong sense of courtesy
suggested that she must laugh, or at least smile politely, in
appreciation of his strained humor; on the other hand, his
every word was so offensive to her sense of decency that she
wanted to slap him. One reaction would signify, she feared, an
acquiescence to the worst kind of racism; the other, in anyone's book, would appear to be the self-conscious, self-
righteous posturing of a professional liberal. For the first time,
it suddenly struck Katie Lee that Hockby might intend to sock
her with this dilemma. Perhaps, despite his long years in the
role of the "white Negro," perhaps Hockby had his own
cancerous resentment, and perhaps he had finally found his
own way of getting back at whitey.

Katie was startled at the thought.

Somehow, she had never allowed herself to consider the
strange misfit as a fellow human being. Certainly, she had
never thought of him as a man. If something had happened, if,
but for the misfortune of experience, he could have grown
into . . . Katie shook her head violently. She cut her thoughts
short.

"No time," she mumbled.

"What?" Hockby asked involuntarily. "No time for what?"

"Nothing," she quickly replied, coming back to her senses.
No time to get involved; Lesson Number One for the Seventies
for Miss Katie Lee. Too late, too late. Nothing to be done. Not
about Hockby, not about Beverly, not about anyone. No time.
For a moment, it had seemed so simple just to reach out and

say, "Floyd. Floyd, I'm sorry." But she had not done so. He would not have understood; she would not have been able to explain. She had kept her mouth shut and moved back to social inanity. And she was damned glad she had.

Floyd was no fool. He caught the whole scene. He stepped back upon his own slippery bank and watched the little paper sailboat whirl awkwardly and sink. The current had been too strong. But, for a moment, his pathetic launch had ridden the waves. That was something.

"I don't know about you," Katie said lightly, "but this chick is bugging out of here. Beverly can run her own show, for once."

"A sound decision." Hockby reassumed his own caricature like an acrobat donning a silk cape. "Might I offer my protection to the safety of your carriage?"

He was happy. For a moment, this woman had begun to see him as a human being, even as a man. What if, years before . . . But the moment had passed. Hockby, if anything had good timing. He sensed when the curtain should be rung down on domestic tragedy; he knew when the comedy should begin.

"Delighted," Katie answered with a strange wink. Her timing wasn't bad, either.

The two teachers walked to the faculty parking lot.

Meanwhile, Beverly wept alone in the conference room adjoining Orson's inner office.

She wanted to wail with the clear shrieks of Ashanti women, as she imagined them, crying to the jungle gods over the polished limbs of their fallen warriors. Then, or so she thought, her misery would take on traditional grandeur. The old chants would make of her grief a symphony, and the chords would strike as deep as the bowels of nature, and the eerie melodies would move delicately or stridently, in answer to the catastrophes and proud victories of a race of kings.

Instead, she feared, she was simply bawling foolishly like

any other middle-class, Westernized, assimilated, breast-bound dentist's wife.

She was alone, and her bright hopes had muddied. Something terrifying had intervened. It moved fast, and with no mercy. It was like a night demon, a fiend of the hurricane, that would not be propitiated. It had its own stealthy ministers, who killed young Benedict and Obadiah, who was not young. It spread hate and fear, which could now be seen and named. But it had no name, and no visible form. And it was moving still.

Shouts and curses from the other office fell unheard through the plywood door. In other times, Beverly would have sat, tense, attuned to every shift of pitch in the hue and cry. She would have been angered when Orson seemed to take the flag, exhilarated when she could hear the students rabid at his throat. Today, it was all a monotonous and low cacophony, like a high school band tuning up. Her sobbing reached its peak and she fell into an exhausted state of despair. The harsh sounds guttered below the limits of her consciousness; she thought blank thoughts.

For several moments, Beverly did not take notice of a curious new instrument banging away with the others. Violent percussion, under the circumstances, would not have been unusual, but this new sound came with a persistent, regular rhythm. Moreover, it was loud, but carried a peculiar flavor of caution. Beverly glanced vaguely toward the window, and then jumped up, startled, at the odd spectacle before her.

Gannett, whose face was not thin, looked even more gross with his red face pressed, like a grouper's, against the glass. She was too stunned to move, but he, with the nervous comic gestures of high farce, began jumping idiotically when he caught her gaze. He continued the dumb show with great enthusiasm, making spasmodic gestures toward the locked window and elaborately drawing a warning figure across pursed lips. Too surprised to reconsider, Beverly walked over, unthinking, and slipped the catch open.

"Well done," the detective whispered with the paternal aplomb of a five-star general. He heaved himself into the room without finesse, leaving scars on his three-piece suit and his respiratory system.

"In these pursuits," he continued, "there comes a time for discretion." He paused to catch his breath with a final mutter about the urgent need for secrecy.

Beverly smiled in spite of herself and closed the window. Across the street, beneath a tree, around a corner—with a quick pan, her eyes swept at least thirty astonished youths still staring, as at an afterimage, at this unusual entrance. The detective, she thought, had attracted no more attention than a cement mixer filled with loose rocks.

Suddenly, the anger and hurt burst back over her. She wheeled on the ludicrous Gannett. "Why you playin' the fool, Mister Man?" she screamed. "This ain't TV; this is the real thing. You got another murder on you hands, or ain't you heard?"

"I am well aware, Miss Minere, that—"

"Oh, Lordy!" she hooted. "So now it's Miss Minere, is it?" She strode over to the stocky detective, who had not yet reassembled his cool, and spit the words in his red face. She dropped one role for another. "It was a quite different salutation some months ago, sir. If memory serves, the term was *you, girl.* Or perhaps, *black bitch.* One or the other, or both. Admittedly, my cruder brain cells (the genetic curse of a benighted race) do not always function accurately."

The detective seemed to reel beneath the unjust accusation. "My dear woman," he started, "surely you are mistaken. I would never—"

"Dear woman, shit!" Beverly screamed. She feinted a quick slap near his heavy jaw and laughed to see him dodge instinctively. And she laughed with still deeper pleasure when, with cruel skill, his fingers snapped around her wrist and something vicious sparked up in his eyes. "Go to it," she gasped, for the words were stifled by the fierce pain of Gannett's professional grip. "Beat me, Mistuh Charley. Get your rocks off, he-man, 'cause your white woman ain't doin' you no good."

They stared, and hatred cracked the air between them like lightning. The man's tense sinews screwed tighter, crushing the slender wrist of the laughing woman. He wanted to throw her to the ground, but the lust was born of sadism. Malevolence boiled in his eardrums and would have exploded, until, at the last instant, a cold rag whipped into his face. It was over. He was himself again. He had, in a weak moment, looked away from the hell-pits of her eyes; the white heat of her savage anger, which had nourished his own, and lost its power. In that chance glimpse, he had seen again the little conference room and scarred oak table and faded green walls that formed a pocket of his pale and ordinary world. And he rushed back, breathless, to the familiar scene like an acid freak coming home to Mother. He jumped back quickly, as if it were Beverly releasing him. He had seen something, and it had shaken him, and he would never speak of it. He covered his obscene nakedness with a ready-to-wear respectability. He changed the subject.

"A man named Obadiah Snatch was killed early today," he said. He brushed imaginary lint from the regular interstices of his natty tweed.

She played along. After all, she had already won a round.

"So what else is new?" she answered jauntily. She fairly skipped around the table and sat down by the window. "You must really have your finger on the pulse . . ." She smirked; he caught the reference. ". . . of the ghetto. Congratulations. No one else knows about that, except everyone around here who isn't deaf and dumb. And most of them probably know, too. Anyway, what's it to me?"

"Could be you knew him."

"Could be."

"Could be you know who might want to do away with him."

"Could be." She smiled warmly, and her voice changed

again. "It would appear," she said primly, "that we watch the same movies, you and I."

"Okay," he said quietly, throwing up his hands helplessly. "Let's play it straight."

"Now that's good," she said mockingly. "That's good. We all drop the funny business and work together. Forget our little differences in pursuit of a common goal. Now where have I heard that tune before? In the last day or two?"

"Miss Minere, I can understand you—"

"You don't understand nothing, white man," she snapped. "But it doesn't matter. I don't need your understanding, or your help. I just want you on your job. I pay taxes, too, and you're a public servant, and that means, whether you like it or not, you're working for me."

"Of course."

"Of course," she sneered. "Well, prove it! You bungled the Benedict case; now you're tripping over your own feet on this one. Yeah, I trust you. You handle things just fine."

A dim bulb began to glow in the unswept recesses of the detective's brain. He almost sidled up to her. "You see a connection?" he breathed.

But Beverly's mood had sunk low again. She had tired of games.

"We let him do it," she answered softly.

"Who?" Gannett, too, was scarcely audible. The cautious angler. "Who is 'we'? Who is 'him'?"

Beverly did not listen. She longed for that clear vision which had led her only two days before. Now it was muddied, polluted with foul substances, and she felt only a slight motion sickness as she floated slowly, dreamily, around the sinking currents of a large whirlpool. She wanted peace. She wanted to pray, as her mother had done, and as Benedict's grandmother had done, but she did not know the language of any god.

"It was justice," she said. "Those who live by the sword . . . I knew. I knew about it." With a cold thrill of horror, she shuddered. "I never thought it was Snatch, but then

Finch . . ." She stiffened with a new wonder. Something was wrong. Something was very wrong.

"Go on," Gannett puffed. He found self-control strenuous.

"Listen," she said.

"What?"

"Listen!" She jumped up. The detective pretended to listen, but he already knew what she had just discovered. There was nothing to hear. No sound flared now from the office next door. Nor from the hall, nor from the grounds outside, nor from the street itself. Beverly shook with fright. What had happened? Her students had been laying it on Orson—minutes ago, not hours. And now, she thought, it was as silent as a virgin's womb.

"What have you done?" She shrank in terror from Gannett.

"Me?" He faltered, then caught her meaning. "Nothing. I swear it. I can't move my men in on a situation like this; there'd be violence. That's Orson's lookout. We let them scream all they want."

"Liar."

"That's just the kind of trouble we don't want. You know that." He had a thought. "Why do you think I was so careful to sneak in here through that window? It was to avoid—"

"Then what has happened? How—"

The answer came from an unexpected source.

"Panthers. They moved in, cooled it." Beverly and Gannett snapped around to meet the baleful stare of Emory Finch.

Both recoiled from the sight of the pitiful figure before them. Finch, who never looked more self-confident than a refugee from a concentration camp, now looked beaten. The current which animated his peculiar jerks and twitches had been cut off. His shoulders had melted into mush beneath his clavicle; his hair, dry and thin, hung in ghastly wisps. Mockery, which had so often gamboled about his lips, had sloughed off and left him nothing but a stalk; his once-quick hands now hung limp.

Beverly recovered first. Weakness bred in her contempt, not

pity. And she was doubly happy to see the arrogant Finch laid low, for she thought she knew why. She forgot the terrors of her own guilt and lusted for the kill of the scapegoat. She meant to dance in the soft mud of his flayed skin.

"Murderer," she coldly whispered. She gripped Gannett's upper arm and then pointed slowly toward the dead little man at the other end of the room. "Murderer." She suddenly whooped, with a frenzy meant to purge her own misery. "Murderer!"

"Finch?" babbled the hapless detective.

Beverly paused, then drew herself up straight. She became as regal and chill as the high priestess of a forbidden mystery. "Finch," she boomed, and her grand voice made the word into a terrifying incantation. "Emory Finch!" She glared down from the high place of her fantasy.

"Killed Benedict? But that's—"

"No, fool." Beverly came back down to the rabble. "Don't you get it? He pulled the wool over your eyes, too. He sneaked around, like some old alley cat scaring the fool out of all us simple-minded gutter rats, and then he struck. Don't you be surprised; that man, he got claws, and they do dig deep."

"You mean, he killed Snatch."

"A wise man in the tribe." Beverly twirled around in affected glee. "You got it. Once you copped out . . ." She snickered. ". . . as it were. Once you copped out—"

"I didn't. I was taken off by—"

"Have it your way, mister; have it your own way. He certainly had it his. He made himself lord and executioner. He made up his little puzzles, and he figured them out. And when all the pieces fit, he walked over, nice as you please, and blew that poor pimp's brains clean out of his head." She turned viciously on the silent Finch. "Ain't that right, boy? You wanted to play with the big guys." The journalism teacher said nothing, nor did he move. There was no wind to stir him.

"That's ridiculous," Gannett sputtered. Unlike Beverly, he

talked as if Finch were not in the room with them. And, in a sense, the man was not.

"You ask him, mister policeman. You just ask him."

"Unbelievable. Besides, he was—"

"Ask him." Beverly took the lead; hatred, like some powerful new amphetamine, scrambled her movements into a nervous dance. She lurched toward Finch. "Did you kill Obadiah Snatch, Mr. Finch?"

The journalism teacher quivered slightly, but did not speak.

"Answer," Beverly shrieked. "Or I'll beat it out of you. Did you, or did you not, kill a poor old nigger named Obadiah Snatch?"

Finch still said nothing. But he nodded slowly, and that was answer enough.

"See? He admits it. Arrest him, lock him up! Here is your fine instrument of justice. Murderer of weak old men."

"You?" Gannett stuttered. He forced himself to look at the shattered specimen in front of him. "Finch? You shot Snatch?"

"No," the man answered hoarsely, and the others jumped at the awful sound of his voice before they saw his meaning. "No," he said again, but just as weakly.

"No?! What do you mean, no?" Beverly did not give up her advantage. "You just said—"

"I killed him." Finch was coming to. The emotion-charged air of the little room seemed to work on him, to revive him. His arms loosened, his hands began to move awkwardly, aimlessly. "I killed him. But I did not shoot him."

"Come off it, Finch," Beverly snapped. "It is too late for your equivocations."

"I agree."

"You murdered that old man because you decided he had murdered Benedict. You made yourself into the law."

"I made myself into the law," Finch repeated without emotion.

"What you're saying," began Gannett, who suddenly saw his way into the breach, "is that you murdered Snatch."

"Yes."

"In that case," the detective beamed triumphantly, "where is the murder weapon? Prove it. Where is the weapon?"

"You don't need it," Beverly was about to say, but she stopped in the face of Finch's manic laughter. The little man doubled over with insane glee and made pitiful gurgling sounds in the silent room.

"The weapon . . . where? . . . where?" His convulsed face struggled with the words that insisted on life. "Here." A laugh choked in his throat. "Right here." He pointed to his sallow skull. "Locked up, where you'll never find it, Gannett. You'll never use. it in court. Isn't that hilarious? Don't you see the joke yet? Beverly does; don't you, Beverly? She's catching on . . . because the weapon, don't you see?" He stopped, for he could take no more, and suddenly Beverly turned away from him and the detective. She turned away as suddenly as she had grasped the meaning in his raving, for the insight was painful. It made her guilt as heavy as his.

Gannett tried the old bluster. "I'm happy you two understand so much," he said cheerfully, "but this poor old flatfoot is still confused. How can you kill, but not kill? And what kind of murder weapon do you carry in your head?"

"Arrogance, Gannett." Finch was now calm in his bitterness. He had suffered a severe injury, a near-fatal one, but he was back on the field. His voice was harsh and strong. "I know who killed Benedict, but I waited. I wanted to be sure. There was no proof. I waited, and the murderer killed again, because Snatch was the gateway to that proof. I waited, and Snatch died."

"Who is it?" the detective eagerly demanded.

"Oh, no," said the little teacher. "You could do nothing. You're helpless."

"Finch," moaned Beverly. "End this thing. Tell him. Let them handle it."

"No."

"You can't do this, Finch," Gannett interrupted, almost shouting. "We'll hold you as—"

"As what? A teller of tales. I have no proof." He smiled. "Consequently, you have no proof."

"But someone else might be killed," Beverly pleaded.

"I made that mistake once. I won't make it again."

The detective tried a new approach. "Hey, man," he said lightly. "We agreed to work together. If you've got something, it's your duty . . ." He realized his mistake.

"My duty," Finch said quietly, "is to Benedict, and now to Snatch. Fear not, Gannett; you won't be implicated. And I promise you, Beverly, I am no longer the white man playing God in the God-forsaken ghetto. I am not the law. This is not my world."

"Finch," she said helplessly.

"The wheels are set in motion. That is why the Panthers moved your children out a few minutes ago. I can't turn back. They won't turn back."

"You're out of your mind," Gannett wheezed. "You can't fool around with that pack of murderers, Finch."

"Why not?" Finch smiled. "Now I have murdered."

"But that's not the—"

"It is out of my hands. I observe. Others will act. The voice of this miserable community will be heard, and there will be one more death. A just one."

Light had faded as dusk gathered in the room, and neither Beverly nor Gannett could quite see the strange gleam in Finch's eye. But they knew it was there, and they were oddly frightened.

He smiled, and then vanished through the door into the hall. They did not move to follow. They stood there, stunned, as the gray light made flannel and silk from the sharp highlights of the battered old room.

CHAPTER XXIII

As there is a Colosseum in Rome and pyramids along the Nile, in Los Angeles there are the Watts towers.

Tourists have flocked there since the city fathers declared them a safety hazard years ago.

From the most dispirited, tubercular patch of the Watts ghetto, three bizarre spires rise against the bored skyline of telephone poles and splintered palms. They are not so tall as radio towers, not so colorful as nearby billboards touting beer. Only a tireless tracker can find them amidst the maze of crumbling streets; they do not loom majestically in the distance. They dominate only one already-defeated street.

On this shabby back street, poor as an alley, the sleek white woman shone like the Holy Grail.

Little children, blacker than the mud they played in, stared from their blasted lawns. Dying houses stood sad behind them, as if aware of impotence. Windows had cardboard where glass should have been, as the street lay still where there should be life. The children pretended to play, as they had seen other children do in toy commercials, and made no noise. They stared at the white woman. They listened to the foreign joy in her loud voice.

"Twenty cents for coffee?" she shrieked, as if goosed by someone harmless, like her husband's boss. The young black man with the pushcart shrugged without expression.

"Yes, ma'am," he said quietly.

216

"Well, I don't mind doing my part; I hope you understand that," she went on.

"A coke is only fifteen," he suggested.

"Oh, no," she said. "I want to help out. I just don't want you to think I can be—"

"No, ma'am," he said in the same even tone. He opened the lid on the wooden cart. It was homemade, that cart, but the lid fit exactly, and he was proud of that. The cups were styrofoam, the best that Safeway sold; they were white and sterile beneath plastic wrappings. He knew that customers expected the best, even when they were slumming at the Watts towers. That was business.

"Make that four now, son." She was scarcely thirty; he was seventeen. "I have friends inside, looking at the . . . uh, monuments." She spoke too clearly.

Of course, he thought. *You wouldn't come down here alone.* But he bent about his work without comment. He didn't even glance at the Mexican silver someone had carved into bracelets for her husband to buy. He just brought out the old coffeepot, still warm from the stove in his mother's house down the street, and began to pour.

The woman smiled serenely at the children.

"Aren't they cute?" she said. She radiated the good health and contentment peculiar to those who inherit money. She was happy as a blue-chip stock. By Los Angeles standards, she was very well-dressed, although the dancing colors and teen-age cut of her clothing would be puzzling to anyone from another city.

The young man had not replied.

"Oh, I'm sorry," she said quickly. A faint cloud had blown up on her sunny horizon, but she smoothed it over easily, like an oyster rounding a grain of sand with pearl. "I didn't mean to sound, you know, condescending." She smiled warmly, innocently. *These days,* she thought, *you never can predict what will offend them.* Her slender hand gestured toward the silent children, who continued to stare. "I mean, I just think they're darling. Pretty as a picture."

"Yes, ma'am." He was pouring the fourth, and final, cup.

She waved to one of the little figures. It did not wave back.

"How shy she is!" the woman trilled. "Look at her sucking her fingers and . . . ." She paused, gasped slightly. "Why, she's . . . she's eating that mud. Somebody should—"

"Yes, ma'am." He was counting out paper napkins, quarters carefully cut from the standard table-size. "She's probably hungry."

"What?" The woman didn't know whether to laugh or sympathize. She knew about ghetto humor. She was hip. Yet, you just never knew where you were with these people. Sometimes, they went too far. Surely, he was joking, even if the joke was in very bad taste. But if he wasn't, and she laughed, and he thought she was racist or . . .

Katie Lee could stand it no longer.

She had been sitting, chain-smoking, at the wheel of her parked car, waiting for the woman and her friends to leave. She had not expected to wait so long. The sun was sinking into the brown smog; surely the four ladies of culture would not risk staying in Watts until sundown. It was a thought at which, she had heard, strong men quailed.

This was her place. She had assumed it as her own during her first lonely week in LA the preceding August. Unfortunately, like so many of her fondest treasures, the Watts towers had seduced her under the cover of a misapprehension. She thought she had discovered the black man's sacred shrine. A spring, bursting up through the garbage of the slums, from which would flow the liberated folk art of a liberated people. She saw Africa in its strange spires, "soul" cavorting through the nimble traceries, a black emperor's hoard when the sunlight struck fire from the bits of colored glass embedded in the framework.

And then it turned out to be the work of some Italian nut, a window washer who had wanted to give fat and happy, puzzled American a kind of thank-you present.

Well, so what? It was still her strange and secret place. It was unlike anything she had ever seen, or known. Three graceful towers, fantastic as childhood dreams, but made of soda bottles, old pots, bedsprings, junk. It had stood firm when the City Council had tried to pull it down with a crane, and maybe that was why she loved it. Or because it had taken decades to build, while the neighbors laughed at one man's private dream. Or because that man had finished and then moved away, deserting that dream, as if something that was poetry had died.

In any case, she resented that other woman's interference. The mindless laugh, the careless appraisal to be chewed lightly and belched forth at some cocktail party.

She ground a half-smoked cigarette beneath her heel.

"Marvelous, really marvelous," cooed another young matron, who appeared from within the cement wall that ran around the towers. Two older women twittered closely behind her.

"Here, girls, I have some coffee from this enterprising young man."

"Why, Vicky, how much fun!" This other young woman was the group's wit, it appeared. "A spot of native food, what?"

"Excuse me!" said Miss Lee venomously. She strode through the gay little group toward the wooden gate set in the wall.

"Why, of course," said one of the flustered ladies. She was too well-bred to make much of the incident, although she certainly found it startling.

Miss Lee was already paying fifty cents for her admission when she heard the last of these women.

The stage whisper was very loud.

"I hope, Vicky, you remembered to have him make mine . . ." The breathless giggle could not be suppressed. ". . . black. That's how I like it." The mirth proved infectious.

"Oh, really, dear. Do come on. We'll never push through the

appalling traffic," answered another, trying to keep a properly straight face.

"Fuck," whispered Katie Lee, shocking the old black man who had taken her money. He smiled wryly as she fairly ran off between the towers.

"Miss," he called blandly. "Closing time, fifteen minutes."

She didn't answer, so he went back to counting up the day's receipts. That was his job. He wanted no one else's troubles.

In the shadows left by the fading sunlight, Katie Lee's expression lay hidden, secret, illegible to all but the subtle fingers of the blind.

She sat on one of the cement benches molded by the mysterious Italian. Colored glass, bits of aquamarine and ruby-red crudely faceted, lost its sparkle as the sky grew duller; a night-chill brushed in before the dusk. She looked up at the crazy prayers of the three spires, but she was not at peace.

I despise her! she thought. *I despise that stupid, loud white woman! I despise her for her whiteness, and I despise being white. . . .*

It was comic, for real, but she was not tough enough to laugh.

Where does that leave me? she asked.

She tried to become playful.

I ain't white, ain't black. Ain't nobody's child.

She stiffened at the thought—*and without Chuzz, without Chuzz, the whole thing's a foolish, an obscene imposture. Nobody's fooled, nobody's helped. And here I am, bleating to this madman's castle, because without Chuzz—*

"Time to go, little lady."

Katie jumped up. *Thank God,* she thought. *Next thing, I'd work my way down to a good old-fashioned identity crisis.*

"Time to go home. Sorry."

Home? Buster, you don't know how sorry that would be.

She smiled, nodded, and walked out into the street. *If East Texas could see me now . . .*

The young vendor was still there.

"Like some hot coffee, ma'am? Fresh from the pot."

She winced. *Oh, no, you don't put me in that bag,* she thought. She tried one of her McAdoo ploys.

"Hey, man," she said. "I ain't your mother. You got no call to talk up to me that way. Ain't you together, and proud?"

The young man stayed as blank as before.

"Yes, ma'am," he said mechanically. "Sugar? Cream?"

"Oh, damn it all," said Katie Lee. "Damn."

Exhausted, drained, Finch hung up the phone.

They had listened, like the others. He had been convincing. They were going to act. For him, it was over. He could lean back against the cracked panes of the outdoor booth and drowse to the dying growl of late traffic, as another rush hour dribbled off into the gray desert beyond the off ramps.

Unthinking, he jiggled the change button. It was the reflex of an inveterate optimist, the man who expects something for nothing. Like love in the chance meetings of loose sex, a bent coin returned, the system confounded.

He jiggled in vain.

Nothing. The machine had exacted its due.

Finch stared out at the fumes, at the dusk. There was one more step to be taken before the curtain rang down.

But he would be no more than a disinterested observer.

Power was now back in the hands of the people. Wasn't that it? Or had he, like Gannett, just stepped back and turned the keys of the asylum over to the inmates?

Not for him to decide. None of his business.

He would just watch.

The pompous little mansion in the well-tended forests of Bel-Air had every right to be proud. It had been skillfully copied after a minor French chateau, and because of that, or the pink paint added by its builders, it had been featured in the Sunday magazine section of the Los Angeles *Times.*

Moreover, it was now owned by a very with-it fun couple, who, if they did not speak often to each other, certainly lavished affection on the house. It was expensive; it was tasteful. It had been filled with the rarest Peruvian rugs, the most delicate crystal and porcelain, the most recent forms in leather-chrome-plexiglass furniture. And it was as warmly cosmopolitan as the United Nations.

It smelled, for example, of old-world wonders cooked by an aged Italian signora. Its lawns were pampered by gentle Orientals; the most willing and grateful Mexican maids cared for its insides. A pedigreed Navajo weekly cleaned its pool, smiling to watch the real Danish baker drive around to the kitchen door with fresh, authentic sweets. A Scottish housekeeper kept the workings efficient, and an English social secretary did the same for its mistress' hectic life. Yes, it had certainly given refuge to the huddled masses. An Albanian refugee had once come to dinner, although that was little spoken of since something in the rich food had given his refugee's stomach indigestion.

And now, best of all, the little mansion housed the fabled and very chic Sugawee. Its owners were extremely well-meaning folk.

"It's settled," he whispered in the Toussaint L'Ouverture Bedroom, which had been hung with cheetah and goat hides for his visit.

Ulabenzi, remembering his place, hedged only slightly. He looked down, worried, at a master who lay on a vicuna spread, crushing the fur.

"Can we . . . be sure?" His lowered eyes deprecated the impertinence.

"I am sure," Sugawee intoned. One saurian eye rolled up and fixed his henchman like a gig.

"It is found true?"

"It is found," Sugawee snapped pettishly, as if annoyed that an underling could so well imitate his special rhetoric.

Ulabenzi tried again, the poor functionary willing to stick his neck out for the greater good.

"The Panthers—"

Sugawee groaned; his lips pursed. Obviously, the very name was painful to him.

"They." Ulabenzi stuck to his point. "Can they, in this delicate and embarrassing matter, be trusted?"

"Ulabenzi!" the leader thundered. He shook his great head slowly, evidently wearied by the duller wits, the shallower comprehension of lesser men. He knew, alone, what it is to be Caesar. Tediously, his massive form tensed and bunched in strategic places and he began to rise, chanting as he did:

"It is a night of the gods, a night to be praised with the beating of drums and the roaring of old songs, Ulabenzi, my brave one. Who are we to have the petty suspicions of men? The tribes are coming together; peace at last among warriors of the same blood. What else does Sugawee work for? Pray for? We are better to rejoice. Our brothers will sit round the same council fire, as in the days of our—"

At last, he was up. He sighed and realigned the rolling slabs of flesh.

"But fascists are not our—"

"But? But!" Sugawee spat on the black-and-white marble of the inlaid floor. Someone named Cato Murphy looked out beneath the heavy brows. "What are these, fool?" He patted the revolvers as he slipped them beneath his robes.

Ulabenzi smiled. Everything would be all right.

"Come," Sugawee said. He stopped only to choose a plump persimmon from a Finnish crystal bowl.

"Degenerate," he said, then dashed the bowl to bright slivers on the hard floor. Strange lights glittered among the smashed, wine-red pulp of the bitter fruit.

"Come," he said.

Katie hung up her pastel Princess phone and walked briskly over to her home-entertainment center.

She flicked the selector dial from FM stereo to phono, adjusted treble to a slight advantage over bass, and efficiently put into action her dearest album. She moved swiftly, professionally. When she sat down in the glossy red-vinyl lounge chair by the window, Katie seemed merely to relax, she did not collapse. It was a calm gaze that wafted out into the leafy green avenues of residential Beverly Hills.

The music was all. It washed away all thought, as she had known it would. It was modern, but suggestive of the Elizabethan; Katie had further confused the issue by choosing a version pressed by some string-swamped orchestra of middle-aged men. It didn't matter. She still saw two lovers swathed in ochre glow at midnight. It didn't matter that they were teenagers, and Italian, and slightly addled. It didn't matter that they had never lived, but their love had endured for centuries; and yet she was alive, alive now, and her love had been already . . . The hell it didn't matter.

Chuzz had been plain. He had told it "like it is, baby." She had always hated that expression. Now she knew why. Telling it like it is was like . . . telling nothing; it was just like lying down helpless on the tracks and letting the freight train plow into you.

And now, that's where they were at. As the saying goes.

Helpless.

And here come de train.

Katie Lee wallowed in sad thoughts for several moments. The Panthers had met, and their deliberations were final. Chuzz had to drop her, or they would drop him, and not too gently. She and her man had flown in the face of convention, but their wings had been clipped. Coolly, with precision. No muss, no fuss.

But Katie Lee was too tough an animal to die starving on the moor.

Already, the self-confident voice of her naughty self came blustering through the sentimental violins on her stereo. She saw, in the cool evening beneath the palms on her street, a silver-gray Rolls gliding up the canyon; already, her Texas instincts had accurately calculated how many oil wells the driver carried on his comfortable back. She smiled. Yes, this was her world. What was revolution to her? Or the starving masses? They had their roles to play, she had hers. They needed a strong enemy. She had only complicated the issues by switching sides. As for true love and broken hearts . . . .

A good douche, said the naughty self, *will wash that man right out of your—*

Right on, Katie agreed. A little too quickly. *Uh . . . that is, you're right.* She would have to clean up her language.

Miss Lee was an activist. She made a decision, then moved on it. She snapped her fingers and stood up; she was going to make a telephone call. Maybe she had already known what was coming; maybe she had really made her decision that afternoon when the coffee vendor had said so stubbornly, "Ma'am."

Daddy would be relieved. The Miss Lee of McAdoo High was not the real Katie Lee, and the Miss Katie of East Texas would not be the real Katie Lee, either. But, at the least, the Southern version would be accepted at face value, without question or reservation; it was the part she was trained by experience to play. It would be a good vacation. She would be petted, and admired; a Dallas businessman would try to place her on his formica-surfaced pedestal. No one would think to probe. They would leave her insides alone. And so, after a time, would she.

She would stay there; she would let them all cuddle her until the chirping drivel filled her with vomit and she would be ready to come back.

Oh, not to Chuzz. Not to Watts. Not even to Los Angeles. She didn't see herself recovering that quickly. Not just yet.

But it would not take her long to find her footing again. She had needed Chuzz, but she could not have him; that was over. Now, as if some frightened child within her cried in the dark, she needed East Texas. But it would not imprison her again; that would soon be over, too.

She didn't know when. A month. Several. But she saw how it would happen. She would be smiling as the women chattered away some Sunday afternoon in the kitchen; she would listen with one ear to the men drowsing in another room, loud belchers pretending to watch some ball game on television. Suddenly, she would be free. She would shout and run upstairs to get the bag which would already be packed. And no matter what they said, how they pleaded or made threats, this time she would really leave; she would know her own mind. She would leave their life behind and go—somewhere—to find her own.

The setback was definitely temporary.

Miss Lee picked up the receiver and dialed an area code somewhere in Texas.

She was going home.

Floyd Hockby had declined a certain invitation.

For one thing, he did not have a strong stomach for physical violence. Only emotional pain could titillate his finicky sadism. And for another, not one of his finer feelings could be transmuted into brotherly warmth for the likes of Sugawee, Ulabenzi and Chuzz Jackson. "Soul," Hockby felt, was not in the classical mold. It would have been chauvinistic to pretend otherwise.

Yet he had been tempted to join the party.

It rarely happened that Floyd Hockby was asked out for a night with the boys. In fact, it never happened. He was, after all, no man's idea of a regular guy. On the contrary. He would have ordered a martini to their beers, donned a blue blazer to match their wool sweaters and flannel jackets, offered opera for their roller derbies. He knew; they knew. It was knowledge of the bones, driven in by bullies. Floyd Hockby had dedicated his life to proving himself superior to those bullies. He would not let himself covet their friendship now.

Still, they had the upper hand. They weren't groveling.

Here he was, lost in the dark bowels of a nameless bar, as if hiding from his own face. He was anonymous, and cold. Weak bulbs, scattered about, gave off the dim red glow of an Eastern temple. The other postulants were strangers to him. They stumbled against other strangers in the semidarkness and made ritual demands of the high priest behind the reeking altar. Money clanked, and the fluorescent brews flowed, but their pungent odors fumed into a stale cloud indistinguishable from sweat in a Turkish bath. Cries of the happy hour grew hoarse with the coming of night, and loosened lips made chilly nonsounds on the lonely air.

My life, thought Hockby, *is a waste.* He looked around, but saw no one who might disagree. How could they? He was a brilliant scholar, and he was in his prime, and the doors of academic heaven were being opened to less qualified brothers who shared the curse of Ham.

He swallowed this irony with an olive and signaled for another drink.

Cruelest joke of all, he considered, was the uniformed approbation of his former colleagues. They praised him, from their secure ivies, for going out on the social battlefield. They thought him a brave crusader in the infidel ghetto, the loving son returned to save his downtrodden race.

How bitterly far from this notion was the truth. Floyd Hockby had closeted himself in this wasteland for one reason. *Because,* he smiled to himself, *I can get away with murder. In a manner of speaking, that is. Because, down here, I am just another black punk out on the prowl. Because no one expects anything else. I walk through my eight-to-three, and turn in forms promptly, and that is all the Board of Education wants. And then my nights, and the long weekends, are mine to squander as I choose. And no one asks questions, so long as the gendarmes are kept off the scent.*

A great life, he smirked. And then, in the crimson glow on the table before him, Floyd Hockby suddenly made a great vow. He would change. He would reform. He would rise up from the garbage pit of his decadent life, like a phoenix in the old myths, and leave his diseased body burning to ashes on the dung heap. Yes, oh yes. Let Dr. Hockby emerge. Scholar, savant, epicene wit. A credit to his race, a joy to his aged mother. He would return and wring new poetry from the mildewed classics. He would be the standard-bearer of a new Renaissance, the man who had sprung from the dirt of the cities to discover the ether of classical thought. He might even go on television.

Hockby left his martini. Drunk with the euphoria of these new plans, he fairly danced out of the ratty bar into the cool evening smog.

The bright streetlamps blinded him for a moment. Here was life, here was action. He had only to choose the right turning. He walked full into the crowd, the rags and tatters of a dying civilization. They were the rabble, and he had tarried too long with them. He was headed for Parnassus.

Suddenly, he stopped, and the spurious joy passed. He had seen something, and it had slapped him in the gut. He was sober. He remembered who he was. A poignant thrill unmanned him.

On the curb sat a lone, slim figure.

The Latin teacher glanced a second time at the unknown boy and felt for his wallet. It was there. He was prepared. When fate spoke, she spoke harshly, and no mortal should quarrel with her decisions. Floyd Hockby knew the signs. This was a route he had traveled often before, always in search of the same elusive peace.

He paused and let his limbs relax into the saunter of a casual encounter. He whistled a noncommittal tune and watched his prey, unmoving, imperceptibly tense in answer.

Floyd Hockby forgot the great vow.

"Yes, yes, I know all about it. You're doing a fine job. The board is—" The speaker was trim and healthy. On another coast, he would be tagged a Kennedyite, that attractive combination of expensive schooling and boyish charm. It was a charm all the more wonderful in a man past forty.

"Just a minute. Can you hold on?" He didn't wait for an

answer; he was already signaling his wife, pointing to his watch and then toward the television set.

"Oh," she mouthed, and tiptoed across the yellow plush rug to do his bidding. Her husband turned back to his caller.

"As I was saying, the board couldn't be more pleased, Orson, with the way you're handling a difficult . . . No, no, don't interrupt me with any false modesty, man. You're the new breed." He assumed his most beguiling tones. "And, remember, when you . . . uh, take over some day, I was your strongest supporter on the board. Hey, hey, what is it?" He was more annoyed that his little joke had fallen flat than that Orson kept interrupting, but he was disturbed on both counts.

"What's that?" His voice took on an ugly edge. "Hey, now, I thought you had everything under— Why, man, I just told the press this afternoon that it was all going— Don't tell me you've let those . . . ."

His wife tugged frantically at his soft cardigan.

"Now, darling," she whispered. "It's on now."

"Just a minute, Orson. I'm not finished with you." He held the receiver in his hand and walked over for a better view of the set. Grimly, he watched himself speaking to the cameras; tight-lipped, he saw himself smile.

"Your best angle, darling. You look great."

He said nothing until the screen cut to a film of some cretin spilling chocolate on his jeans at a fraternity picnic.

"Hello? Hello!"

"Well, I thought you looked like the next mayor, really," said the poor woman. She came up and put a sallow arm around his waist.

"Damn! He hung up."

"Who, darling?" She could count the years in her own skin, as it puddled next to his firm lines; she knew she had to try harder now to keep him.

"He can wait all night if he thinks I'm going to call him. Who does he think he is, anyway? He'd be nothing without me."

"Who?" she asked timidly.

"Orson, damn it! Don't you ever listen?"

"Oh," she replied.

"He promised to clean up that mess down there. I fell for it; oh, I admit that! A black leader for the black school, qualified or not. Now look at it! Our own little Viet Nam, right in the heart of Los Angeles."

"No one can blame you."

"Hell no, woman! Who said they would?"

She waited for his anger to spend itself; she smiled and tried to hold her belly firmer beneath the tight cocktail dress.

"It just goes to show," her husband continued. "First sign of real trouble and they're ready to run out, leave the real work to us."

"That's their problem," she ventured.

"Theirs? What about me? Do you ever think of me? How do you think I feel? I've just made an ass of myself on television, don't you realize that? I said the whole thing was calmed down, and now he says it's starting again. Something—I don't know what—about meetings, phone calls; I don't think he knows, but he's fucking scared. It's starting again, and I just told the people of Los Angeles there is nothing to worry about. How do you think I feel? Don't you ever think of me?"

His wife drew her breath in sharply. Her answer wasn't quite ready.

She walked without music down the long rusty canals of her ghetto neighborhood.

Beverly had been banished. Somehow. Silently. She was a stranger in the land she loved, as if the gods had set a curse on her brow. She had thought herself a vestal of the revolutionary flame, but she was suddenly locked out of the temple.

Since the mysterious stillness of the afternoon, no student had answered her call. Street friends nodded curtly and passed quickly on. Tight knots of leather-jacketed youths did not cluster on the street corners tonight. At the market, her clenched-fist salute was answered with a down-home wave.

Tonight, she did not hear the gay banter of black power slogans; there were no secret smiles at conspiratorial insinuations. Children did not follow her, laughing with joy. Their intuition, which had sensed her magnetic power the day before, now shrank before an unspoken warning.

"Cool it" was the new watchword in Dogtown. The people knew it. The very gutters knew it. Even stray mongrels seemed to slink away warily as she approached. But if anyone knew why the word had gone out, he did not step forward to tell her. The people bowed, as they had often, before the heavy hand of a silent threat.

Beverly was terrified. She finally realized that she had never been alone before.

She had always had hate to keep her warm. But now she was too confused to direct her venom. She had always found pride in her exotic lineage, in the heritage of forgotten tribes who had first worked gold and made marriage bowers in a savage jungle. But now she was just another HEW statistic; she was a tally-mark on a dead, littered street. The broken glass in the alleys did not make a king's jewelry, and there were no gods in the trash cans. Yet her deepest misery was indefinable. She had never deserted her people, but now they turned a stone eye toward her. She had returned from the white man's university, determined to spread his magic freely. Now she was rejected. She, who had given up all the glittering promises of a guilt-ridden society, she, who had turned up her nose at money and security and the chance to be the pampered darling of philanthropic Mister Charlies, had been betrayed.

So be it, thought Beverly Minere. She had always been tough, far tougher than any man. So be it.

She stopped on the dark sidewalk and raised both fists to the polluted sky. It had a sour-milk glow from the night lights of the vomited city. But she saw beyond the petty instant. She remembered her pagan kings, murdered by self-righteous white missionaries; she remembered her field hands, hard-muscled and tall, castrated by towns of Southern bookkeepers; she remembered her destiny. She swore to wrench grandeur from the seamy slum around her.

No wonder she fairly choked with disgust at the sudden intrusion of a familiar whine.

"I thought I recognized the fists," said Emory Finch. He wore a shapeless trench coat and an open white shirt with a shredded collar; he looked like an out-of-work grocery clerk.

"Jesus," Beverly replied. This was the last insult. Had he come to gloat? She definitely preferred tragic loneliness to the company of this pablum-fed white man.

"I've been calling you for hours," Finch said. "You're about to miss the party." The words were casual enough, but he did not speak lightly. There was a grim decision in his voice which she had not suspected until that afternoon. He was calmer now; he was harder, too.

"Fine time for a celebration, Emory," she sneered, but her thrust missed the mark. She had taken his sally at face value, but he would not be stalled. He briskly took her arm.

"Be grateful. Your uh, brothers didn't think you belonged; they didn't think this was a party for the ladies. I begged leave to differ," he said simply.

Momentarily off balance, Beverly allowed him to lead her away. For one thing, she had already made one scene in the street; she did not want to make another. But she was not defeated.

"I can walk," she hissed.

"Of course." He dropped her arm, but stayed close beside her. Although he walked swiftly, she found herself automatically keeping pace with him.

For some minutes, they strode in silence. Finch wove an intricate pattern through the maze of deserted back alleys, and Beverly followed. Breathing became difficult, and her heels stumbled through the heaps of refuse, but she did not lag behind. If this was a contest, she would not lose. At last, they ran into an apparent dead end; a buckling chain fence blocked their way to an abandoned factory.

"Great!" she shouted. "Follow the leader, the inimitable—"

"Shut up!" Finch snapped. His hand shot up, as if to restrain her. For a moment, she thought he had tricked her down here to—

"You bastard!" She pushed him away and fell back against a slimy brick wall. "What is this? I'll scream bloody murder if you so much as touch me again."

But he was ignoring her. He had found what he wanted.

"Here," he said, pointing to the fence. On the far left, behind a pile of rotting crates, was a small opening. It looked as if the links had simply fallen apart from shoddy maintenance and old age. "Here," he said, and it was an order.

Slowly, cautiously, Beverly obeyed. She crawled through while Finch held the sharp flanges apart for her.

Curiosity had shoved her through, but curiosity could induce her no farther. Not without explanation. The sickly glow of the city barely illuminated the cold scene before her. Twenty yards away loomed the stale brick façade of the dead building. As her eyes adjusted to the gloom, she could make out the jagged stars of broken windows. There was no sound. Even Finch, behind her, knelt mute as a sinner's shade.

Abruptly, she turned to question him, to see what he was doing to the fence. It was then she caught sight of the bayonet, a sliver like an icicle.

"Halt!" said a terrible voice from the dark silence. "Brother, or devil?"

Beverly shook, but grabbed desperately for a reply. "Sister," she stammered. "Yes, I'm a sister."

The voice was not convinced. The delicate icicle poised near her quivering throat. "Kuu elise . . ." The voice was impatient. "Kuu elise . . ." Instinctively, Beverly looked for a way to run out, but she was trapped. And she could see little in the unfamiliar enclosure.

"Malis."

"Brother Finch?"

"The same."

"Hey, man, you had me jumpin'. Why you keep you mouth closed like that, huh?"

"Sorry," laughed Emory Finch. "Just a little joke between the sister and me. Right, Beverly?"

"Sure," she said. She got the joke, but she wasn't laughing.

"Well, you better watch out. Man get his throat cut funnin' like that. And nobody to blame but hisself."

"Sorry," Finch answered, but he sounded less than contrite. There was a gentle exhilaration in his voice which had not been heard for some time. Beverly was almost touched.

"That's all right," the other voice relented. "Everybody pretty nervous tonight."

"I expect so."

"She all right? You sure?"

"Word of honor. Invited by Sugawee himself."

"Okay, but you better hurry." The voice deteriorated from its former majesty into a hideous gargle that seemed to represent laughter. "You gonna miss the party. From what I hear, they's just about finished carvin' up the turkey. Know what I mean?"

"Yeah," said Finch with sudden grimness. "I know what you mean. Come on, Beverly. No use making this trip for nothing. Take my hand; we go this way."

"Finch, what is all this?" She was fighting a growing dread; the one hint had been ominous enough.

"Come on."

She went. She had no choice. As she clung to the white man's slender hand, one particular worry chewed at her more viciously than the others: Why was she a stranger in her own house? The black sentinel had challenged her, but accepted Finch. Wherever they were going, Finch knew the way; and apparently Sugawee, the most fearsome of leaders in the black man's world, had given him the nod. And yet Finch, for some reason of his own, had insisted that she be allowed to come. She gave it up. Besides, the answer lay closer than she suspected.

Confident as a cat, the little journalism teacher took her through an open entranceway. He guided her skillfully around great lumps of discarded metal strewn crazily across the vast floor; they passed into a cluster of dusty cubbyholes that must once have served as offices. Now alerted, Beverly searched the musty emptiness for further bayoneteers. None appeared. She bumped into Finch, who had stopped in front of a blank wall. He took her hand and let it graze against a deep grove; she recoiled at the warm ooze of fresh oil.

"Industrial rehabilitation, BAM-style," he said. She didn't understand. "Freight elevator, *circa* 1930," he explained. "Only equipment left in this shell when the business moved to the suburbs. But it works."

He pushed something, and the door must have slid open. Beverly didn't see it do so; she felt it. A cold hand, like a medium's trick, brushed at her as air rushed from the shaft of the rickety old machine. She let Finch guide her in. She heard the doors close ponderously and wondered how she could have missed that terrible noise before. Yes, she definitely must pull herself together. She wasn't thinking clearly. She was vulnerable.

The descent was slow and spasmodic. Irregular creaking noises jerked at Beverly's raw nerves; the crude platform swayed as corroded pulleys slipped out of sequence. There were no walls to the ancient device, only a latticework of filthy metals, and she set her feet wide apart to keep balance; she would not risk reaching out a hand to find support in that awesome darkness. She forgot Finch; she was alone.

As slowly as they descended, so slowly did Beverly begin to sense noise and heat from several yards below. She lost her bearings. It seemed she was merely walking through a tunnel, rather than sinking into a pit, and there would be daylight at the other end. Instantly, she saw her mistake. With a sudden flash, as if an outside barrier had been penetrated by the pitiable elevator, hot light cut through the cracks in the old wooden floor. It shot up, in ghastly parody of sunlight through venetian blinds, and laid yellow bars across the little cage. Finch, like an evil djinn, seemed to undulate horribly as the tarnished glows danced in the dusty air near his face.

Beverly wanted to shatter the menacing silence. She didn't have time. She was interrupted.

And the new sound made her think, ludicrously, of trolls. Workmen in the bowels of the earth. Regular, insistent, a distant hammering. And, barely perceptible but necessary to the illusion, an irregular sound, like the deep, involuntary groans of exhausted miners. The fantasy amused her. How long had they been in the elevator? She couldn't tell. It was like a moment in a dream, or under pot; it could have been a few seconds, or an hour, and it really didn't matter. Beverly began to enjoy herself. Whatever Finch was up to, this was—

She gasped in horror. Her hands clutched wildly at her temples. She bit her tongue, hard, against the involuntary scream.

"Beverly. Steady." Finch could discern her convulsions in the eerie light.

"Oh, no, no." She shrank from him, like a frightened animal. Her terror became a painful moan.

For they were almost there. They were a few feet away. And now she knew. The gentle, regular hammering was no longer the tinkering of picturesque elves. It was a pounding; it was a monstrous, relentless pounding, and the low groans were not the weary sighs of industrious workmen. She had heard of such things. In theory, she would have condoned such things. But now, face to face with the—

"Finch," she hoarsely whispered, "I can't. Not now . . . ."

The elevator bumped to a halt.

"Last stop," Finch sang out. He was determined to be inexorable; the decision was made. "Bargain basement." He almost shouted, for the chilling noise now beat exuberantly through their cage. "This week's special—"

"Don't!"

"—Black Unity." Maniacally, as if exhilarated by the young

woman's hysteria, Finch lunged for the heavy iron bar that locked the sliding door to the basement. The cage was dark again, for they were now on a level with the source of light. Yet Beverly threw herself drunkenly toward the crack of Finch's voice; she found him and bit at him; her sharp nails slit his pale skin. She was insane with horror and disgust. The sliding door held back all illumination, but it could not shut out that final pounding. It could not shut out, or even muffle, those irrevocable groans. Finch finally pushed her away and got a firm grasp on the metal bolt. With a desperate push, he flung the heavy door open, and the hot breath of that terrible basement broke into the elevator shaft to reveal his victory; Finch stood, breathless, by the door, and Beverly, hiding her face with frenzied hands, huddled miserably on the rank flooring.

Hands, firm and gentle, took Beverly at the elbows and lifted her up. She took no notice. It was only that sound, that mechanical sound, which could penetrate her consciousness. Did it continue? She could not tell. She would not look. In her brain, it pounded still, and she feared it would never stop.

The hands led her out into the room. They were diplomatic; they were sensitive to her cringing, and they brought her to a makeshift sofa against the wall. It was an old mattress, stained and torn, but to Beverly it was a sultan's divan. She lay down, drained of spirit, and buried her head in the tatty fabric.

"It's over," said Finch.

"No," she said. She would not be tricked. It was not over. It had just begun, for she would never forget. They would lie to her. She heard the pounding still. It was more horrible than the searing smell which scorched her struggling lungs.

"Dear princess," came the voluptuous tones, "let it be known, I protested your coming here." Sugawee heaved one of his volcanic sighs. Beverly shuddered; it was too much like one of those other sighs. "I am duly sensitive to the tragic susceptibility of the feminine organism." He sounded calm, as if nothing unusual had occurred in that deserted basement.

"Beverly," said Finch. "I'm sorry. It was my idea. I thought you should—"

"And you were right, Finch." Chuzz spoke slowly, but it was the ruse of a shaken man. "We all have to share . . . the credit. These are the credentials." He stopped, and thought of Katie. This was a credit he would not let her share. He had given her no choice. He had sent her home. "No one will lead us," he continued, "who was not here tonight." It was stagy, rhetorical. It was a speech made to rally his broken nerves.

To Beverly, these were disembodied voices that came from very far away. What were they to her? She wanted to go to sleep. She wanted her pills. Tele-phone, she thought. From the Greek, *tele,* for "Far away." *Tele, tele, tele.* She repeated the syllables over and over, like an incantation to drive out the demons of madness. *Tele, tele, tele.*

"It's all over," Finch said again. "I'll take you home."

"Yes, it is finished. The just have triumphed, as they shall in the great—"

"Come on, Beverly." Chuzz was a man again. "Let the black man take care of his sister."

Yes, thought Beverly, I asked for this. I will stick it out.

She turned over on the faded mattress and looked into their weary faces. Even the smooth hills of Sugawee's magnificence slumped slightly under strain. Chuzz looked grave and solid; Finch looked bilious, but sympathetic. She seemed to draw strength from the steadiness of their several gazes; she took a deep breath. Impulsively, she jumped to her feet and stared at the medieval scene behind them.

The large brown hulk hung, like a side of flayed beef, from a hook in the center of the well-lighted room. It was an insignificant, sagging lump. It no longer moved. Only the ooze of the red network across its back broke the still monotony of death.

Beverly did not know it, but she was seeing a replay of what Finch had seen on Polaroid two nights before.

It was the murderer. This time, she knew, they were right.

It was the ravaged body of a man who had been tortured to death. It had once been named Orson.

Beverly fainted.

CHAPTER XXIV

SCUM from the offshore drilling had not discouraged several thousand wistful Angelenos. Neither had a brisk November breeze, nor the heavy tributes demanded by parking-lot barons, nor the general litter of musty, flaking bodies spread out to dry. It was, in fact, cold. But the sky was clear, and the sun was out, and this misery, after all, was the point of moving to southern California from grimmer climes.

There are not many colors in that arid landscape. The sky, on days like these, gave off a weak shimmer that resembled blue. The ocean surged brown, like a giant vat of castor oil; fetid whitecaps crashed and died out among picturesque humps of garbage on the beach. Pale bodies, under a pale sun, gradually assumed a protective coloration so that they blended with the jaundiced sand.

It was the fulfillment of the Great Dream.

Little old ladies and little old men, speaking strange tongues, grew leathery where they squatted on bright Indian blankets. They put thick eastern European sandwiches into their thick eastern European gullets and sipped cheap Gallo from a marked-down thermos bought at K-Mart. They had their ritual. They played cards as an occupation, not a diversion. They were no less avaricious than they had been at thirty.

Pairs of young boys prowled through nests laid by pairs of young girls. And some, on both sides, were not so young.

The Anglos wore little, but according to strict code: tight-fitting shreds on the female, loose hangings on the male. Chicanos wore heels and sat quietly with their families; black young men wore faded gym clothes.

To the layman, there was no order in this apparent heterogeneity. Beach denizens knew better. There was a certain volleyball game for red-blooded, sun-bleached college kids; another one for aging, sun-bleached fags. There was a lifeguard station where bored surfers gathered, suited in black rubber, to wait until the swimming crowd thinned; beneath another, folk songs were sung in a mist of marijuana smoke. Invisible lines divided young mothers from idle cruisers, weekend swingers from professional dopers. And everyone knew the rules.

Not far out, a covey of gregarious little sailboats bobbed in the predictable gusts. Their white triangles skipped silently back and forth, a study in futile motion. Their skippers, semiliterate drunks, had inherited used-car lots in Orange County and fried-chicken franchises. They were the cream of the new society.

It was not, in short, the proper setting for deep discussion. The halcyon day, like southern California itself, was a lotus that blanked out the higher thought processes. Philosophy choked before the massive onslaught of meaninglessness; Descartes would have lain down and gone to sleep, the better part of valor.

In this respect, there was one couple that did not differ from the others. They lay, unthinking, in the meager sun. She would be called slender; he was skinny. She languished, like a drugged sacrifice; he squinted.

But there was a lot to be said. Finally, she spoke.

"No doubt, you wonder why I haven't left yet." There was a peculiar kind of privacy in that mob. It was universally revered; anything could be said.

"You had to pack?" Finch ventured. Neither moved for the conversation. They lay prone on the ridiculous griddle.

Katie laughed, but not easily. She didn't want to crack the smooth patina of suntan cream that glistened on her face.

"I didn't acquire that much in three months," she continued. "At least, not in material possessions." The slight cloud, on this sunny day, passed quickly. "By the way, can you use a stack of secondhand books on the black revolution? Going cheap."

"Free?"

"Miser."

"Underpaid teacher."

"Dig. You can pick them up when you take me to the airport."

"Deal."

They paused and let themselves doze briefly to the tubercular rattle of the polluted surf. Friendly cries, like the small talk of piping dolphins, broke indistinguishable on the air. Katie tried again.

"Since you insist," she said, "it's because of horror movies."

"I insist?"

"You have a very insistent silence."

"Horror movies? I thought you just wanted to brighten up the tan for the folks back home. Make them suffer."

"That, too."

"I understand what you mean, you know. About the horror movies."

"Damn it, Finch. You always understand. It's disgusting." She shifted a little. One thigh had fallen into the shade of a nearby squatter. "Maybe that's why . . ." She edited the thought. "Why you find life so difficult."

He ignored the remark. He had understood. *Maybe that's why, little Emory, you are alone; maybe that's why you are impossible to live with.*

"Particularly if it's a late movie on television."

"Right."

"It's a dark and stormy night. For two hours of unrelieved horror, it's been a dark and stormy night. Finally, they kill the monster. All's well. But you can't quite go to bed, you can't quite shake it off, unless there's a last scene in the afternoon sunlight. All good men gather under the olive trees; brave boy kisses golden girl. And the nightmare's really over. You can feel it."

"You making a proposal, brave boy?"

He took it in the proper spirit. "Little late for that."

"Yeah." It certainly was.

Neither raced to the topic uppermost in their minds. They sniffed around it cautiously, like old mongrels.

"You going back tomorrow?"

Finch smiled. In direct sunlight, it seemed a frown. "Why not? I'm still employed as a teacher. I have to eat."

"And if they don't want you?"

"They? What kind of racist are you?"

"They. What other pronoun is there?" It was a tired old argument. It took up time.

"They don't need a white knight. As it were." With his eyes closed tight against the glare, he had almost forgotten what she looked like. Even his own voice seemed far away. They talked from opposite banks of a flooded stream. "But they do need a journalism teacher. Especially with a new administration coming in. I'll stay. It's nothing but a job. A little good, a little moral lesson," he said quite seriously, "comes out of the fray. Although not worth . . ."

She waited. After a moment, he went on.

"Not worth Benedict's life." He glared, for some reason, at his own weak hands. "Emory Finch, it seems, has to be kicked in the face before he catches on." His mouth was a taut line. "But he gets the point, in the end. My students don't need love; they don't need me, except as a means."

She protested. "That's too cynical, and too easy."

"A better word is 'practical'; for them, and for me." He smiled in his special way. "Hold on now, I'm not looking for a devious copout. I wish . . ." His words were less audible, less sure. ". . . I had my illusions still. That would be nice. I wish I saw myself again as a kind of Dr. Dooley in the wilderness." He looked at her frankly. "But it won't wash. My students, if they are ever to win, will win out on their own. And they will. They need me to teach school, and that's it. I will be a good teacher, but only that. The other things, the spiritual things, must come from the source; from Beverly, for example. They'll make it without me. Just you wait."

"But can you divide yourself that way? Leave it at the door?"

"Society can. Why can't I?"

"Because . . . it's heartless, Finch."

"No. As I said before, it's only practical. The ghetto needs my knowledge; it doesn't need me." He laughed. "And it's time I spent my emotional energies on Number One. I don't want to wind up, beached in a rest home at seventy-five, living off the memories of other men's children, clucking piteously, 'They were all *my* children.' "

"How horrible."

"Right on, sister."

She got the message; in a way, she changed the subject.

"What's Gannett going to do?"

"Accept a promotion."

"Come again?"

"To West Los Angeles. The soft life. Teen-aged acid freaks in Brentwood; middle-aged drunk drivers. Maybe a hatchet murder now and then, some lawyer's wife who deserves it."

"The system."

"Uh-uh. Naughty, naughty. You better wash your mouth out before you get back to Texas. They don't like talk like—"

"You know it. And longer hemlines."

"The new Katie Lee."

"On the contrary. The old Katie Lee. All made up and smelling pretty."

"With teased hair?"

"That much, I'll fight. My one corruption." Operating on a secret timing mechanism, she suddenly turned over; skillfully, without dislodging a single item in the paraphernalia on her blanket. Her head lay toward Finch, but her eyes remained

closed. "All the rest, return to form. Talk quietly and let the
men discuss politics. Cook and simper. Not a brain in my
pretty little head."

"Sounds just . . . ."

"Yeah." It was a weak enough protest, and she knew it.
Better than staying here and . . . . She buried the nasty
thought. Rule number one for the Southern Belle. Think
happy thoughts. It was going to be hard for a while, but she
would manage. Did she not have more than twenty years of
rigorous training behind her?

Finch, following her lead, also turned over. He was not so
practiced as she. He kicked his shoes into the sand. Nearby
sunbathers smiled indulgently at the novice as he scrambled
awkwardly to retrieve the ragged tennis shoes. He didn't flush
with embarrassment. He always felt like a vulgarian among the
polite elite, even when the elite were vulgarians; at least, they
had their agreed-upon standards, and he obviously didn't mea-
sure up.

Settled, he decided to go straight to the point. After all, he
wanted his sunny afternoon, too. The horror had ended.

"Chuzz was right," he said with sudden relevance. "It was
not a pleasant party. Even Beverly—"

"I know." She shuddered, and the sun's rays fell like snow-
flakes. But she wanted to hear. She wanted to hear it all. Only
then would it finally be over.

Finch understood.

"There will be a quiet funeral this afternoon. Not well-at-
tended. But there will be a representative from the Board of
Education, someone very old and very white, hoary with
respectability. And there will be some bright-eyed delegate
from the Police Department. Between sobs, they can synchro-
nize their watches."

"Meaning?" She wiggled daintily, just enough to lower the
back of her bikini pantlets to the forbidden zone. A final
ribbon of white flesh was revealed for the frying.

"Meaning, they've reconnoitered, and decided to wear

blinders. The body, suitably dressed, was found on the steps of that great institution, McAdoo High; the body of a valiant soldier cut—"

"What steps?"

"A figure of speech. Anyway, Gannett got there first and ventured a dime, luckily for him, on a phone call downtown. Alert, he made a lightning dash to the emergency room of a certain hospital and scooped the story: fearless black leader, overworked and under severe strain, collapsed under the inhuman pressures of a thankless job. Body undiscovered for hours. Pronounced dead on arrival at hospital. Verdict: heart attack." Finch almost mumbled against the scratchy lumps of his blanket, an olive-drab remnant from an army surplus store.

"A cover-up," Katie said without emotion. "For the common weal."

"Actually," Finch answered clinically, "that verdict is probably accurate. The death itself, I mean. Brought on by the beating, and the burns."

"God!" Sure, she felt removed from it all. But not that removed.

"The rest," he went on, "is . . . mechanical, predictable. It falls into place. Even if they didn't see the wisdom of discretion, even if they weren't sure this was the end of it, they couldn't move against all of us."

"Us?"

"I was there. I was . . . invited. Cruel as it must seem, that's also why Beverly had—"

"Yes. That makes sense." Katie had not been invited. And that made sense, too. "She asked for it."

"In a way."

Katie still did not move, but she perceptibly tensed. Finch saw it. There was one question, and it was more important than any others. Not a happy thought. And what an inconsequential ogre it seemed, after all, on this sunny afternoon in the best of all possible worlds. How out of place. She needed all her powers of concentration to remember what it was, to remember why it should be important, to remember that this golden throng of happy people was not, and never would be, the fibrous misery of which real human beings are made.

Who could think of moral questions in this land of milk and honey? She had to grit her teeth.

"Was he . . ." she faltered. "Are you sure?"

His answer was simple enough. And assured.

"Yes," he said.

At that, she opened her eyes. She was momentarily surprised to find his looking soberly into hers. She smiled. On impulse, she suddenly flipped out one arm and pinched the soft flesh of his waist.

"Tell me," she said, laughing, "and be quick about it." He laughed. Neither took note of a greasy old lady with drooping breasts who rotted near them in the sun. She was watching them mournfully; her *Ladies' Home Journal* had dropped, unnoticed, on her cheap rubber go-aheads. And has it been so long ago, she thought, that my smelly old man and I, on the beach at Coney Island, like those two young lovers, played little games of love?

"You have a bizarre passion for gore."

"Just . . . make it quick." She relaxed sensuously on the towel, and the old lady sighed.

"First of all, our man confessed."

Katie stared at him. "Well, big deal," she said with annoyance. "Who wouldn't? He was . . . well, coerced . . . That wouldn't stand up in court, Emory."

"It was not overruled in ours."

"For real."

"He was very convincing."

"I'll bet. You vigilantes were . . . uh, persuasive."

"True."

"And you enjoyed . . ." Calm down, she thought. No scenes. Not on such a sunny day. "Not in the best traditions of American justice."

"Maybe." He fidgeted a little in the unaccustomed sun. He

hated the ritual of the tanning bath; he had never understood how women could stand it, could thrive on it. "And yet, from one philosophic point of view, the criminal was punished by those who suffered most from his crime. Ain't that justice?" He smiled.

"Not a good blueprint for democracy . . . or something."

"Perhaps. Peace in our time. Bad precedent. But the traitor was killed by the people he betrayed; the harsh rules of wartime."

Is that what it really is? she wondered. *A war?*

"Besides," he continued, "it wasn't my decision. It wasn't any one man's decision. The sweep of a historical force. For one grand moment, we were all one."

Yeah, she thought. But not this chick. Uh-uh.

"And how long will that touching unity last?"

"Who knows?" Idly, he made random holes in the yielding sand. "Not my business. Not my world. Not yet, anyway. That's one thing I learned. Who am I to say? It is a world with its own rules, and they are rules which are the product of necessity. Who am I to impose my—"

"White middle-class morality?"

"Something like that."

Okay, Finch, the girl mused. *You say it. You live with it. I can't, and that's why I'm taking a seven o'clock plane for Dallas, and points south. My little resolution: Forget it. All of it.*

Again, Finch understood.

"This is unbearable," he said, changing the subject. "My Anglo-Saxon Protestant forebears breathe down my neck. Emory Finch, they shout, you are living a decadent life. You lie on the beach like a depraved sultan; you neither reap nor sow. I've got to do something productive. How about a hot dog, or something? A goal-oriented mission. I'll go get it, or whatever you desire. You can lie there, sweltering, like some jet-set flotsam on the Costa del Sol."

"The what?"

"Spain." He made as if to stand, but she was too quick.

"Oh, no, you don't!" Katie grabbed his sloping shoulder and pulled him down.

"Ouch!" Her fingers left naked white circles in the tender pink embarrassment of his basting flesh. "Oh, no, I don't what?"

"You know very well. You haven't told me ... how you knew."

"About Orson?"

"You want a smack in the jaw, smart-ass?"

"Okay, okay. I guess that's what you mean."

"Genius."

"It was ... simple."

"I figured you'd say that."

"Ouch!" She had clutched the tender spot again. "It was, it was! Anyway, you must forgive my old ploy."

"I must." She saluted him. "Deliver me from ignorance."

"Gladly. It's the least— No, no." He jumped out of her reach, shielding his assaulted shoulder

"Keep a civil tongue."

"You're a hard woman." Katie laughed. Some days, she wished it were true. Like Friday, for instance. "Actually," said Finch, not unconscious of his drop into a lecturer's monotone, "there were only two important ... uh, facts. I avoid the word clues because it sounds so pompous and seems to suggest that I—"

Katie nodded with apparent patience, but her eyes lidded threateningly. She wrinkled her nose.

"Uh, you see the point." Finch smiled. He was, strangely, grateful that she had turned this business into a coquettish parlor game. No doubt, a virtue peculiar to the Southern belle. Not all bad, that lace-and-petticoat stuff. "First, the simple fact. File it away."

"Thanks."

"If we weren't all such racists, we might have seen it right away. There's a tendency, you know, to assume that all ghetto blacks come from the Deep South; specifically, Georgia, Mississippi and Alabama. To be fair to us poor dedicated liberals struggling with our stereotypes, even the black bourgeois—"

"Public Enemy Number One."

"According to Chuzz and . . . Sorry." His apology fell, unregarded. Her smile had not wavered; he went on. "Even educated blacks, that is to say, wouldn't see anything strange, or particularly significant, in the fact that both Benedict and our late principal grew up—"

She jumped on it. "In Alabama!" A dozing teen-ager started at the exclamation. Was it a new song?

"So they were both from Alabama," Finch went on. "At McAdoo, who isn't? In any case, or, to be specific, in this case, that was the simple fact. And Obadiah Snatch knew what it meant."

"That poor old man," Katie said, almost involuntarily. Then she shrugged, the hard woman. "He should have kept his mouth shut."

"Or opened it sooner. And that was my fault. You see, I had called him Friday morning; he was the logical source, after all. But I had to play games . . . ." He paused.

"You couldn't have—"

"I could have done something. But I didn't. I wanted to be sure. I didn't know that Orson, who had a paranoid fear of student plots—"

"With reason."

"Agreed. Anyway, he had a tap in his office on the students' pay telephone."

"Damn."

"Exactly. He heard. He took action. It wasn't difficult for him to slip across the street that morning, as if on an errand to juvenile court, and . . ." Finch stopped; he took a deep breath. "I thought of that, you see, when things got pretty ugly in the old factory."

"Go on." This was a rough spot Katie wanted to skip over.

"The old pimp's story gave me the motive, and I'll get to

that. But first, you may ask, why suspect Orson? And that's the more complicated fact. Intuition, more than anything else. Something else that wouldn't stand up in court. The murderer, whoever he was, had gone to Byzantine lengths to implicate most of us. It was the work of an imaginative but slightly crazy human being. Naturally, he let one ·strand wind around himself."

"The paralyzed finger."

"And yet . . . when the move was made, some last instinct of self-preservation, or maybe a streak of overcaution, made him too wary. The fingerprints, to anyone else, were an obvious frame-up. But Orson couldn't be sure. It might just boomerang. And so he took one step too many."

"I won't try to guess."

"Don't. You're at a disadvantage. You see, I saw the prints. And that morning, before our meeting, before my call to Snatch, I also saw Orson's hand. The prints were fake. That was his mistake. It seemed that he had been implicated, but, if Gannett had closed in, there was one important hitch. One factor didn't jibe."

"You mean . . . the prints wouldn't match. It was the wrong finger."

"Close. It was the wrong hand."

"That bastard. But clever." She laughed. "But not, it seems, clever enough for Emory Finch."

"Thanks, but it would have come out in the end. Even Gannett might have noticed, although he never suspected Orson, or any black man, of possessing much intelligence. I just got there first."

"Admirable modesty."

"Fat lot of good it did me. Here was a murderer, in the classic sense, without a motive. And Snatch was just a stab in the dark, as it were." He winked.

She groaned. "Spare us such puns," she pleaded. "Just tell me the juicy story."

"It's a short one. You will remember, without pleasure, that

Orson liked to entertain the students with dreary stories of his miserable youth on a dirt farm in Alabama." She nodded. "He told them that he ran away early in his teens, struck out on his own. And that was true enough, according to Snatch. Except that Orson didn't get very far. He reached the big city, Montgomery, Alabama, and hied himself from one menial job to another."

"Orson pushing a broom? That's hard to imagine."

"It is. And that's to his credit. He came a long way."

"And I bet he was on the make, even then."

"He was. He had to be. He did all the things the poor do in government reports, and then some. He went to night school; he got a job as a bricklayer's helper, or whatever it's called— meant he did a lot of carrying for a little money. By the time he was twenty, he had a high school diploma and—"

"Twenty?"

"Surprising, isn't it? Off to a slow start. And by the time he . . . died, Orson was near completion of his doctoral thesis. He meant to succeed; there's no question of that. But he needed a break, and he didn't get it. Scholarships for overall-clad Negroes, about ten years ago, didn't exactly—"

"Ten?" Katie sat up. She was beginning to see the connection.

"More like twelve."

"Twelve." She was working it out.

"The nice young black man, who knew his place, had lucked into a nighttime job in one of the factories in Montgomery. Even got to work a machine in the back shop, although he was officially employed as a custodian. It didn't matter. He got a little more money. It was at night, after all, and there was no union to worry about."

"Not in the South."

"The boss was short-handed, and Orson was willing to do white man's work for black man's wages. It was a step. And then the wheel of fortune turned. One day, Orson had skipped. They looked for him, but nobody seemed to know anything definite. There was just one crazy story— something about a sudden legacy, and some rumor that the young man had taken the money and gone up North looking for college. Of course, no one really believed it. Where would that kid get money? And if he had it, wouldn't he spend it, more likely, on a year-old Cadillac?"

"I know the reasoning." She frowned. "But, of course, there wasn't a legacy."

"Not in the usual sense. But it was a legacy for Orson. The night before he disappeared, he had cut the nerves of his finger on the machine he worked. Nobody at the plant knew, because he didn't tell them. The equipment was probably dangerous as hell, but he was afraid he'd get the blame, and lose his job. White is right."

"I know." Katie, inadvertently, thought of home.

"After work, early in the morning, he sneaked over to the emergency room of the nearby hospital. It was a city facility, with white doctors and separate waiting rooms for blacks. And the word waiting was no misnomer. Oh, he knew his place, all right, but the pain, like fear, made him lose his unfailing sense of caution. There was no nurse on duty, they were needed on the other side, I suppose, so he slipped into a room marked Treatment, or something like that, and there he found his train ticket to the promised land."

"Benedict. Four years old . . ."

"He saw a drunk young resident butchering the kid. And that's where the ironies begin. You see, Orson didn't really know what he was seeing. The man's drunk. So what? And maybe the lung was lost from the beginning. But the doctor knew. He was the son of a prominent industrialist, and so on, but he had neared the end of the hospital's patience. In fact, why else would he be assigned to nighttime duty in the Negro emergency ward?"

"Why, indeed?" A dangerous anger rose in Katie that must be stifled, she knew. This was nothing to her. The world is full of misery. It was no business of hers. No longer. Still, she listened.

"The doctor was alone. He hadn't waited for a nurse, although they are well-trained in covering up such indiscretions. He was not too drunk to be canny, and he sobered quickly. Alabama, even in those days, was not Mississippi. Somebody might listen, even to a young black man half-crazed with the pain of his torn finger. Besides, that doctor's career was at the point where the weight of a feather would mean anything. A chance remark, a rumor, and that would be the end. Maybe he really wouldn't have cared; he had money. But Daddy cared, and Daddy would write the will."

Again, Katie nodded. She knew the importance of Daddy in the South; he was the solemn institution from which all others sprang.

"And so the young Orson, who had come looking for a Band-Aid, found himself holding a check. A generous check. Next morning, it cleared, and he cleared with it."

"But how did Benedict . . . ?"

"I'm not sure. Maybe his grandmother had heard something; maybe the street-corner gossips had done their Monday morning deductions. As Snatch said time and again, there are no secrets in the ghetto. In some mysterious way, he was right. After all, how did he know? The grapevine. It would not be hid."

"But what was he afraid of? Revenge? Disclosure? After all these years, what could be done? Or proved? It really wasn't even a criminal act, not by law."

"It was immoral."

"It was shameful, but what could be done now? Orson was safe."

"That's the tragedy. Orson lived in constant fear, like an escaped convict; he was in hiding. Not because of the Benedict thing; that was a minor incident. It was his whole screwed-up psychology. He had spent his lifetime trying to better himself. Despite what he said, he hated his past; he hated being black. As protection, he built a very strong wall of respectability and, in a sense, cleanliness. Beverly was right about one thing;

Orson was the quintessential Uncle Tom, ashamed of his origins and seeking salvation in the acceptance of white society. Benedict's tale would be a crack in that polished facade. Orson couldn't face it; he was driven, by his obsession, to murder."

"That's a horrible way for a man to live."

"His death wasn't pretty, either." She did not reply. "And they were both taught at the same little schoolhouse, at the knee of some grinning redneck with a whip in his hand. That's where he learned how to live, and that's where his brothers learned how to kill him."

"Straight-A students, every one of them."

"The best."

"And yet . . . that's no excuse . . . for it all."

"No."

"And yet . . . I feel sorry for him."

"And . . . for them?"

Again, she did not, or would not, reply. No, she thought, my mind's made up. She looked at her watch. It lay at her side, because she had not wanted a white ribbon at her browned wrist.

"Two o'clock," she announced. "These are the crucial hours. At this time of year, the tannies die out at three; after that, it's only bennies." She smiled at his puzzled grin. "For the uninitiated, that's tanning rays and beneficial rays."

"Oh," he said. And again, he understood. And gave in. For a moment, he had thought: *I could do it; I could change her mind. I could reach out in some way, and pull her back.*

But he didn't. It was noisy and hot, and the beach was stuffy with sweating joy. It was not the place and the time. There would never be a place and a time. In his books, maybe. But not here. Not with her. The casting was all wrong. This time, he stood up, and she made no move to stop him.

"Can I get you a coke?" he asked simply.

And she understood, too. "Love you," she said. "But make it a Diet Pepsi."

Emory Finch, journalism teacher at William McAdoo High School, picked his way through the jumble of shiny limbs and headed toward the makeshift hot-dog stand near the parking lot. He was definitely not one of the Beautiful People, but he had no complaints. He was satisfied with himself, although he couldn't say why. Perhaps it was just the warm Santa Monica sun.

And Katie Lee, a former colleague, lay still and wondered lazily why she thought nothing, felt nothing.

She had enjoyed the little man's story, as if it were a tale set in a foreign land. But it was light reading, a diversion. The characters did not resemble the good-hearted citizens of the America she came from. It was all fantasy, and she knew about real life. It was strong, silent men and pretty women. It was happy families and children who minded their manners. She was returning to that real life. Home. She would clutch it to her breast until the pain made her faint. And then she would be ready to return to the fantasy.

The invisible timer buzzed again, and Katie turned over on her back. She closed her eyes. She warmed, like a lizard, in the afternoon sun.